PR[AISE FOR]

THIS W[AS ALWAYS]

ABOUT BASKETBALL

"With his latest book, Leener delivers an astonishing three-peat! This adventure is as triumphant and fun as the first two, taking us to the interplanetary depths of basketball, and even deeper into the heart and soul of its hero, Zeke Archer."

CLARK PETERSON
Film and Television Producer
Academy Award Winner for *Monster*

"The book neatly wraps up this supremely engaging and satisfying trilogy. Leener's sense of story and his ear for dialogue make this series perfectly poised for the big screen."

THEO GLUCK
Director of Library Restoration and Preservation
The Walt Disney Studios

"With *This Was Always About Basketball*, Craig Leener steers his trilogy to an ambitious and immensely satisfying conclusion. Richly imagined and skillfully told, this final volume is not easy to put down, even though you'll wish you could slow down long enough to savor the experience. But fear not. This story's true heartbeat—its deeper lessons about life's journey and the power of friendship—will stay with you long after you've turned the last page."

DR. ROBERT DICKSON
Chairperson, Communication Department &
Associate Professor of Communication
The Master's University

"Zeke and Lawrence commit a traveling violation, but it's not a turnover. Instead, it's an action-packed fast break to the origins of the game—a play drawn up on a mystical clipboard that honors the power of friendship and teaches young people about the seven tenet tools for a successful life. A 3-pointer by Craig Leener ... nothing but net!"

HOWARD FISHER
Head Coach
Youth Men's Basketball Team for Team USA

"I liked the first two in the series, but I really think the author found his stride in the third. It was emotional, really grabbing your attention and holding on."

TODD GILMORE
Co-Creator, "Beware of the Phog" Banner at Allen Fieldhouse
The University of Kansas

"The final installment of Craig Leener's basketball trilogy is expressive, absorbing, and teeming with wit. Along with colorful characters and an intricate journey, Zeke Archer's story of growth, within both his basketball career and in his maturity, brings readers to an impassioned conclusion. *This Was Always About Basketball* is inventive, almost as inventive as the infamous 'Deckerball.'"

CHRIS MEYER
Author of *Life in 20 Lessons*, *The 'Wood*,
and the upcoming *Four Months ... And A Lifetime*

"*This Was Always About Basketball* is an amazing story with cool twists and turns! This book will keep blowing your socks off right after you put them back on!"

SANTOS RODRIGUEZ
Avid reader and youth basketball player
Murrieta, California

"This is the capstone of a literary achievement—a trilogy so emotionally powerful and heartwarming, so rich in detail and thought, and so deeply profound. Craig has woven a truly unique and incomparable book with imagination, heart, soul, and creativity. It left me on the edge of my seat, spun me around, and settled me into a joyful end to a wonderful ride."

"Craig Leener is a wonderfully gifted teller of tales and spinner of yarns. The three books that comprise his Zeke Archer basketball trilogy are barn-burners and page-turners, where flights of fantasy and life lessons are offered up in equal and highly entertaining doses. Reading these books is like listening to great music—you don't want it to end."

"The author's narrative has a real-world feel to it, even despite the far-out adventures the characters are experiencing. Zeke and Lawrence and their colorful cohorts are tackling some of the same issues that young readers will no doubt have to face, or have already experienced, and this makes the trilogy both relatable and immensely satisfying. Craig Leener has quickly become a master of his craft."

"I think that readers tend to become less interested as future books in a series are released. But following the adventures of Zeke has kept me absorbed for three books straight. As a basketball player myself, Zeke's passion for the game made it effortless to connect with such a genuine character. It was yet again a page-turning experience full of life lessons and character growth that inspired me to follow my heart. I found this third book of the trilogy to be my favorite of them all, and hopefully readers from all walks of life will feel the same way."

HAILEY STAR DOWTHWAITE
Avid reader and high school basketball player
Los Angeles

"*This Was Always About Basketball* is a wonderful and fitting end to the trilogy while also being a thoroughly engaging read as a stand-alone story. Hoops fans will enjoy seeing Zeke and his crew's moves on the court, though the book is also a clinic on the power of friendship and building relationships that last through thick and thin."

JOEY HELD
Founder, Crisp Bounce Pass Newsletter

"Leener's smooth and textured writing, coupled with an addictive story, kept me page-turning right to the end. The author has managed to encapsulate what's good in the world while writing a truly memorable and sublime series of books. *This Was Always About Basketball* was not just a fantastically enjoyable read—knitted throughout all three books may just be the tenet for how we might live our lives."

CHRIS COPPEL
Author of *Luck* and *The Lodge*

THIS WAS ALWAYS ABOUT BASKETBALL

THIS WAS ALWAYS ABOUT BASKETBALL

CRAIG LEENER

GREEN BUFFALO
PRESS

Rules photos, courtesy of The University of Kansas

Cover design by Tabitha Lahr
Designed by Brent Wilcox

A catalog record is available from the Library of Congress.
ISBN: 978-0-9905489-6-6 (print)
ISBN: 978-0-9905489-7-3 (e-book)

10 9 8 7 6 5 4 3 2 1

To you, dear reader,

for joining Zeke, Lawrence, and me

on our strange journeys—

I hope you enjoy all of the well-meaning

weirdness and quirky life lessons

And to Andrea,

for believing in me always

CONTENTS

CONTENTS

CONTENTS

THIS WAS ALWAYS ABOUT BASKETBALL

1

Maybe I Had the Wrong Storage Unit

My name is Ezekiel Archer. Most people call me Zeke, except when I'm in trouble. Then they call me Ezekiel, and it's usually in a stern tone, and there's a lecture involved.

I was busy finishing up things in Los Angeles as I prepared to move in the next twenty-four hours to the University of Kansas, KU, some 1,600 miles from the only home I had ever known.

I was leaving L.A. to pursue my basketball dream.

I had earned an AA degree at Jefferson Community College and had enrolled at the University of Kansas to continue my education as a journalism major. But a respected journalism program wasn't the only reason why I had chosen KU.

My goal was to earn a spot on the Jayhawks basketball team as a walk-on point guard.

The time had come to measure my talent against some of the top players in the country.

I had a busy day lined up. I had to settle up my account at Biffmann Self-Storage and drive my pickup truck out of there in preparation for the trip to the Midwest. Then I needed to punch in for my final shift at Chip's Sporting Goods, where I'd been working all summer to earn enough money to make the move.

I also wanted to visit my father at the West Los Angeles VA Medical Center so I could see how he was getting along and say goodbye.

I slipped into my company-issued Chip's polo shirt, grabbed my bike, and zoomed down the apartment building stairs.

"Cheese and crackers, Zeke! Where's the fire?" That was Mrs. Fenner, the building's self-appointed security guard and CGO (Chief Gossip Officer). I knew she cared about my safety and well-being, but she had a nosy way of expressing it.

Mrs. Fenner was standing in front of her mailbox leafing through a stack of envelopes, so I knew that the mail had arrived.

"Nothing of consequence for the Archer family today, just some junk mail and a bill from that Biffmann place, where you keep that old jalopy of yours."

"And you know this how, Mrs. Fenner?"

"I accidentally caught a glimpse over the mailman's shoulder when I brought him a glass of iced tea."

That had to be at least a flagrant 1 foul. Mrs. Fenner resorting to beverage bribery in order to gain valueless apartment building intelligence was a new low, even for her.

"What did that letter say, the one you got a couple of weeks ago from *that girl?*"

Okay, so that question had just elevated Mrs. Fenner's status at the apartment building from nosy to meddlesome.

"She's not a girl, Mrs. Fenner. Rebecca Tuesday is my ex-girlfriend."

At the time, I had stuffed Rebecca's letter into my backpack. I hadn't wanted to read it because I had a feeling it was going to be more bad news.

"Thank you for looking after me, Mrs. Fenner. I don't know what I'd do without you." *But I'd probably start by having more of a private life.*

The last time I had ridden to Biffmann Self-Storage was a few weeks before, when I was met there by Curtis Short, who comprised one-third of my best-friend posse. Curtis and I had pulled my truck out of storage to help Best Friend No. 2, Roland "Stretch" Puckett, move some painting equipment across town.

Back then, I had trouble coaxing the engine to turn over because of the truck's unreliable battery. If the battery were now dead, I'd have to put *the arm* on the storage company's owner, Chett Biffmann, to swing by in the facility's golf cart, the one with a set of jumper cables aboard and a car battery custom-mounted on the rear bumper.

I pulled open the door to Biffmann's main entrance and walked my bike inside.

"Where you been, padnah?" Chett Biffmann swiveled his head to the side and aimed a slobbery wad of brown sputum in the general direction of the brass spittoon he kept on the spongy brown carpeting behind the counter. It was one of the reasons—and there were many—why no one else was ever seen behind that counter.

"I'm leaving for Kansas tomorrow, sir. I need to get my pickup truck out of space 1046 and settle my account."

"That space has been popular lately, *real* popular."

"Sir?"

"Coupla young gents stopped by a few hours ago. Said they had your permission to work on your truck. I figured they might be changing out that hinky old battery of yours."

That was weird. I couldn't remember giving anyone the okay to go inside my storage unit.

"Who were they?"

"Tarnation, son, hold yer horses. I've got their names on this here sign-in log." Chett Biffmann's chubby sausage fingers thumbed through the three-ring binder he kept on the countertop. "Got it right here: Sherman 'Lawrence' Tuckerman. Boy's only got one *n* at the end of his last name, unlike most folk, who've got at least two. Say, isn't he that squirrely friend o' yours? I thought his name was *Larry*."

I knew Sherman Tuckerman simply as Lawrence. He was a kid I had befriended at Ernest T. McDerney Continuation School. "Lawrence" was the nickname he had acquired as a four-year-old after his parents got him a map of the United States for his birthday. Sherman inexplicably became obsessed with the city of Lawrence in northeastern Kansas, where KU is located. After that, everyone except his parents started calling him Lawrence, and the name just stuck.

Lawrence had autism. He didn't often speak, preferring instead to communicate through notes he wrote using a No. 2 pencil and his trusty writing pad. He was a wizard with maps and mathematical calculations, and he routinely received coded messages from something he called an interdimensional energy being. Normal stuff.

Lawrence rounded out my trio of best friends. What he was doing at my storage space was anybody's guess. It had to be a mistake.

"You said there were two people, sir?"

"You don't miss a trick, do ya, son," Chett bellowed, chins jiggling underneath his scraggly, tobacco-encrusted beard.

"Yes, sir—I mean, no, sir."

"I think his name was Brick Dorker, somethin' like that. Wait, here it is: Brock Decker."

Brock was Rebecca's cement-head stepbrother, a former teammate, and an on-again, off-again friend. Brock and Lawrence gaining access to my storage unit together was a troubling development, and in a day that was already so jam-packed, I couldn't afford any surprises that would slow me down.

"Gotta say, I didn't much care for the cut of that Decker fella's jib. I reckon he has more muscles than brains."

Despite certain questionable aspects of Chett Biffmann's personal hygiene regimen, not only was he a savvy businessman, he was also a keen judge of character.

"You said they stopped by a few hours ago. Are they still here?"

"The one with the head in the shape of a cement block, he took off 'bout an hour ago. Big ol' limousine pulled up right there at the entrance and whisked him away. Car musta been a city block long. Left me gasted in the flabber regions—darnedest thing I ever saw."

What in the world was Brock doing riding in a limo?

"What about Sherman Tuckerman?"

"Didn't see him leave, son. I reckon the young fella is still in there."

I said goodbye to Chett Biffmann and pedaled the rest of the way to space 1046, not knowing what I would find when I went inside. I leaned my bike against the corrugated steel wall and soon realized I wouldn't need my key to get inside because the padlock that once guarded the roll-up door was missing. That meant Lawrence had either snuck out without locking the door or was still inside.

I grabbed hold of the door's rusty handle and pulled it up. The familiar smell of unburned gasoline drifted out of the storage space and scraped across my throat.

It was dark inside. I reached in to flip on the light switch and stared in disbelief. I could feel my eyes widening on their own. I felt lightheaded, and I didn't know whether my vertigo was caused by the sharp fuel smell or by what my eyes and my mind were struggling to piece together.

Maybe I had the wrong storage unit. I double-checked the number on the outside. Yep, 1046. I took a step inside.

My vintage 1965 Chevrolet Fleetside shortbed pickup truck was still in there.

But it was dismantled.

The truck bed, hood, fenders, side panels, chrome bumpers, and sideview mirrors were neatly stacked on the oily concrete floor on one end of the storage unit. On the other end was the Chevy's chassis, or what was left of it, wheels still attached but missing one key component: the truck cab.

That truck cab was sitting on the ground all by itself in the middle of the room, windows, doors, and steering wheel still attached.

I was supposed to drive that truck to the University of Kansas the next morning.

2

All Roads Lead to Brock

I could feel hot blood rushing to my face. For the life of me, I had no idea why Lawrence would have taken apart my truck. Even Brock Decker, complete jerk that he was, wouldn't have done that to me on purpose, even if he knew how.

I surveyed the rest of the room. The storage unit's padlock was lying on the floor a few feet from the door. The shackle was disengaged from the padlock's body, and there was a hairpin stuck inside the keyhole.

Lawrence was a fan of TV crime dramas. Picking a lock with a hairpin was no doubt in his wheelhouse of important stuff to know how to do. If the police were later called to the scene, it would be unnecessary for them to dust the lock for fingerprints.

I noticed the Chevy's weather-beaten canvas tarp lying in a heap in the corner.

Wait a second. It was moving. There was something alive underneath it.

I was sweating buckets, and not just because it was nearly one hundred degrees in the windowless room. It was the kind of perspiration that pours from your body when anger joins hands with fear.

I inched over to the tarp, held my breath, and yanked it off the ground.

It was Lawrence. He was sprawled out on the floor sur-rounded by hand tools—a ratchet set, screwdrivers, a cres-cent wrench, and a small electric grinder with a steel cutting disc.

The evidence was circumstantial, but overwhelming. If this were the trial scene from one of Lawrence's crime dra-mas, he would have been convicted unanimously by a jury of his peers, all of whom would've been wearing pocket pro-tectors that housed precisely measured and beveled No. 2 pencils.

I reached down to pull Lawrence to his feet, but he ig-nored me, instead helping himself up before cracking me across the face with the open palm of his right hand.

It was the umpteenth time since we'd become friends that Lawrence had smacked me, but that one stung the most—like a nest of angry bees simultaneously pummeling the side of my face with tiny, white-hot frying pans.

"WHY'D YOU DO THAT?"

No answer. None expected. Lawrence brushed himself off. His eyes darted everywhere around the storage unit, but they refused to meet mine.

He reached into the back pocket of his jeans and pulled out a short stack of folded-up pieces of paper. He took one off the top and handed it to me.

I was no stranger to Lawrence's handwritten messages. He had given me dozens of them in the couple of years since we became best friends while doing time together at McDerney Penitentiary. The kid's notes ranged from baffling to blunt and were generally about as useful as they were odd.

I unfolded the slip of paper and immediately recognized Lawrence's handwriting—rigid and purposeful, letters carefully sketched and slanted in an easterly direction, like the sun rising outside his bedroom's lone window.

I read the note silently:

I wanted to make sure you knew it was me.

We were making progress. The last time Lawrence had slapped me, his follow-up note argued that if more people greeted their friends like that, the world would have fewer friendships, but the ones that managed to survive the violence would be stronger.

I was trying to make sense of why Lawrence would have destroyed my truck without my knowledge. Had Brock Decker talked him into it on a dare? Maybe when I drove Lawrence to NASA's Jet Propulsion Laboratory for his summer internship, he had accidentally dropped one of his cherished No. 2 pencils behind a seat cushion and later became obsessed with rescuing it.

I gathered myself and stuffed down my anger. The whiz kid was a lot of things, but first and foremost, he was my best friend and trusted ally.

"Care to tell me what's going on here?"

Lawrence rocked back and forth as he peeled off another slip of paper.

No.

"I need some answers, Lawrence. You need to tell me what happened."

Another note soon followed.

The answer is still no.

It was as if he'd already figured out what I would ask.

"Listen, I'm giving you one more chance, but that's it," I said, sounding as menacing as my conscience would allow.

Lawrence's rocking intensified. He handed me yet another note. After that one, I noticed he had only one left.

I've done the math.

"What math?"

Lawrence grabbed the piece of paper from my hand and studied it. "Oops, how'd that one get in there?" He actually said those words out loud before cracking a smile. "It's humor, Zeke. Look it up in the dictionary."

Lawrence's reference was to a similar note he'd handed me a year earlier at the funeral for my big brother, Wade, a Marine Corps staff sergeant who was killed in action in Afghanistan. Lawrence had tried to convince me back then that Wade hadn't really died, despite ample evidence to the contrary. At the time, Lawrence said he'd simply done the math. But the translation was he had found a way to connect his research on advanced biomathematics to the communications network of a top-secret, otherworldly interdimensional energy being he called the 7th Dimension, all in an effort to prove that human consciousness wasn't tethered to the human brain.

Therefore, Lawrence had theorized, Wade wasn't really dead because his consciousness was a form of energy that existed as a fundamental element of the universe and outside the constraints of time and space. And since energy could neither be created nor destroyed, Lawrence had concluded that Wade's consciousness had simply transformed itself.

Simple stuff. He'd done the math.

Lawrence slipping an old note into the sequence of new ones as some sort of joke was weird and confusing because everything in his life was highly calculated. He never left anything to chance.

"I need to know why you carved my truck into pieces. Why don't you just tell me what's going on."

Lawrence handed me his stack's final note. I opened it.

All roads lead to Brock.

"Not funny, Lawrence."

"I'm not joking."

Lawrence stepped past me and pulled open the door to the passenger side of the truck cab. He reached in and grabbed the handle of the metal suitcase that served as his travel lunchbox. It was where he kept his bowl and spoon, a thermos of hot water, and several foil-wrapped brick pouches of freeze-dried chili mac 'n' beef.

Lawrence's career aspiration was the loftiest of all my best friends; he wanted to be the mathematics specialist on NASA's first-ever manned expedition to Mars. Lawrence ate that space-age meal three times a day because he was in training around the clock.

Lawrence opened the metal chest and dug around underneath the foil pouches until he located his writing pad. He plucked one of his seven No. 2 pencils from his pocket protector and scribbled out a note. Then he performed the ceremonial fold in half and handed it to me.

You need to find Brock. I'll stay here and put your truck back together.

"You can do that?"

Another note soon followed.

Yeah, as far as YOU know.

3

My Heart Sank

I knew from past experience that there was no use in arguing with Lawrence because he never gave up detailed information freely. And since I now had to ride my bike rather than drive to Chip's, there was simply no time to lose.

I closed the roll-up door behind me, told Chett Biffmann I'd be back in a little while, and raced across town to Chip's Sporting Goods as fast as my legs could pedal. I hadn't counted on the truck being undriveable, so I was in danger of being late for my final shift.

I locked up my bike at the front of the store and zipped inside. Chip's was in the middle of its annual summer sale, so it was jam-packed with customers. I sprinted to the time clock to punch in. The sound of the machine's emphatic *click-thump!* drew my boss, junior college chess champion Nathan Freeman, out of the break room, half-eaten bologna sandwich in hand.

My eyes widened when I saw my clock-in time.

"You're late, rookie," Nathan said. "If I didn't think I'd get mustard all over the paperwork, I would write you up."

I heard a different but more familiar voice from behind me as I was stuffing my backpack into my locker.

"That's an and-one, Nate—count it, and a foul." It was Curtis, taking Nathan baseline. "I've got important company business to transact with Ezekiel."

Curtis must have fallen from the sky. He had a knack for showing up when I needed him most, which was usually in the closing moments of a big game when he would knock down a three-ball to lift our team to victory. Walking into Chip's in the nick of time to put *the blocker* on Nathan was an added bonus in our friendship.

Nathan's normally elevated anger level seemed to increase as he disappeared back into the break room.

Curtis was wearing an aloha shirt and a pair of board shorts—and he was toting his surfboard under his arm. Chip's had a well-stocked surfing section, so I figured Curtis was there to pick up supplies or even get his board repaired.

"What do you need?" I said.

"I need to sell Chipper this primo board."

I felt my stomach lurch toward my throat. I had hoped Curtis was playing a joke on me, but I knew that look all too well.

"What's going on?" I asked.

"Totally lost my mojo, bro. Can't do it anymore."

Curtis loved to surf way more than shoot hoops, but he stayed close to the game so he could spend quality hang time

with me and Stretch. That made it straight-up bad news that
he had walked into Chip's to sell his surfboard.

Curtis had been a customer of Chip's for as long as I had,
so he knew that the store carried a wide assortment of surfboards, both new and used. Sometimes Chip would do a
trade-in deal or even buy a good customer's used board and
put it up for sale in the store.

Curtis leaned his board against the wall and ran a hand
through his shaggy, sun-bleached hair. He seemed to be drawing his focus inward.

"I thought you were doing better," I said.

Earlier in the year, Curtis had been crushed under the
weight of a humongous rogue wave at a desolate beach up
north near the Ventura County line. He was miraculously
saved from certain death by a dolphin that happened to be
swimming by. When I finally managed to pull Curtis to shore,
he wasn't breathing.

Luckily, Rebecca had come with me to watch Curtis surf.
At the time, Rebecca was a sports medicine student in the
Kinesiology Department of Jefferson Community College,
where we all went to school. Rebecca had since left Jefferson
and transferred to the University of Kansas after telling me,
for reasons I barely understood even to this day, that she
needed to break up with me.

Anyway, I ran for help while Rebecca saved Curtis's life by
performing CPR. Curtis eventually worked his way back onto
the Jefferson basketball team for our sophomore season. But
he had never fully recovered from the accident, at least emotionally, and he'd developed a mortal fear of the ocean.

THIS WAS ALWAYS ABOUT BASKETBALL

I never thought I'd live to see the day when Curtis would be trading in his most prized possession.

The board's deck was scuffed and its rails were pitted, but there was a lot of history in that thick sandwich of polyurethane foam, fiberglass cloth, and epoxy resin.

"That's a handsome surfboard, young man. Did you bring it in for repairs?"

That was Chip Spears, the store's owner. Nathan was following close behind.

"Nah, Mr. Spears. It's time for me to sell The Duke."

Curtis had named his surfboard The Duke in memory of Duke Paoa Kahinu Mokoe Hulikohola Kahanamoku, who is considered by most wave-riding aficionados to be the father of modern surfing. Curtis had originally bestowed Duke's full name on his board, but Stretch and I had trouble remembering all those tricky Hawaiian syllables, so Curtis shortened it.

Curtis handed his board to Chip, who ran a skilled hand over the surface and inspected the fins. Chip glanced uneasily at Curtis and grimaced.

"I'm afraid I won't be able to give you much for it. There just isn't a profitable market for used surfboards these days."

Curtis sighed. His eyes went dull. "I understand, sir."

"Fifty bucks is the best I can do," Chip said.

Curtis dropped his head and offered a halfhearted shrug. "Guess I'll take it."

My heart sank. Curtis selling off his coveted surfboard for next to nothing would be like me trading in my vintage pickup—at least while it was still intact—for a moped with an empty gas tank and a flat tire.

Chip whispered something to Nathan as he handed him the board and pointed toward the stockroom. Nathan nodded and hustled it away.

"I asked Nathan to store the board in the back until we can clean it up and clear some rack space on the sales floor." Then Chip told me to walk Curtis to the cash register to complete the transaction.

I filled out a receipt and pointed to where Curtis needed to sign. He picked up a pen, wrinkled his forehead, and looked at that piece of paper as if he were staring down a towering wave. He scrawled his signature and took a step back. I thought I saw my best friend's eyes well up, but he put on his sunglasses before I could be sure.

I rang up the transaction and dug two wrinkled twenties and a ten from the cash drawer.

"You still good for pizza tonight with me and Stretch before I split for KU?"

"Yep, and it looks like I'm buying," Curtis said as he stuffed the money into his pocket. "Got nothing else to do now, bro."

4

I'll Put On My Thinking Cap

I walked Curtis to the door and watched as he shuffled, shoulders drooping, across the parking lot to his surfmobile—a rusty old station wagon with an even rustier roof rack—and drove off.

When I went back inside the store, I saw that Nathan had planted himself next to the cash register. He was performing his daily ritual of drafting a list of tedious duties for my shift. The checklist seemed longer than usual. That was the kind of day it was shaping up to be.

Nathan was going over the details with me when I suddenly sensed a hulking presence approaching.

"Can you direct me to the private-eye section?"

It was Stretch. At seven feet, four inches tall, Stretch had been the starting center on our team at Jefferson for both seasons. His career aspiration was to be a private investigator.

So, first Curtis drops in unexpectedly. Then Stretch makes a secretly welcome appearance. I made a mental note to check the calendar on my break to see if it was Get Your Best Friend in Trouble at Work Day.

"You *know* Chip's doesn't carry any private detective gear," Nathan said. "Zeke's on the clock, so if you came here to screw around, you can turn around and leave—and be careful not to hit your head on the doorframe on your way out."

After Curtis's delivery of somber news, I was hoping Stretch had stopped by to cheer me up, but his long face seemed longer than usual. I led him back through the main lobby and onto the sidewalk outside.

"What's up?"

"You probably won't see me around the rec center much when you come home from KU on Christmas break," Stretch said.

"What's that supposed to mean?"

Stretch adjusted his crusty painter's cap and told me that his father's company was in a tailspin. He explained that if the downward spiral continued for much longer, Puckett Painting would go out of business.

"If that happens, we'll be homeless and living out of the company van. It's already way too cramped in there." Stretch was trying to keep it light, but his elongated face was unable to disguise his look of impending doom. "I've got to come up with something to jumpstart Dad's business, or we're sunk. There's no time for hoops anymore."

I tried to think of something to say but came up blank. I knew virtually nothing about the painting biz beyond the fact that Stretch's access to the company van allowed him to drive to the rec center on weekends to practice his skyhook.

"I'll put on my thinking cap and try to come up with something," I said halfheartedly, knowing full well there was little I could do to help my friend. "I hope you can still make it to the pizza place tonight. Curtis and I would hate to eat all that food by ourselves."

"Hard to say. Dad's got me pretty busy. Might be best if you don't count on me."

That was tough to hear coming from a guy I could always count on. After Stretch took off, I got to my restocking duties. I started in the surfing section by making sure there was plenty of sunscreen and board wax on the shelves. It was the least I could do to honor Curtis, who would've appreciated my diligence on his behalf, had he needed gear.

I figured Nathan might go easier on me if I focused my attention on the chess and checkers aisle next, so I went back to the stockroom and loaded up the cart with game boards, score sheets, and strategy books.

I was organizing the main chess shelves when I looked up and noticed a limousine pulling up to the front of the store. That was unusual for Chip's Sporting Goods. The store had a reputation as the place in Los Angeles where the common man could go to purchase athletic gear.

The limo driver got out, hustled around to the passenger side, and opened the door.

And out stepped Brock Decker.

5

Maybe the Basketball Gods Were Playing a Cruel Trick on Me

"What's going on, dweeb?"

That was Brock's favorite nickname for me, which I considered to be less original and less accurate than my nickname for him: cement head.

Brock looked different from usual. *Way* different. His clothes were preppy. His haircut was angular and precise. I caught the overwhelming scent of his cologne. It reeked of burned cloves and beached seaweed. It made my eyes water.

"What's with the limo?" Nathan said as I reached for a box of tissues.

"I'm having the tires on my Lamborghini rotated, so

Jeeves is chauffeuring me around today in one of my backup rides."

If Brock had won the lottery or had a rich uncle who'd died the week before, the news hadn't traveled all the way to my apartment.

"Hey, cement head, what do you know about my truck?"

Brock ignored my question and disappeared into the store. He strolled back moments later with a shiny new leather basketball.

He walked the ball to the cash register and set it down on the counter. After Nathan rang up the purchase, Brock reached into his pocket and pulled out a wad of cash that would've choked a horse, had one been standing unattended in the store's equestrian section. Brock peeled off a crisp hundred-dollar bill and told Nathan to keep the change.

"That's against store policy," Nathan said as he counted out a fistful of cash and coins to complete the purchase.

"Suit yourself," Brock said. All this was coming from a guy with a reputation for borrowing money from Rebecca and never paying it back.

Brock stuffed the change into the pocket of his designer cardigan sweater. He tucked the ball under his arm and headed for the exit.

"C'mon, man, I need some answers," I said as I followed him.

When Brock got to the lobby, he turned around and smiled. "After your shift is over in this minimum-wage job, you should stop by for the ribbon-cutting ceremony at the rec center," he said. "I'm buying the place."

Wait, what?

Brock was suddenly and unexpectedly wealthy, and he was going to purchase the only sanctuary I had ever had in this town beyond my apartment.

"Later, losers. Jeeves is taking me to the bank so I can cash another royalty check."

What in the world was he talking about? A royalty, I remembered, is a payment made to the creator or owner of a product based on the amount of the product's sales. The only thing Brock had ever created was a spit-wad launcher he fashioned from a ballpoint pen when we were stuck in detention at McDerney Continuation, where Brock, Curtis, Stretch, and I were banished because of the awful decision I had made at the high school basketball city finals.

Then came the clincher. Something caught my eye as Brock was exiting the store. I took a hard look at the ball he'd just purchased. On the place where it usually says BASKETBALL, there was a different word there: DECKERBALL.

Deckerball?

Just then, a new wave of customers scurried through the front door. I whipped around to gauge Nathan's reaction, but the look on his face indicated that everything was normal. I turned to take a second look at the ball, but Brock was already back inside the limousine, and Jeeves was pulling away from the curb.

A bark of laughter escaped my throat. I slapped myself hard across the face to make sure I wasn't in some sort of dream state. *Ouch, that hurt.*

Maybe the basketball gods were playing a cruel trick on me. Or maybe Brock's secret plan to use his noxious cologne to overpower all six of my senses had succeeded.

6

Wade's Trying to Tell Me Something

Nathan brought me back to reality.

"Mr. Tuckerman called the store just before you arrived late for work," Nathan said. "He wanted to know if either one of us has seen Lawrence. Apparently, our young friend never came home last night."

That bit of information only added to the mystery of what had happened to my pickup truck.

"Lawrence is fine," I said. "He's over at Biffmann Self-Storage helping me, um, get my Chevy ready for the drive to Kansas."

"I'll give Mr. T a call to let him know. He sounded pretty worried. He said Lawrence has been behaving rather peculiar lately."

Acting strange was Lawrence's calling card. It had started long before I met him.

Lawrence had told me that when he was four years old, he'd used the ancient Greek geometric technique of neusis construction to create a heptagonal antenna out of seven No. 2 pencils. He claimed to have used the device to intercept communiqués from the 7th Dimension.

Lawrence had learned that the 7th Dimension brought basketball to Earth in 1891 through its secret envoy, a Canadian physical educator, medical doctor, and minister named James Naismith. But the Entity had decided to take away the game for good because of my terrible decision to slug Brock Decker during the high school city finals.

That's what got all of us tossed into McDerney Continuation. It wasn't as if Brock didn't have it coming. He had taken a cheap shot at Stretch as I was driving our team downcourt for the winning bucket. Stretch went up for a dunk that would have clinched it, but before he could jam the ball down, Brock clotheslined him, hooking the big man's throat with an outstretched arm.

Brock had ducked, and I ended up walloping one of the referees instead. A melee ensued, my team from Southland Central High forfeited the game, and the University of Kansas revoked my full-ride scholarship.

All of us were expelled and subsequently dumped into McDerney. That was how we all ended up playing together for two seasons at Jefferson Community College under Coach Kincaid.

Lawrence had later learned that the 7th Dimension brought basketball to Earth as a means of fostering peace and brotherhood among all planet dwellers. After my regrettable judgment, Lawrence found out that the Entity had decided to take away the game for good.

But thanks to Lawrence's remarkable powers and abilities, he and I were able to reason with the Entity, saving basketball for all humankind.

So, yeah, the pencil maven was no stranger to the theater of the weird.

Nathan went to the front counter to phone Mr. Tuckerman while I got back to work. Part of me wanted to clock out early on my last day so I could help Lawrence reassemble my truck and then get him home to put his father at ease. And I still needed to visit my dad at the VA hospital.

But I felt it was important to work my entire final shift. At the beginning of the summer, Chip Spears had given me more hours and a raise, which had come in handy because I was socking away the money I would need to transfer to KU. So not only was it a matter of integrity, but I needed every dime of pay because I was about to move halfway across the country.

I finished out my shift and said goodbye to Nathan on my way out. "I'll stop by tomorrow to pick up my paycheck and turn in my polo shirt," I said as I scrambled toward the bike rack at the store's entrance. I was surprised to see Coach Kincaid walking up to the front door.

Coach Kincaid was the head coach of Jefferson Community College's basketball team for the two seasons I played there. I hadn't seen him since graduating at the beginning of summer.

I waved at Coach as I unlocked my bike.

"I stopped by to pick up some gear for summer practice," he said. "And I need to buy a new—"

Just then, a passing car blared its horn, so I was unable to hear the last word out of Coach's mouth, but I could have sworn it sounded like "Deckerball."

"What?"

Coach didn't answer. There was no way he could have said the word *Deckerball*. Coach seemed to be in a hurry. That made two of us. He waved goodbye and went inside the store.

I put it out of my mind as I hopped onto my bike and rode to the VA hospital.

The Archers were collectively a two-car family, but I was riding my bike around town that summer because I was trying to stay in shape. Making the team at KU was a long shot, and I was leaving nothing to chance.

My parents were divorced. I was living with my mom. My dad had suffered a severe emotional breakdown while driving in nonstop from his home in Denver to attend the championship game in my sophomore season at Jefferson. Doctors at the VA hospital had recently upgraded Dad's condition from critical to stable and told us that his road to recovery would be a long one.

We actually had two pickup trucks. One was my father's. Mom and I had left it parked at the VA hospital. Dad was not currently permitted to drive, but we believed he took comfort in knowing that his ride was sitting in the infantry position in the hospital's parking lot, just waiting for him to get well.

The other pickup was my '65 Chevy Fleetside shortbed. It was a junker my dad had bought from an old army buddy years before and restored with Wade when we were still a family of four living under the same apartment roof.

Before Wade enlisted in the Marine Corps, he locked up the old Chevy at Biffmann Self-Storage because he knew that Chett Biffmann ran a tight ship and would look after the vehicle. Chett stashed the Chevy's keys in the company safe. Two weeks after Wade's funeral, Chett handed me those keys.

I didn't drive the truck much, as I said, because I needed to spend every waking hour exercising.

My mom had never learned to drive, so she rode the bus everywhere. She was working a double shift across town at Mikan Memorial Hospital, where she was a trauma nurse in the emergency room.

I had a lot of asphalt to cover to visit my dad. I criss-crossed the series of busy streets that led to the VA hospital, and I locked up my bike at the entrance. I checked in with the security guard at the hospital's front desk.

"What's up, Officer Nordquist? How's my dad doing?"

Ricardo Nordquist worked the desk on the swing shift, which was normally when I visited my dad. I always asked Officer Nordquist for an update on Dad so that I knew what to expect when I got to his room.

"I haven't seen Kenton up and around for a few days now. Want me to call him for you?"

"No, thanks. I'd like to surprise him."

I made my way through the hospital's network of brightly lit white corridors as my nostrils picked up the stink of industrial disinfectant that lingered in the air.

I knocked on my father's door, even though it was open. It was at least ninety degrees in the room, but Dad was co-cooned from chin to toe in the olive-green wool army blanket he always traveled with.

The walls inside were stark white. The air carried the blunt scent of overbleached sheets and towels. There was a hospital robe hanging from a metal hook on the outside of the bath-room door. The whiteboard behind my dad's bed listed his medications and occupational therapy schedule.

Dad was sitting in a battered lounge chair staring out at the parking lot through the hospital room's lone window. He looked like he hadn't shaved in days.

"Dad." No answer. "*Dad!* It's me, Zeke." Still nothing. It was as if he were hypnotized, caught up in the spell of the bleak concrete vista outside and the hazy brown L.A. skyline beyond it. I shook his shoulder, hoping it would snap him out of it. He blinked and squinted. He seemed to be trying to fo-cus his eyes.

"I keep seeing him," my father said.

"Who?"

"Wade."

I felt the hairs on the back of my neck jiggling. My heart was smacking up against the inside of my ribcage.

"My brother?" I needed to make sure I had heard my dad correctly.

"Uh-huh."

My father had been a sergeant in the army and was a dec-orated combat veteran of the Iraq War.

When he had finally shipped home, the military doctors told my mom that Dad was suffering from posttraumatic stress disorder. After that, my dad had to endure years of nightmares and flashbacks of the gruesome things he'd witnessed in combat.

It left him feeling alone and disconnected from our family. By the time Wade had joined the Marines and shipped off to boot camp, my mom and dad were fighting so much that they divorced. Dad left Los Angeles, transferring to an army installation eighty miles outside of Denver.

Now he was back home in L.A.—or at least his physical body was—and probably for good.

I was having second thoughts about probing deeper, but he was my dad. There was no way I could avoid it.

"Wade is in . . . your dreams?"

"No. I see him inside my head sometimes when I close my eyes."

My father's hands were shaking. That made my stomach muscles clench. I knew that my dad was having mental issues, but this was next-level.

"I don't know what that means, Dad."

"Looks like you have a visitor, sergeant." The nurse in the doorway startled me. If my father heard her, he didn't react. She was standing beside an empty wheelchair. "It's time for your medication, Kenton. Then we're going to physical therapy."

The nurse asked if I wanted to come along. I told her I had some important stuff to take care of.

I squeezed my dad's shoulder. "We can finish this conversation later," I whispered. "I'll drop by on my way to KU."

Before I could back away, Dad grabbed my arm and pulled me close. His hand was unsteady, but his grip was tight. "Wade's trying to tell me something," he whispered hoarsely, right in my ear, "but I can't understand what he's saying because of all the gunfire."

7

You Won't Be Able to Play Full Court Here Anymore

I bolted out of the VA hospital, jumped onto my bike, and flew down McGill Road. It was already the middle of the afternoon.

My time in Los Angeles was running short. If I hustled, I would have just enough time to figure out what was really going on with the limo and Brock's claim of buying the rec center before I had to deal with Lawrence and my disassembled truck.

Of course, it could be no coincidence that Brock's name was on the Biffmann Self-Storage sign-in sheet next to Lawrence's, so the cement head needed to answer for that as well.

The obvious place to look for Brock was his house, where he would likely be hanging out with his cronies watching cartoons and eating spicy pork rinds.

Then I remembered that he had stopped by Chip's to pur-chase a custom-made basketball with his very own name stamped onto it. I knew Brock well enough to assume that he would have taken that ball to the rec center to show it off.

I pedaled across miles of hot, rutted blacktop, dodging cars and pedestrians on that smoggy, windless summer after-noon until I arrived at Bird Parkway and rolled into the rec center parking lot.

There was a massive construction crane stationed in front of the building. It looked as though the worker operating the crane was attempting to install a sign atop the brick structure.

That seemed unnecessary. The rec center already had a perfectly good sign. It had been installed months earlier when the facility was christened the Vernon Shields Community Recreation Center, renamed to honor the club's longtime director.

Vernon Shields had served as head basketball coach at Jef-ferson Community College for twenty-five years before retir-ing and joining the rec center. He had led Jefferson to the only state title in the school's history.

Coach Kincaid, who guided me for two seasons at Jeffer-son, had been the all-conference point guard on Mr. Shields's championship team.

Mr. Shields knew more about basketball than anyone I had ever known. He looked after Wade in the years before my brother joined the Marine Corps, and he was a trusted friend to Curtis and Stretch and me, as well as to Rebecca, Law-rence, Nathan, and even Brock Decker.

I parked my bike by the entrance and walked inside. Mr. Shields was standing in the hallway with a couple of men in business suits. He wasn't saying much, and I could see sadness in his eyes.

One of the men handed Mr. Shields a clipboard. He leafed through some paperwork, appeared to sign his name, and handed the clipboard back to the businessman. Then Mr. Shields turned and hung his head as he walked away.

"What's going on, Mr. Shields?" I asked after tracking him to his office. That office was a museum of artifacts from his career as a coach and community leader: trophies, plaques, team photos, the works.

"I hear you're planning to walk on at KU," Mr. Shields said. "Is that true?"

"Yes, sir. I've worked extra hours at Chip's all summer so I could afford to move to Kansas."

"Are you staying in shape?"

Mr. Shields was always concerned about whether I was taking good care of my health. "I put the Chevy in storage after I graduated from Jefferson so I would ride my bike everywhere I went all summer. I think it worked. My legs feel strong."

"Have you been playing much ball?" Mr. Shields asked.

"Just here at the rec center, mostly full court with Curtis and Stretch." I chose not to burden Mr. Shields with Curtis's decision to walk away from surfing, or Stretch's need to give up basketball in hopes of saving the family painting business. Mr. Shields seemed down in the dumps enough without having to deal with my recent, unfavorable news.

"Anything else, Zeke?"

"I was wondering what's up with the sign on the building."

Mr. Shields repositioned the tattered baseball cap atop his head and shrugged his shoulders. "You might want to ask your friend Mr. Decker about that. You can find him in the back, outside by the Deckerball court."

The what?

I was running out of time. I thanked Mr. Shields and made my way across the rec center toward the court. Mr. Shields's voice stopped me before I got far.

"I'm sorry to say you won't be able to play full court here anymore—just three-on-three."

"Sir?"

"Ask Brock."

8

That's When I Saw It, Spelled Out in Bright Plastic Letters

I walked through the double doors leading to the outdoor basketball court.

That court was the club's centerpiece. It had also been my second home and the focal point of my life for as long as I could remember.

The court had everything: a polished concrete floor, regulation lines, and identical NBA-size glass backboards with steel-chain nets hanging from the rims.

Heaven on Earth.

At least it *had been* heaven.

The rec center's basketball court was now only a half-court.

Half. Of. A. Court!

The midcourt strip was still there, but just beyond it stood a ten-foot-high wall that ran the entire width of the outdoor recreation area, cordoning off the other half of the basketball court. There was a door in the middle of that wall leading to the other side.

That must've been what Mr. Shields was referring to when he said I wouldn't be able to play full court anymore—and that somehow Brock Decker was at the bottom of it. All of a sudden, the fact that I was planning to leave town for KU the next morning had taken a back seat. This was a matter of principle.

The day was already a nightmare. How much worse could it get?

I wouldn't wait long to find out. I opened the door and peered inside.

The basketball court's other pole and backboard were gone. The concrete floor was covered over with black paint. There were three shiny sports cars parked in the area above where the three-point arc used to be. That area was no longer the sacred real estate where Curtis would rain three-balls on unsuspecting opponents.

The driver side door on one of the sports cars flung open. Out stepped Brock Decker, dressed in the same expensive clothes he'd been wearing when I saw him at Chip's earlier in the day.

"This is private property, dweeb. You're trespassing," Brock said as he swaggered toward me, his repugnant cologne arriving a few steps ahead, causing me to gag.

"I need to get to the bottom of what happened to my pickup truck, but it'll have to wait. What have you done to the court?"

"Parking is at a premium in this one-horse town. I bought the rec center so I'd have a place to store my fleet."

I was losing touch with reality. Sweat was forming on the palms of my hands. I could feel my knees wobbling, the way they used to whenever Mr. Appleton, my math teacher at McDerney, would call on me in class and I didn't have the right answer.

First, Lawrence breaks into my storage unit and dismantles my truck. When I ask him why he did it, he tells me that all roads lead to that numbskull, Brock, who carries a "Deckerball" from Chip's to a waiting limo. Then Mr. Shields concedes that full-court games are no longer an option at the rec center, and his only explanation is for me to check with Brock, who has just converted half of my personal safe zone into his very own overflow parking garage.

"I guess you and your pantywaist friends will have to settle for three-on-three from now on," Brock said. "Gotta say, that's no way to stay in shape if you've got any prayer of walking on and being a Jayhawk."

It was clear I wasn't going to get anywhere with Brock. I needed to go someplace where I could think. I went back through the door and saw a group of kids starting up a game of threes on the half of the court Brock had spared.

Brock followed close behind. "Hey, chump," he said. "I spoke with Rebecca." That sent the hairs on the back of my neck in motion. "She seems to be getting along just fine without you."

What did Brock mean by that?

That did it. I snapped.

I took a running leap at Brock and tackled him to the floor of his new parking garage. I was about to pummel his cement head with the fist of my nonshooting hand when Mr. Shields pried me off.

"That's enough!" I'd never seen Mr. Shields so angry. There were veins popping from his leathery neck. "This is supposed to be a safe place for kids as well as cars."

"Sorry, Mr. Shields," I said.

What was happening to me? I'd never done that before at the rec center.

"Don't let that happen again, Shields, or I'll have you scrubbing toilets for the rest of the summer."

Hearing Brock disrespect Mr. Shields like that caused my stomach muscles to squeeze and cramp. I thought I was going to hurl, right there on the court—I mean, in the parking lot.

The squeaking of sneakers had abruptly halted when the kids on the court stopped to watch, mouths agape. I walked past them toward the rec center's rear door. One of the kids shouted at me.

"Hey, Zeke, you got next? Mr. Shields says you're the best Deckerball player at the rec center."

Deckerball? I needed to get out of there. I shot back through the building to the entrance, hopped onto my bike, and pedaled down the driveway. When I got to the street, I turned and saw that the worker operating the mammoth construction crane was about to lift the tarpaulin off what looked like a new sign installed on the roof of the building. There it was:

DECKER ENTERPRISES

I turned my attention to the mini message sign that stood atop the grass at the rec center's driveway entrance. It was the place where Mr. Shields announced upcoming rec center activities to Angeleños in passing cars. That's when I saw it, spelled out in bright plastic letters:

DECKERBALL FALL YOUTH LEAGUE
SIGN-UPS START TODAY

9

I Chickened Out

I was wide awake and trapped inside my own personal nightmare. I glanced down at my watch, knowing full well the world wasn't going to operate on my timetable.

I heard footsteps coming up behind me.

"What's up, champ?"

No one had called me that since Rebecca did after our basketball team had won the regional title. Reliving that moment just then made my stomach churn.

I swung my bike around and was face to face with Darla Davenport.

Darla and I had studied journalism together at the *Jefferson Journal*, the college's newspaper. She was always the reporter who interviewed me after basketball games in high school and college.

Darla went in for a handshake, locking onto my sweaty shooting hand with what Stretch referred to as her "iron grip of death." That was how Darla would attempt to put me at ease before an interview, but it was unnecessary because I secretly liked being around her, even though her presence at that moment was unwelcome.

When the pain subsided, I wiggled my fingers to restart the circulation and make sure nothing was broken.

"It's just my luck that I would bump into you here. What are the odds?"

Lawrence wasn't around to help me calculate them, but I knew it wasn't a long shot. "What's going on?"

"I'm in summer school to pick up the extra units I need to graduate," she said. "I'm working on a follow-up story to the one I filed after you won the championship."

I had known Darla since elementary school. She was smart and cute and had a silky voice and a provocative smile that revealed a narrow gap between her two front teeth. She had a habit of cracking her knuckles in class, which was annoying to me at first, but it later became one of her more endearing qualities.

And she was also the only girl to ever beat me in a game of Horse. It had happened in middle school on the playground in front of the guys, and I've been trying to forget about it to this day.

"I don't mean to be rude, but I don't have a lot of time right now," I said.

I liked Darla as a sportswriting colleague, even though she was awkwardly pushy whenever she was writing on a deadline.

I think her pushiness came from growing up as the youngest of seven children—she'd had to learn ways of getting noticed. Darla's six older siblings were all brothers. That meant she'd always enjoyed a layer of protection at school, and she knew how to defend herself.

"Don't worry, this won't take long."

Darla had a spray of freckles and spiky red hair that made her stand out in a crowd, which helped me to avoid her postgame interview attempts if the team had lost and I was in a lousy mood.

"Okay, just a couple of questions. I really have to get going."

"In our postgame interview after the big game, I remember saying it looked as though you hesitated on that fast break before dishing the ball off to Brock for the winning basket."

At the time, I had tried to brush off Darla's question by telling her I had paused in that split second to explore my options.

But there was a lot more going on that she didn't know about.

A year earlier in my freshman season, I was in the exact same situation—running the break with the SoCal regional title on the line. I chose to take the shot back then because I didn't want Brock to have to live with the outcome if he'd missed it and cost us the championship. As Jefferson Jackrabbits team captain, I felt I should bear that burden—and that's exactly what happened after I airballed the potential game winner as time expired.

"Is there a question in there somewhere?" I said as I picked up a whiff of Darla's perfume, which smelled as if someone had dragged a weathered basketball across a bed of spring wildflowers and then rinsed it off with mint-flavored lemonade. Smelling that good was a new and unexpected development for the shapely, intrepid reporter. It made me feel kind of warm inside.

"Did you pass the ball to Brock because he had a better look, or had you lost confidence in yourself after what happened in the finals the year before?"

Wow. Really, Darla?

I felt my body heating up from the inside even more. I took a moment to compose myself before staring long and hard into Darla's fierce green eyes.

"I think we're done here," I said, instantly regretting my words.

"You taught me that."

I had no idea what she was talking about. Even though I liked being around Darla a lot, I felt like I needed to cut our impromptu interview short.

If it were a year earlier, I would have started pedaling. But I was a lot older and wiser after my sophomore season. I knew I couldn't leave things with Darla that way because of our friendship and the journalist's code of ethics.

"Taught you what, exactly?" I asked.

"To ask the tough questions—to tell readers what you think is important for them to know."

Darla was right. We had worked side by side for two years at Jefferson's school paper. She taught me how to write with empathy and compassion. I showed her how to dig a story out of a reluctant subject.

"I make that shot nine times out of ten when I'm not being blitzed by a six-eleven linebacker. Brock was wide open, so I dished it off. End of story."

Darla's pointy shoots of flaming scarlet hair bobbed up and down above her freckled forehead as she scribbled my words onto the pages of her reporter's notebook.

"Anything else?" she said.

I took a deep breath and wondered silently how Brock was still able to torture me, even when he wasn't standing there being a major tool. "Maybe it was just Brock's time."

Darla sorted through her notes while I studied the laces of my high-tops. "Just one more question," she said. "What's up with you and Rebecca?"

The question made my ears turn hot and sent a nervous ripple across the lining of my stomach. I had arrived at the point of a media interview where most athletes would have simply said, "No comment!" and walked away.

But Darla was a trusted friend, so running and hiding wasn't much of an option.

"Is that part of your story?"

"Nah, I was just curious," she said.

I wanted to open up to Darla and tell her I was as confused as ever about where things stood between Rebecca and me and how our lives seemed to be on different paths. I thought about asking for her help in figuring out what was going on inside Rebecca's head and what my chances were of ever getting back together with her. But I chickened out.

"Just one more question: What are you going to do if you don't make the team at KU? Are you coming back to Los Angeles?"

I didn't know what Darla's motivation was for asking that question, but I had a ready answer for her.

"Not going to happen. Anything else?"

"No, I think I've got everything I need."

10

I Never Meant to Hurt You

The uncertainty surrounding my breakup with Rebecca was a constant dark cloud that hung over me. And it didn't help that Darla Davenport, who I really liked being around, was asking questions that had less to do with basketball each time she interviewed me.

If I didn't know better, I would have thought that Darla had just asked those easy-layup questions to distract me from the real one she wanted answered.

I pedaled down Summitt Street as fast as my legs could move. By then, I was obsessed with that numbskull Brock Decker, how he might be behind the dismantling of my truck, and how he had resorted to such an elaborate scheme to make it seem that he was suddenly and unexpectedly so rich that the game of basketball would be named Deckerball in his honor—and to his profit.

I was riding to the one place in town where I would be guaranteed to find answers. I thumped my tires onto the public library's entryway and lowered my kickstand.

If basketball's name and history had somehow been altered, then the library would have a detailed account of it—and there could be no doubt that Lawrence, Brock, and for sure the time-hopping 7th Dimension were behind it.

I pulled the library's brass door handle. The chilly air rushed against the perspiration on my face as I walked inside. That icy blast brought much-needed relief, but the enjoyable feeling didn't last long—like most of the enjoyable feelings in my life over the past couple of years.

I was met by the grassy, musty aroma of several thousand books, many of which were older than Mrs. Vanderhorst, the branch's kindly but stern librarian.

Mrs. Vanderhorst, standing guard at the checkout counter, was also the librarian at McDerney Continuation, as well as that school's study hall magistrate and detention bailiff.

Her blue-gray hair was coiled up into a tight bun the size of a softball. She wore a bulky wool sweater buttoned up to the base of her chin, no doubt to counteract the effects of the library's efficient air conditioning system.

"*S-s-sh!* Not so loud, Ezekiel," she hissed.

"I haven't said anything, Mrs. Vanderhorst," I whispered.

"Maybe, but you were about to. Consider this a preemptive warning."

"Yes, ma'am."

I tiptoed past Mrs. Vanderhorst to the History section, where I browsed through dozens of volumes until I located

The World History of Games and Sports, which I had checked out of the library many times before. That encyclopedia of recreational know-how was as reliable as it was thick. I figured it would hold answers to the questions that were coursing through my brain, starting with: *What in the world had happened to basketball?*

I picked up the book and settled in at a nearby table. I knew I needed to find answers, but I was having trouble focusing because I was haunted by my conversation with Darla about Rebecca.

Then I remembered that I still hadn't read Rebecca's letter. I couldn't stall any longer. I pulled it from my backpack.

I anticipated the subtle aroma of Rebecca's perfume escaping from the envelope as I opened it.

Not there.

I figured Rebecca had written to update me on summer school and her new job. And I thought she might at least ask me what my plans were after Jefferson.

> *Dear Zeke:*
> *This is a hard letter for me to write. I know it won't be an easy one for you to read.*

Uh-oh.

> *I've had to deal with so much here at KU. I studied day and night to get good grades in summer school while holding down three part-time jobs to pay for food, tuition, school books, and my shoebox of a studio apartment.*

THIS WAS ALWAYS ABOUT BASKETBALL

I know it was my own decision to move to here, but I didn't expect my life to be consumed by so much loneliness once I arrived. And knowing we couldn't hang out hasn't helped much.

I considered that last part to be a compliment of sorts that, for a fleeting moment, enabled me to feel okay about Rebecca's letter, which seemed to be headed in the opposite direction of what I had been hoping for. I considered stuffing the letter back inside the envelope to finish reading it once I arrived on campus, but I knew I had to continue to the end.

So the real reason why I'm writing this letter is to tell you that I'm joining the Peace Corps.

Gut punch.

I'm putting my studies on hold to serve as a volunteer in West Africa helping with children's health, nutrition, and water sanitation. As soon as everything is approved, I'll be flying out of Kansas City International Airport to undergo three months of preservice training in the Philippines prior to fulfilling my assignment in Senegal.

Brock told me you're really planning to transfer to KU. I'm happy for you and proud of you. I wanted you to know my status before you moved to campus so you could make plans that don't include me for now.

I felt a spasm in my jaw and realized it was from clenching my teeth.

I'm so sorry, Zeke. I never meant to hurt you. I know you will have a great year at KU.

Rebecca

11

The Building Started to Spin

I swallowed hard and lowered my forehead to the table. I was devastated. But I was also running out of time. Feeling sorry for myself would have to wait.

I flipped to the index at the back of the sports history book, scanning it to see on which page the basketball chapter started.

AIR HOCKEY
ARCHERY
BACKGAMMON
BADMINTON
BASEBALL
BILLIARDS

Wait. What?

The number-one sports reference guide in the entire library just skipped over BASKETBALL by going from BASEBALL straight

to BILLIARDS. That couldn't be. A book's index was supposed
to be an arrangement of its contents in alphabetical order.

I skimmed farther down the index.

BOWLING
BOXING
CYCLING
DARTS
DECATHLON
DECKERBALL

Uh-oh. I ignored DECKERBALL and continued down the
page, hoping that when I scanned back up, the word would
have magically disappeared.

DODGEBALL
DOMINOES
FENCING
FIELD HOCKEY
FOOTBALL
GO FISH

I ran my finger back up along the smooth page. DECKER-
BALL was still there. BASKETBALL was nowhere to be found.

I crossed and uncrossed my arms a few times, as if that
might make everything all right despite mounting evidence to
the contrary. I noticed a couple of kids staring at me and giggling from a nearby table. It felt like the library's four walls
were closing in on me.

I squeezed my eyes shut and tried to steady myself by exhaling every bit of nervous energy from my lungs. I knew the noise I made was audible because I heard Mrs. Vanderhorst's attempt to restore order from the other side of the library.

"*S-s-s-s-s-sh!*"

That sent those two kids into a giggling frenzy.

Quit stalling, Zeke.

The time had come. I had to know.

I flipped through several chapters until I landed on the first page of the section on DECKERBALL. I glared at the word. It felt as though someone had cranked up the tightness knob that controlled my chest muscles. The world around me seemed to be grinding to a halt.

I read silently.

> *Deckerball was invented by Phineas Bartholomew Decker at the International YMCA Training School in Springfield, Massachusetts, on December 21, 1891.*

The date and place were accurate enough, but in addition to the horribly wrong name for the game, there was no mention of James Naismith, who, as far as I knew, was the game's actual inventor. I continued reading.

> *Decker, a notorious grifter and braggart of the era, was granted parole in December of 1891 and released from the Massachusetts Reformatory, a state prison in the city of Concord, after serving a five-year sentence for swindling an elderly librarian out of her life savings.*

None of that information came as a surprise.

Upon Decker's release from prison, he was purportedly greeted at the reformatory gates on that bitterly cold winter's day by an unnamed relative who arranged for a horse-drawn carriage to transport Decker ninety miles west to the Springfield-based International YMCA Training School.

Decker, nearly frozen to death and with nothing more than the clothes on his back and a nickel and two pennies in his pocket, is reported to have wandered onto the YMCA grounds, where he was warmly greeted by a faculty member, identified only as a Christian minister with rounded spectacles, neatly parted hair, and a bristling but well-kempt mustache.

The good-hearted faculty member reminded me of someone.

Upon learning of Decker's unexpected arrival and dire circumstances, Dr. Luther Halsey Gulick, Jr., the International YMCA Training School's dean of physical education, offered the wayfaring soul a hot meal and temporary housing until he could get back on his feet.

I skipped down to the part that described the physical education challenges Dr. Gulick was facing as the weather in Springfield worsened.

THIS WAS ALWAYS ABOUT BASKETBALL

The cold winter had forced the training school's young students indoors for their exercise. Football had proven to be too rough, and the students soon became bored with calisthenics and gymnastics.

Weeks earlier, Dr. Gulick assertedly challenged his faculty members to invent a new winter game that could maintain student interest while reducing the risk of injury normally associated with football, rugby, soccer, and lacrosse.

Decker, after finishing his meal, reportedly barged his way into Dr. Gulick's office unannounced to tell the dean of his invention, a new game that needed only a soccer ball and two half-bushel peach baskets hung at opposite ends of the YMCA gymnasium's railing.

The game was an instant international sensation. The savvy Decker, his life's path now restored and set on its proper course by the mysterious, bespectacled faculty member, sought to profit from his invention by naming his new game Deckerball. He went on to secure all legal rights in perpetuity and later founded Decker Enterprises, the monolithic global empire that oversees the game worldwide to this day.

I slammed the book shut. I had been under the impression that Lawrence and I saved basketball from permanent extinction when we were attending McDerney Continuation together.

Had the 7th Dimension reversed its decision because of something I had said or done, then elected to chastise me by traveling back in time to the 1890s and using one of Lawrence's

No. 2 pencils to sign an exclusive licensing deal with Decker Enterprises? And what of Dr. Naismith's legacy, his life's work and desire to never profit from the game because he wanted it to be owned not by any one person but by *the world?*

I flipped back to the index again in search of Dr. Naismith's name or any mention of his remarkable contribution to humankind.

MONOPOLY
NORDIC SKIING
OLD MAID

Nothing there. It was as if Dr. Naismith and his wonderful invention had never existed.

"Maybe the boy wonder can tap back into the 7th Dimension's communications network to ask where basketball has dribbled off to," I muttered under my breath, hoping those words wouldn't seem nearly as absurd if I were hearing them through my own ears.

Lawrence had to know what was going on, I thought. I needed to hurry back to Biffmann Self-Storage to confront him without hampering his progress as he reassembled my truck.

I must have sprung up from my chair too quickly. I felt dizzy and lightheaded. The building started to spin. I slid off my chair and conked my head on the library's unforgiving linoleum floor.

Then everything went black.

12

We Need to *Talk*

Someone must have switched off the lights because all I could see was murky blackness. I blinked and fluttered my eyelids. The light filtered back in. I was flat on my back on the floor. I must have passed out.

I stared at the meaty hand reaching down to help me up. I didn't remember there being a defensive lineman reading at a nearby table. I grabbed hold with both my hands, and someone pulled me to my feet.

"I'm sure there must be more comfortable places to take a nap than the floor of the library, Ezekiel." It was Mrs. Vanderhorst. She had a more powerful grip than I had imagined.

"Thank you, ma'am. I haven't eaten since breakfast. Guess my blood sugar must be a bit low. I felt a little woozy."

I dusted myself off, put the book back on the shelf, and tore out of there. I arrived back at Biffmann Self-Storage and walked my bike through the office entrance. Chett Biffmann was fast asleep at his desk, feet up, snoring as loudly as a lumberjack chain-sawing a redwood. I wondered whether Mrs. Vanderhorst would have approved of how quietly I scooted out the side door on my way to space 1046.

The roll-up door's handle wouldn't budge. I banged on the corrugated steel with my fist.

"Lawrence, it's me. Open up." No response. "C'mon, Lawrence. I need some answers. Open the dang door."

I heard shuffling coming from inside the storage unit. Then a folded-up piece of paper materialized on the ground below. I opened it.

What's the password?

"The password is: if you don't open this door right now, I'm going to ask Brock to buy up all the Bazooka bubblegum in the country, wholesale, every last piece of it, Bazooka Joe comics too, and I'll ask him to hire me as Decker Enterprises bubblegum distribution supervisor and put me in charge of rationing bubblegum to customers, and I won't be in a good mood, ever, so I'm going to take my time doling it out, especially to future astronauts-in-training who don't unlock doors *to their friends' own rented storage spaces when someone asks them to!* How's that? Did I get it right?"

A follow-up note soon followed.

Close enough.

I heard what seemed like a metal latch scraping across the concrete floor inside. That was followed by what sounded like one of the Chevy's doors slamming.

I threw open the roll-up door. The light bulb was off, but enough sunlight had flooded into the room for me to see that my truck—the last remaining evidence of a big brother who had lost his life on a desert battlefield on the other side of the world—was no closer to being put back together than when I had left.

I had been gone for several precious hours, but it looked like Lawrence hadn't lifted a finger.

I walked over to the driver side door. Lawrence was behind the wheel, gazing through the windshield at the darkened space in front of him.

"You didn't get as much done as I thought you would."

Lawrence responded by hand-cranking the window closed. It was clear the process of getting the pencil warlock to open up might take longer than expected. I noticed a goofy-looking contraption made of pencils stuck to the inside of the windshield.

"What's that?" I said as I flipped on the light and secured the roll-up door and latch behind me.

Lawrence responded by scribbling out a fresh note. Then he cracked the window a fraction and tossed the slip of paper through it. He shut the window as I caught the note in mid-flight and opened it.

I can't hear you because my window is closed.

Then he locked his door.

I still needed to meet up with Curtis and Stretch for pizza and then pack up my stuff at the apartment. "We don't have time for this, Lawrence. Lots of weird things are happening out here, and all fingers are pointing to you." Technically, it was only Brock's finger, plus maybe one of Chett Biffmann's chubby digits, but I felt as though I had made my point.

I walked around the truck cab to the passenger side, flopped onto the Chevy's bench seat, and slammed the door. Then, in a gesture of solidarity and brotherhood, I rolled up my window.

"It's just you and me now, buddy," I said as I stared straight ahead through the windshield, just like Lawrence. "No more notes. We need to *talk*."

13

I Had Come Too Far
to Turn Back

"Let's start with an easy one," I said. "Would you mind telling me what *that* is?"

I motioned to the doohickey affixed to the inside of the windshield. I reached out to examine it more carefully, but Lawrence smacked my hand away.

"Don't touch that!"

I was relieved to hear Lawrence's voice, even if there was panic in it. It meant we had a better chance to move the conversation along at a brisker pace. "Sorry, friend. I guess my curiosity got the better of me."

I took a closer look at the object. I couldn't believe I had missed it earlier. It was clearly Lawrence's heptagonal gadget taken to the next level. As usual, Lawrence had assembled it

from seven interconnected and precisely measured and beveled No. 2 pencils. But this device was different. In addition
to the familiar seven pencils making up the heptagon's exterior, there were another seven arrayed in the center like the
spokes of a bicycle wheel.

Lawrence once claimed to have created the original device
using the principles of what he called neusis construction.
Beyond that, I knew its presence meant the 7th Dimension
was in the mix because that antenna thingamabob stuck onto
the windshield was how Lawrence said he intercepted Entity
communiqués.

Wait. There was something else unusual about this version
of the Entity antenna. The original relied on a set of notches
that enabled the pencils to be snapped into place like Lincoln
Logs. The apparatus I was staring at had a familiar pink,
putty-like substance at the joints.

"What's *that* stuff?" As if I didn't know.

"Bubblegum."

"You're using already-chewed bubblegum to glue the pencils together?"

"Something wrong with that?" I hadn't anticipated Lawrence's strategic tactic of answering my question with one of
his own.

"Aside from not being very sanitary, I think it's fine." I
didn't know where our conversation was headed, but I doubted
it would intersect with Deckerball anytime soon.

My eyes had adjusted enough to the dim lighting in the
storage unit to notice another odd feature in the truck cab.

The steering wheel was wrapped in what appeared to be the outer surface of a basketball.

I inched my hand toward the wheel, remaining vigilant as to whether Lawrence would knock my hand away—or worse. Lawrence sat there like a statue.

I gripped onto the steering wheel and ran my fingers over the orange, pebbly surface of its cover. It seemed as though someone had cut apart a well-worn basketball and recrafted it as a steering wheel cover.

"Nice, isn't it? Made it myself." Lawrence was proud of his handiwork.

"Where'd you get the ball for that?"

It was a legitimate question. Lawrence's main interest in the game to that point had been in statistical analysis and mathematical probabilities. His demeanor abruptly shifted with the question. He scratched out a note, folded it in half, and set it on the dashboard.

Brock borrowed it from the rec center. He said he would replace it later.

"He *borrowed* it?"

Another note soon followed.

I took him at his word. That's what friends do.

There was a great deal of information in the note that needed to be unpacked and verified. Brock buying a new basketball earlier in the day at Chip's seemed to validate the cement head's keeping his promise to Lawrence. But Lawrence referring to Brock as his friend was a generous and likely misguided assessment of reality. In my experience, Brock was friends mostly with himself. And now, with a giant pile of cash.

The longer we sat there, the less sense anything made. Every time Lawrence offered up new details, it only led to more questions that had vague answers stuck to them like gum on the bottom of my high-tops.

"Got any more Bazooka?" I asked. Injecting the subject of bubblegum into our time together often served to ease the tension and focus the conversation.

Lawrence got out of the cab and retrieved his aluminum lunchbox. He set it onto the truck's floorboard, sat back down, and slammed the door. Then he snapped open the security latches, pulled out a fresh bag of bubblegum, and tore off the top with his teeth.

"Take two, they're small."

I peeled off the waxy wrapping and popped the gum into my mouth. Lawrence took a pair for himself. That leveled the playing field. We chewed. Time passed. Tensions eased.

Then I made another run at him.

"There were probably better options for fastening those pencils together—wood glue, epoxy, rubber cement, and pine resin all come to mind. Why'd you use bubblegum?"

"For the DNA," he said, wringing his hands.

"For the *what*?"

Lawrence's breathing became deeper and more deliberate. Inhale. Exhale. Repeat. He seemed to be preparing for something. Several moments passed before he spoke again.

"It's time to get this show on the road," Lawrence said. *Finally.* "We'd better strap in." His tone turned serious.

Even though we were sitting in a steel-and-glass box that had no wheels or propulsion system, I thought it was best to comply. I knew it was important to keep Lawrence calm, and I wasn't interested in getting slapped again.

I picked up both ends of the passenger-side seatbelt straps and snapped the metal tongue into the buckle. Lawrence followed suit.

"Pay attention. I'm only going to say this once." Either Lawrence's confidence was on the rise or his patience was wearing thin. In either case, his warning came as welcome news because I had a feeling I wouldn't want to hear what he had to say a second time.

"I'm all ears, buddy."

"Most people know that DNA stands for deoxyribonucleic acid."

Oh, great. A review of high school biology. My favorite subject.

"DNA is the self-replicating chemical building block present in all living organisms and the main component of chromosomes. It contains the instructions organisms need to develop, survive, and reproduce. We scientists and mathematicians know it to be the carrier of genetic information."

I remembered all that, more or less, from biology class. But

I had no idea of how it could possibly relate to basketball's disappearance, Brock's newfound wealth, or my truck's dismemberment.

"So, you interconnected the pencils with your own ABC bubblegum in order to mix in your DNA?"

"Precisely."

I didn't want to ask, but I had come too far to turn back.

"Why?"

"Simple. The laws of Sacred Geometry."

14

Coincidence?
I Think Not,
My Friend

I wondered if I'd had a mild stroke, or was stranded inside a nightmare that had somehow become permanent, or had been suddenly and mysteriously catapulted into a parallel universe.

I covered my face with my hands and shook my head. "I don't know what Sacred Geometry is. You need to help me out here."

"I'll spell it out for you," he said.

Lawrence filled up another sheet of paper as I braced myself for the familiar deluge of words beyond my comprehension.

Let's go to the dictionary:
Sacred. Something worthy of or regarded
with reverence, awe, or respect.

Okay, no surprises there. I read the rest of Lawrence's note.

Geometry. Branch of mathematics dealing
with properties and relations of points, lines,
angles, surfaces, solids, and higher-
dimensional analogs. Mathematicians such
as the little-known but highly regarded
Sherman Tuckerman (that's me, in case
you've forgotten) study these concepts using
deductive logic in assuming certain properties
of space.

Even though Lawrence wasn't looking at me as I read, he seemed to know that, despite a couple semesters of high school geometry, I didn't really understand what he was driving at—especially with that "higher-dimensional analogs" part, which I definitely did *not* remember from the word problems about triangles and cones and stuff I had waded through in class. The only geometry that had ever mattered to me involved shots and passes on the court.

Lawrence wrote a follow-up note.

Geometry comes from the Greek words
gee, meaning "related to the Earth," and
metria, meaning "measuring." Together, they

literally translate to "the measuring of the Earth." Get it?

I wasn't sure whether either one of us had enough bubble-gum in the truck cab to make it through the rest of this conversation.

"I don't understand what any of it has to do with why you took my truck apart. Maybe I should take you home now on the back of my bike."

SMACK!

Lawrence had slapped me again. Hard. Too dark in there. Never saw it coming. The side of my face felt like it was running a whistle drill on the surface of the sun.

"WHAT'D YOU DO *THAT* FOR?"

"I'm not going home yet. We're not done here."

Correction. *I* was done here.

No truck. No basketball. No answers, at least not any I understood. I decided to cut my losses.

"Grab your gear, marine. We're bugging out."

Wade used to say that to me at the conclusion of basketball practice when he coached my park league team. It's an order to retreat in a hurry during a military action, but Lawrence wasn't having it. He didn't budge. I sensed a confrontation brewing.

"C'mon, it's getting late. Your dad is going to be pissed—he's probably already worried about you," I said as Lawrence pulled another sheet of paper from his pad. "That's your final note, bud. Better make it a good one because it needs to last us all the way home."

Lawrence jotted something down and handed me the note.

Sacred Geometry led me to the Flower of Life.

"The *what*?" We'd gone from chemical building blocks that self-replicate, to a reverent subsection of ancient math, to what, gardening? "Make it quick, Lawrence."

Lawrence started drafting another note, but after a few words, he crumpled up the piece of paper and rang it off the windshield.

"Did you see that?" he said.

"Yeah, it was hard to miss. If we were sitting in the Mc-Derney bleachers at a track meet watching the hundred-yard dash, it would've been called a false start."

"No, the way it bounced. The *angle*."

Here we go again. "Sorry, I didn't notice. What can you tell me about it?" I wasn't confident I'd understand what would follow.

"The '65 Chevy Fleetside shortbed pickup truck is the only motor vehicle ever manufactured that has a windshield angled at precisely 51.83 degrees at the center point. And each side of the Great Pyramid of Giza in Egypt rises to the top at an angle of—wait for it—51.83 degrees."

"And that's important why?"

"Because the two are interconnected through Sacred Geometry. Coincidence? I think not, my friend."

15

Tell Me What It All Means

At that point, I understood less of what Lawrence was talking about than when our conversation had started moments earlier. And my pickup truck, the center attraction in Lawrence's circus of madness, remained hopelessly in sections on the ground. I needed to put that Chevy on a highway bound for Kansas the next morning.

"Get out of the truck right now, or I'm going to call the Sacred Geometry police and ask them for the correct angle to yank you out that window."

Lawrence made his familiar talk-to-the-hand gesture before putting pencil to paper again.

Do you want to know more about the Flower of Life?

Not really, but I didn't think I could stop him unless I had a bag of zip ties and a roll of duct tape in my backpack, which I didn't.

"Sure, go ahead."

Lawrence must have sensed we had both reached the limits of my patience. He scribbled furiously.

The Flower of Life: Sacred Geometry's most basic shape, consisting of seven overlapping circles. That's right, seven. Does the seven remind you of anything?

Yeah, it reminded me that what was about to follow would be beyond my comprehension and wouldn't bring my truck any closer to being reunited with itself. Normal high school geometry I understood pretty well. Basketball geometry—the sweetest arcs and angles in the universe—I understood to the depths of my soul. But the idea that geometry could be a religion made no sense to me at all.

Those seven spheres, propelled on their journey by consciousness, build infinitely outward, forming a flower-like pattern that has been used in cultures around the world since the beginning of time.

The Flower of Life is thought to be the gateway to the divine, the universal geometry for all species of creation, connecting all that is present in the universe—from construction of the two trillion galaxies that are known to exist, to our solar system (including Pluto, which I contend is still a planet, not a dwarf planet, despite scientific evidence to the contrary), to the tiniest living things on Earth—especially DNA.

It means that you and I are built from the same blueprint. Brock too. Maybe even Chett Biffmann.

I saw Lawrence crack a rare smile when I paused after reading that last sentence. Lawrence had long held a fascination with the mathematically improbable number of consonants in Chett Biffmann's full name, so it was only a matter of time before he weaved the self-storage facility magnate into the conversation.

"I suppose this will all lead somewhere?" I said.

"It will, but I think we need to stop here. I don't think you can handle the truth."

Lawrence was actually speaking again, so I knew he had calmed down enough for his left hand to no longer pose a threat.

I analyzed the facts. First there was my Chevy, separated into sections, its steering wheel cloaked in a protective basketball-skin cover. Then there was the expanded version of Lawrence's 7th Dimension communication device, held together by DNA-fortified bubblegum and stuck onto the windshield using the principles of Sacred Geometry so that it would rest at the exact angle of the sides of the Greatest Pyramid of All

Time. Finally, there was the Flower of Life, a symbolic reference to Lawrence's imagination and the universal template that glued it all together in a maze of ancient patterns generated by—what else?—consciousness.

It was all one big word salad, nothing more than nonsensical gibberish, which, as far as I knew, was the highest level of gibberishness there was.

It was time to cry uncle.

"I give, Lawrence. Tell me what it all means."

Lawrence reached down to the floorboard to retrieve the note he'd ricocheted off the windshield. I unwrinkled it.

Time Travel

If it were possible for something to make no sense and perfect sense all at the same time, this was it. I was now forced to accept the fact that Lawrence and Brock must have somehow traveled to the past—and changed basketball history when they got there.

16

The Pieces to the Puzzle Were Starting to Come Together

The gap between basketball's abrupt disappearance and Brock's building a parking garage atop the rec center's court was a wide one. Lawrence seemed to know about all the weird stuff that had happened in between, but his hedgy explanation included complex mathematical theories that apparently involved time travel.

The Deckerball explanation in the sports history book at the library was a sizable clue, but I had a sense Lawrence was keeping crucial details from me, likely out of friendship, possibly for my own protection, and maybe out of guilt too.

Lawrence reached back inside his lunch case and extracted another folded-up note.

"I guess I should show you this one now," he said. "I wrote it to my dad, but I never gave it to him because I didn't want him to worry."

The words *to Dad from Lawrence* were written in pencil on the outside of the note. I opened it and read it silently.

> Dear Dad:
> It's me, Sherman—or as I like to refer
> to myself whenever I'm in the presence of
> both my friends: Lawrence.

I took the liberty of assuming Lawrence was referring to Nathan and me. I knew that Lawrence and Brock were not on the best of terms, and I wasn't aware of any other friends the pencil jockey had.

> I know you prefer to call me Sherman, but
> I wanted you to have the option, especially
> since what you're about to read may be
> upsetting to you, and I thought it would be
> best if you had the choice to think about me
> using whichever name helped you to be marginally
> less worried than you might otherwise be.

Lawrence, as usual, was leaving little to chance. I was hoping his lengthy self-introduction would soon give way to the actual reason why he had written his father the letter.

By the time you read this, I expect to have gone missing. I hope to return soon, but I have to admit, odds are I might not be coming back at all, and I don't have time to explain why.

I could feel cold beads of sweat forming on my upper lip. The pieces to the puzzle were starting to come together.

I won't be around to serve my punishment if I'm grounded for life for not coming home, so my inability to return will not have been in vain. (That's humor, Dad. Look it up in the dictionary.)

Lawrence had casually been developing a sense of humor in the time I had known him, but I didn't think Mr. Tuckerman would have appreciated his son's wit in that moment.

Last thing: Please tell Zeke I'm really sorry. I hope he'll still be my friend, especially if I make it back, which, as I said, is unlikely.
Sincerely yours,
Sherman "Lawrence" Tuckerman (a.k.a. your son)
Future Mars Astronaut-in-Training
Los Angeles, California

17

This Was *Always* About Basketball

I stared at Lawrence. I tried to think of something to say but came up blank. I ran possible scenarios through my head about what might actually be going on.

Maybe a clandestine quantum physics cult that needed a mission-to-Mars mathematics flight specialist with exceptional geography skills had threatened to kidnap him, but not before allowing him to write a vague but intriguing letter of explanation to his father, so as to throw the eventual search party off the scent, and then Lawrence had somehow escaped and headed over to Biffmann's.

Or maybe Lawrence had momentarily run out of ways to cope with a world that didn't understand his developmental disorder—or worse, one that understood why his social interactions were awkward but was indifferent and cast him aside anyway.

"I think I can fix everything." Lawrence was speaking again, but I took no comfort in those words. Every time he had ever set some scheme into motion that was connected to the 7th Dimension, danger lurked and shadowed us at every turn. Plus, Lawrence's plans had historically always involved a lot of me driving us somewhere, which was currently impossible.

I was down to my final two options: seek the truth or walk away altogether and deal the best I could with a world that had changed overnight, and not for the better.

I had traveled this path with Lawrence twice before. Both times, he had leveled with me, and he had never let me down. There had been ample risk, but we'd always managed to emerge unscathed.

I paused to consider my responsibility to get Lawrence home safely. I wondered whether pursuing the truth would jeopardize my ability to do that.

I turned to my friend and gave him my bottom line.

"Lawrence, what you have done to my truck and what you and Brock appear to have done to the history of basket-ball is as wrong as wrong can be. I have no idea how you can possibly fix this mess, but I need you to give me your *personal guarantee* that no harm will come to you if we attempt to undo whatever it was that you and Brock cooked up."

That must have increased the stress level in the truck cab because Lawrence reached for his pad again and slammed out another note.

I regret to inform you that I am unable to make said guarantee.

He repeated the process, drawing up a fresh note before sliding his No. 2 pencil back inside his pocket protector. When he peeled off the sheet of paper, the only thing behind it was the pad's cardboard backing. Lawrence had run out of paper, so after that note, he either had to talk to me or put a sock in it.

I can, however, give you my personal guarantee that I would be brokenhearted if anything unfortunate happened to YOU.

That gave me pause. *Brokenhearted* was not really a Lawrence-type word. Certainly dramatic, but not exactly what I was looking for.

It was clear we had slammed into the wall. It wasn't worth risking life or limb. I decided it was time to pull the plug.

I very much doubted that Lawrence could turn back the hands of time again. That meant asking Chett Biffmann for the name of a salvage company that could haul away the Chevy's chopped-up parts because the storage contract I had signed was going to expire at the end of the month. The bottom line was I wouldn't have enough money to extend the rental agreement after I bought a bus ticket to Kansas.

Abundant questions. Zero answers.

I stepped out of the cab, unlatched the roll-up door, and flung it open. It was late in the afternoon. The sun had dropped below the horizon, but enough light had penetrated the storage space to allow for one last mental inventory of the carnage that used to be my cool truck. Wade's truck.

That caused me to think about what my dad had said at the VA hospital, about how Wade was trying to tell him something, but he couldn't understand Wade's words because of the gunfire.

"C'mon, Lawrence. Maybe we can catch a ride home with Chett Biffmann." Lawrence didn't move a muscle. I was losing my patience. "Darn it, Lawrence, it's getting dark. Chett needs to lock the place up. Let's go."

I still had a ton of stuff to do, not the least of which was getting together with Curtis and Stretch for our farewell dinner.

I walked to the driver side of the cab and motioned for Lawrence to roll down the window. He turned the hand crank until the glass dropped down out of sight.

"Step out, please."

"I'm sorry," Lawrence said. "I should have asked for your permission."

"That would've been an excellent idea. Probably would have saved us both a lot of time and trouble."

"I really think I can fix everything. Please give me a chance."

By this point in our odd friendship, Lawrence and I had experienced a lifetime of peril together, and we had both lived to tell about it. I felt I should at least hear him out before taking him home. "Okay, start from the beginning, make it snappy, and don't leave anything out."

Lawrence took me back in time to the rec center a week earlier, when he had been wrapping up a research project for his summer internship at the Jet Propulsion Laboratory.

He said he was taking a breather the way most people do, by assembling his heptagonal antenna device to scan for random 7th Dimension interstellar communiqués. Lawrence said he knew that picking up anything would be a long shot because, months earlier, the 7th Dimension had altered its spectral broadcast subcarrier to keep him at arm's length. He said he hadn't been able to tap into the Entity's revised nonneutral linear half frequency ever since.

But in leveraging his JPL research findings, he had formulated a process for reestablishing the communication link by introducing a secondary heptagonal set of pencils into the design as an interior cluster.

Lawrence said that as soon as he snapped the final rung of the seven-pencil internal pattern into place, data downloaded into his head, just as it had before, and he recorded it onto his writing pad as fast as his nonslapping hand could move. He said he had taken it all down—DNA, Sacred Geometry, the Flower of Life, every word of it.

Lawrence said none of it made any sense at first, but soon after, he theorized that he must have stumbled onto the Entity's top-secret blueprint for time travel.

At the same time, Brock Decker was at the rec center annoying kids who were trying to study. Brock must have noticed the whirlwind of activity surrounding Lawrence as he peeled off more and more sheets of paper to document the evidence.

Lawrence said that Brock grabbed the pencil-and-gum gizmo and threatened to slather it with mustard, put it between two slices of egg bread, and take a huge bite out of it if Lawrence didn't tell him what he was using it for.

"And you believed him?"

"Wouldn't you?"

I let that go and probed deeper. "Then what happened?"

"I told Brock that my advances in quantum theory enabled me to reconcile and then overcome time travel paradoxes." Lawrence paused to pop a fresh piece of bubblegum into his mouth. "Then I told him I could build a time machine, but I'd have to take your truck apart to make it work."

"What did he say?"

"Nothing. He just started laughing. He went on for a long time. Mr. Shields finally came over and told him to stop because he was disturbing the other kids. After that, Brock said he had some research of his own to conduct, and he took off."

Lawrence explained that Brock returned to the rec center the next day to say he'd combed through the Decker family archives and was bragging about an old relative from five generations ago who was about to become famous.

That had to be connected to what I had read in the sports history book!

"I told Brock I was having second thoughts about dismantling your truck without asking you first, but he said you wouldn't mind because we'd be doing it in the interests of science."

Leave it to Brock Decker to have the world's best interests at heart.

"Then, he said if I didn't comply, he'd write a letter to NASA explaining why the first manned flight to Mars didn't need an onboard mathematics specialist after all."

I didn't want to ask again, but I felt duty-bound. "And you believed him?"

"I couldn't risk my future, so I decided to take Brock at his word."

Of all Lawrence's quirky traits, faith in his fellow man was his most endearing. It was also the one most likely to plunge him into hot water. I'd heard enough about the cement head to last me a lifetime, so I swung the conversation back to time travel.

My head was already swimming. I was looking for easy answers.

"How does it work?"

"First, you must understand the concept of time."

I understood it just fine. We were spending a whole bunch of it discussing Lawrence's fantasy about journeying to another realm.

Lawrence continued: "*The American Heritage Dictionary of the English Language* defines time as a nonspatial continuum in which events occur in apparently irreversible succession from the past through the present to the future."

So far, so good.

"Right now, you are in the present," he said. "When you remember the basketball championship you won at Jefferson, you're in the past. When you imagine starting as point guard at the University of Kansas, you're in the future. To go back and forth in your mind is to travel in time."

Most of that made sense, except for the back-and-forth part. "I think I'm with you so far, buddy."

"Consider time to be a measured portion of what we know to be eternity. For example, when you imagine your future at

KU, in a sense you are seeing what the present might look like when it had become the past."

With that, I exited the truck cab, shut the roll-up door, and flipped the latch. I thought the momentary break might give my mind a chance to unmelt itself, but it didn't help. And the clock was ticking.

I got back into the truck cab. "Where are you taking us?" I was only half serious, but Lawrence took it as his cue to expound his theories.

"Our first destination is the space-time continuum."

My head was throbbing the way it might if someone were dribbling a basketball inside it. "Don't bother wasting time to explain that. It's best you keep going."

"When I used my newly created dual-heptagon antenna to infiltrate the 7th Dimension's communications network, I learned that the Entity is at once the gatekeeper of time and the ruler of its traffic in both directions. That's when I discovered a traversable wormhole."

That nervous, untethered-from-reality feeling, the one I would get whenever Lawrence, in his logical, reasonable way, pulled the rug out from under all logic and reason, had crept back in.

Lawrence said the concept of a traversable wormhole was consistent with Albert Einstein's general theory of relativity. At that point, I knew our conversation would take longer and be more complicated than I had anticipated.

"Imagine a wormhole as a tunnel with two ends at separate points in the space-time continuum. I figured out how to travel through it in the truck cab using the principles of

Sacred Geometry and the Flower of Life. My breakthrough was in creating a dual-purpose wormhole generator that could also open the gates. I did it by harnessing an alternative form of matter that contains negative energy density."

I was totally lost. It felt like everyone on Earth was in on some celestial practical joke but me.

"Negative *what*?"

"Try to keep up, Zeke. Negative energy density is the chemical hairpin that picks the universal padlock. I created it by binding together the elements of Bazooka bubblegum with my own DNA. Then I used it to activate the double-heptagon antenna."

I scratched my head and tried to look less dimwitted than I felt. Lawrence unwrapped yet another piece of bubblegum before squeezing both hands onto the orange scraps of leather covering the steering wheel.

My world was like a basketball spinning on my fingertip—oftentimes whirling, other times wobbling, but always refusing to fall off its axis. The game was how I made sense of the world, especially in those times when I was completely in over my head, which seemed to happen more often the older I got. And especially when I was in the pencil wizard's orbit.

I was desperate to understand, well, anything Lawrence had just said.

I pointed toward the steering wheel. "What's the connection between basketball and time travel?"

"It's *you*, Zeke. Don't you see? *You're* the connection. This was *always* about basketball."

18

I Was Running Out of Time

BAM! BAM! BAM!
Something banging on the corrugated steel roll-up door jolted me back to reality. All that talk of dense negativity and timely traveling would have to wait.

"You boys in there?"

It was Chett Biffmann. That sound of rattling metal was likely caused by his fleshy fist.

"Yes, sir!" I shouted through the door. I looked at my watch. It was 6:45 p.m. "I'm in here with Larry Tuckerman. We're working on my truck."

Technically, that was true. There wasn't much work going on, but I reasoned that since my truck remained chopped up into pieces, the possibility existed that work might still take place—even if it consisted of heaving truck parts into a dumpster.

Chett was a stickler for the rules. "Biffmann Self-Storage rolls up the sidewalks at precisely seven p.m., and the missus don't much cotton to me being late for supper. You fellas best be outta there soon, or else."

"Or else *what?*" Lawrence had picked an inopportune time to come out of his shell.

"Well, son, that'll be between you and ol' Gus."

Gus was Chett Biffmann's ornery guard dog. That mutt had a reputation for taking a sizable chunk out of the butt of anyone who hopped the barbed-wire fence after closing. I had little interest in getting to know Gus on a personal level.

"Sorry, Mr. Biffmann. We're just wrapping everything up. We'll be out in a jiffy."

I heard the sound of wheels crunching over the asphalt and fading away. There wasn't much time. Understanding how I had landed at the intersection of basketball and time travel would have to wait. I needed to know exactly what stunt Brock had pulled.

"We've only got a few minutes. Why don't you fill me in on your adventure with Mr. Decker."

"I can't."

"C'mon, Lawrence, I'm not going to get mad. Just tell me."

"Mr. Biffmann reminded me that I'm late for my training dinner."

Lawrence was obsessive about eating freeze-dried chili mac 'n' beef at predetermined times. If he were later rejected from NASA's mission to Mars program, it wouldn't be because he couldn't keep to a regular meal regimen.

Lawrence flipped open his traveling metal lunch case, extracted a foil-wrapped brick pouch, and mixed its contents together with steaming water from his thermos while I wondered whether Chett Biffmann would enforce the ultimate tardy lockout.

"Want some?"

"I'm not very hungry. I'll pass."

"Suit yourself."

I was running out of time. "Do you think you can eat that stuff while you tell me what happened with Brock?"

Lawrence said he could, as long as he spaced out his words evenly between spoonfuls. Then he swallowed and said Brock had driven him to Biffmann Self-Storage and helped him take apart the truck.

Once they had finished dismantling the Chevy, Lawrence said Brock handed him two pieces of paper. The first one contained the precise latitudinal and longitudinal coordinates of an abandoned building in Concord, Massachusetts, seven blocks from the Massachusetts Reformatory. I recognized that institution from the sports history book as the same state prison from which Phineas Bartholomew Decker was released after he was granted parole.

The second slip of paper had the specific date to which Brock wanted to travel back in time: December 20, 1891. Anyone who followed basketball knew that date to be exactly one day prior to James Naismith's invention of the game.

Lawrence said Brock had asked him for assurances that his makeshift time machine might actually work. Lawrence said he'd explained to Brock that it would, because he'd done the math. He'd even gone as far as to convince Brock that while the space-time continuum was an unchanging four-dimensional block, he'd developed a way to bend the self-consistency principle so that their journey into the past would be minimally disruptive.

I would have expected no less from my brainiac pal. Everything was coming together in a way that made my stomach bubble.

I was convinced that Lawrence and Brock had somehow gone back in time to enable Brock's distant relative, the notorious grifter Phineas Bartholomew Decker, to stake an ill-gotten claim to the invention of basketball.

That meant Dr. Naismith's legacy had been erased from the history books—and from the world—for all time.

19

Might as Well Go for Broke

Lawrence was finishing up the last of his space meal when we heard the approaching sound of wheels gliding over asphalt, followed by more banging against the roll-up door.

Bam, bam! BAM!

I pressed my finger to my lips. "*S-s-s-s-s-s-sh.*" Lawrence froze in place. We waited for what would happen next.

"Durn kids. Where are their manners? Must have snuck out without saying goodbye when I went to go see a man about a horse."

Then we heard a click.

"*Uh-oh,*" Lawrence whispered after sizing up our predicament.

"Those boys left in such a hurry, they forgot to secure the premises. That temp padlock and ol' Gus will just have to keep that Chevy secure till morning."

The sound of wheels rolling away was replaced by the feeling of my chest muscles tightening.

We were locked in—me, the kid with the pencils, and a glass-enclosed steel box manufactured according to the exact same angular specifications as the oldest of the Seven Wonders of the Ancient World.

Just another summer night in the City of Angels. But in that moment, I felt as though I were living in the City of *Angles*.

"I'm probably going to regret asking, but how does your DNA fit into all this?"

With that, Lawrence carefully pulled the dual-heptagon antenna off the windshield. Sizing it up with a wary eye, he removed a wad of bubblegum from inside his cheek and ground the shiny pink clump into one of the device's joints.

"I needed to reinforce the seventh notch point," he said. "Those two pencils must have separated during reentry."

"Reentry from *what*?"

Lawrence didn't answer the question, so I asked my DNA-source pal again to keep things moving.

"It's complicated," he said.

"Try me."

Lawrence said he'd learned that the 7th Dimension existed within the structure of Sacred Geometry by using the universal codes of the Flower of Life. He explained that the first time he intercepted and decoded Entity communiqués, the 7th Dimension had identified him by sequencing his unique DNA.

"After the 7th Dimension judged my actions to be pure and ethical, it designated me as an Earth Affiliate. That is what enables me to perform certain tasks normally considered to be outside of Earth's commonly accepted four-dimensional space-time constraints."

I nodded to indicate I'd understood everything he said, which I hadn't. Then I took stock of the looming disaster I had walked us into.

We were stranded inside the storage unit until daybreak. Our only sustenance would be bubblegum and space rations. Mr. Tuckerman would no doubt be worried out of his skull. My truck was still in pieces, and I doubted whether it could ever be resurrected. I was supposed to drive myself to KU the next morning. Playing full-court hoops was no longer an option at the rec center.

Topping it all off, my nerdy, well-meaning friend had become Brock Decker's unwitting accomplice in the destruction of Dr. James Naismith's basketball legacy.

There was nothing left to do but call Lawrence's bluff.

"You need to make this right," I said. "Let's go."

"Go where? We're locked in till morning."

"Let's take this thing on the cosmic open road."

"Where to?"

"What the heck. Might as well go for broke. Take us somewhere safe near the International YMCA Training School, northeast corner of State and Sherman streets in Springfield, Massachusetts."

"What date?"

"December 21, 1891."

20

I Felt Less Stupid, But Not by Much

Lawrence reached into his lunch case for the Bazooka bag and plunked three pink blocks of sweet joy into his mouth. I waited while he worked that gum into the proper consistency for a reality-bending road trip.

"Whamp whum?"

"Sure, buddy."

"Goob. Yah gomma neebit." I wasn't sure if Lawrence was giving me friendly but garbled advice, or warning me of imminent danger. Or both. He plucked two pieces of gum from his precious stash and handed them over.

I popped the gum into my mouth, adding to the chewed-out chunk I had been absentmindedly grinding for what already felt like hours.

Lawrence put away his dinner tools and fastened the metal box's lid. "It's going to be a bumpy ride," he said. "We need to secure the cabin. Strap yourself in. Lock your door."

Lawrence reached forward to adjust the rearview mirror. I had no idea what he would be looking for back there, but I chose not to question his preparations. My friend appeared ready to accept his fate. I was worried about mine.

"I need to dial in the coordinates," Lawrence said as he gripped the basketball-encrusted steering wheel and spun it seven times to the left. Once he had it in the exact position he was seeking, he rotated the helm seven full orbits in the opposite direction.

There was scant light in the storage unit and no air circulating in the truck cab. My hands were sweaty and shaking.

"I need you to give me a countdown from ten," Lawrence ordered.

"Why?"

"Just do it." Lawrence seemed agitated. I thought it was best to comply.

"Ten. Nine. Eight. Seven. Six." I felt stupid. "Five. Four. Three. Two. One. Liftoff!" Stupider.

Nothing.

"What happened?" I asked.

"Not much."

"Why not?"

"I didn't turn on the time machine yet."

"How come?"

"I was waiting for you to finish counting."

Good grief. "So the counting wasn't really doing anything?"

"Right."

"Then why did you ask me for a countdown?"

"I wanted to see if you'd actually do it."

"REALLY?" I wondered if I sounded angry when I said that. I felt my pulse rate increasing with each steamy breath.

"It's humor, Zeke. Look it up in the dictionary."

"We don't have time for this, Lawrence."

Lawrence fiddled with his pocket protector, possibly to make sure all seven pencils were secured and accounted for.

"I asked Brock to count down from ten too."

"Did he do it?"

"Nope."

"Did he say why?"

"Nope. But he *did* say he'd slug me in the arm really hard if I asked him a second time."

We were back to square one. It was the square I had become most familiar with whenever Lawrence was practicing his craft.

The boy wonder was locked into position on the Chevy's bench seat. He was staring straight ahead and not moving a muscle. I waited for him to, I don't know, send the truck cab hurtling back in time, or something.

"What's going on, Lawrence?"

"*Hello?* It should be obvious to you why I asked for a countdown. I'm in training." The faint light from the room's lone incandescent bulb reflected off the tears streaming down Lawrence's cheeks. He wiped them with his sleeve. "NASA intends to utilize a countdown when it launches the first-ever spacecraft to Mars, just as it has for all previous space flights. I plan to be on that spacecraft as the mathematics flight specialist. I need to be ready."

I had almost never seen Lawrence cry before. I didn't know what to say. It seemed like the pressure was getting to him. I attempted to calm him down.

"My bad. No excuses. I should have known that." I thought it was best to take personal responsibility. That always worked out well on the basketball court whenever I flubbed up and let my teammates down.

"It's all right," he said. "I know you're doing the best you can."

It was cool of Lawrence to let me off the hook like that. I seized the momentum and tried to get the issue of time travel back on track. "Let's give it another go. I'll do the countdown again."

Lawrence fidgeted with the knobs and controls in the truck cab. I didn't know if he was doing that for my benefit, or was actually dialing us in for the trip to another realm.

"Ten. Nine. Eight. Seven. Six." I felt less stupid, but not by much. "Five. Four. Three. Two. One. *Liftoff!*"

Lawrence released the parking brake and pressed down on the clutch pedal until it hit the floorboard. Then he clicked the steering column's three-on-the-tree gearshift into first gear before simultaneously easing up on the clutch with one foot and pressing down on the accelerator pedal with the other. It was a fluid knee, elbow, wrist workflow—the universal language of basketball—just as Wade had taught me, and just as

Lawrence had used to operate the aging Chevy during our otherworldly road trip to Kansas two years earlier.

Only this time we weren't headed for 7th Dimension headquarters within the intertwined root system of a grove of oak, sycamore, and pine trees living adjacent to Allen Fieldhouse on the campus of the University of Kansas. Our destination was the International YMCA Training School in Springfield, Massachusetts, otherwise known as the birthplace of basketball.

I sat nervously and waited. And waited.

For nothing.

"What happened?"

Lawrence ignored me, choosing instead to blow a gargantuan bubble that ultimately gave way to the laws of physics, shattering the silence in a deafening pressure wave that discharged sticky bits of bubblegum onto the windshield.

"That's gonna leave a mark, bro," said Lawrence, channeling his inner Curtis Short, or at least the Curtis Short I knew before a gigantic wave had stolen away his confidence. "Better check the tool kit for a putty knife."

"Lawrence, I don't think your time machine works. What happened?"

"Dead battery."

21

A Pilgrimage Backward in Time via a Cosmic Tunnel

Lawrence collected bubblegum shrapnel from the windshield while I gazed across the storage unit at the metal chassis that the truck cab had once been bolted onto.

I understood little about the inner workings of an internal combustion engine or how a motor vehicle's hundreds of parts all worked in synchronous harmony to convert fuel into motion. But I was intelligent enough to know that the Chevy's battery was no longer connected to the truck cab because that battery was bolted to the inside of the engine compartment next to the engine block—and all of that was sitting atop the chassis at the other end of the room.

"Dead battery?"

"Yep," Lawrence said. "Dead as a doornail."

"I don't understand. Isn't the battery over there?"

Lawrence shook his head in disapproval. "You need to get some battery knowledge. You need to go to battery college."

With that, Lawrence plucked his dual-heptagon antenna device from the windshield and removed the center hub's bubblegum plug, revealing a 9-volt battery nestled inside. He detached it from the snap connector and brought the battery's two terminals to the tip of his tongue.

"Unfortunately," Lawrence said, "I must report that this battery has been fully discharged. It is dead to us. Get it?"

I nodded in agreement, even though none of it made any sense. By then, my sanity was hanging on by its fingernails. "So what you're saying is our ability to travel back in time hinges on whether or not that thing's 9-volt battery has a strong-enough charge?"

"That surprises you?"

"Yeah, I guess." It all seemed so random. Reality was hand-cranking down the window and floating out the truck cab.

"Did you know that the 9-volt battery was invented in 1956?"

"Are you stalling?" The time had come to give Lawrence some tough love. "Look, if this fantasy time-travel thing of yours isn't going to work, maybe it's best we concentrate on how to get out of here without landing in ol' Gus's crosshairs."

Lawrence unbuckled his seatbelt. I took that to mean he was waving the white flag. With the storage unit locked from the outside, the only way out would be to somehow cut through the corrugated steel roll-up door.

Boy, was Chett Biffmann going to be pissed.

But instead of reaching for the truck cab's door handle, Lawrence snapped open the lid to his utility lunchbox and rummaged underneath his reserve brick pouches of freeze-dried chili mac 'n' beef. He emerged with a replacement 9-volt battery.

"Found it. Last one." He touched the battery to the tip of his tongue. "YOWCH!"

"Lawrence, I think we should call it a day and look for a way to get out of here."

"Nuh-uh. We're back in business."

I was beginning to miss the process of Lawrence committing his thoughts to paper, which gave us both more time to think things through. Now everything was happening so fast.

Lawrence rebuckled his seatbelt and repositioned the rearview mirror. I finally had to ask.

"Why are you adjusting that?"

"Duh. We're traveling *back* in time, right?"

"Wow, what was I thinking?"

I decided right then and there to let Lawrence's time-travel fantasy play out. The truth would come hard for one of us, and the other one would eventually go back to Chip's Sporting Goods to turn in his company property and collect his final paycheck before boarding a Greyhound bound for Kansas.

"I give, Lawrence. Let's just do this."

Lawrence snapped the fresh 9-volt battery onto the connector and used the original wad of bubblegum to hold it in place at the hub of the dual-heptagon antenna. Then he stuck the device back onto the windshield.

"Ready for preflight check," he said before readjusting all the dashboard controls. Then he did something he hadn't done before—he clicked the radio's power knob to the *on* position. "Initiate the countdown sequence!"

I decided to play along. "Ten. Nine. Eight. Seven. Six." I went from feeling less stupid to feeling sorry for Lawrence because we were running out of graceful ways to face the inevitable. "Five. Four. Three. Two. One. *Liftoff!* Fire the rockets, commander!"

Lawrence released the emergency brake and pushed down on the clutch. He slid the shifter into first, pulled back the clutch, and pressed down on the gas.

"Roger, going with throttle up."

Lawrence took hold of the steering wheel, his hands in the ten-and-two position, just as they'd taught us in driver education class at McDerney Continuation.

"SEE YOU IN HELL, COPPER!" Lawrence shrieked at the top of his lungs. "You'll never take us alive!"

Those were the exact words Lawrence had screamed while piloting the pickup to Allen Fieldhouse two years earlier. Back then, a Kansas Highway Patrol officer was in hot pursuit, red lights flashing, siren blaring. At the time, Lawrence had the Chevy doing 120 miles per hour as he struggled to keep it from veering off the highway and into the rocky ravine below.

I remember thinking we were going to die in a fiery mass of tangled metal—kind of like the feeling I was experiencing now, sitting in the truck cab as we were about to test the immutable laws of physics.

Then it happened.

First, a familiar leathery aroma drifted in through the air vents. It smelled like a brand-new basketball. I immediately felt the same sense of calm I always experienced standing at the free-throw line at the front end of a one-and-one. But then that beautiful alert calm downshifted into a weird drowsy feeling. My whole body felt fuzzy. All my senses were dulled.

Next, I felt the floor vibrating. Moderately at first. Then more intensely.

We were in Los Angeles, also known as earthquake country, so my first thought was that we were experiencing a mild temblor. Routine stuff. After all, the San Andreas Fault was only about thirty-five miles northeast of downtown Los Angeles.

But the vibration didn't fade away as normal earthquakes do. It grew in severity, sending the truck cab into a violent rocking motion.

And there was a loud humming noise, the kind you'd hear if you held a magnet next to an old AM tabletop radio.

"Hold on." There was no panic in Lawrence's voice. Just a simple command. The kid was the picture of calm. "I've pinpointed the wormhole."

Lawrence shifted into second gear. My chest muscles contracted so tightly, I was unable to speak. My knuckles turned pasty white from my hands squeezing onto the lip of the bench seat.

I had no way of knowing whether traveling back in time would allow us to fix what Brock and his distant relative had set into motion.

The rocking and humming gradually subsided. When they did, the interior of the storage unit abruptly illuminated, the light so bright it nearly blinded me. Then the room went pitch-black. Then bright white again. Back to black. Light, dark, light, dark—faster and faster, until the two states merged into an oscillating gray.

"No matter what happens, thanks for being my friend," Lawrence said as he threw the truck into third gear.

I felt my larynx lock up, so I acknowledged what Lawrence had said with a thumbs up.

Lawrence's hands remained glued to the steering wheel. Keen sense of purpose. Unflappable. Supreme focus.

Mars-astronaut-level focus.

My brain seemed to have produced this admiring realization all on its own. I understood that I had never taken Lawrence's dearest ambition seriously. I had underestimated my friend, and felt guilty about it—not for the first time.

There we were, unlikely friends encased together in a pulsating, metal-and-glass eternity box on a pilgrimage backward in time via a cosmic tunnel that, for all I knew, looped through the far-flung reaches of the universe to get to Springfield, Massachusetts.

Rocketing to Mars had to be easier than this.

22

That's Gonna Leave a Mark, Bro

My stomach lining delivered the news to my brain that the truck cab had somehow risen off the ground.

It hovered there for a heartbeat before launching us at tremendous speed to lord knows where.

The immense G-force pressure squeezed my body against itself and back against the seat as we accelerated. It must have been what it was like to be strapped inside the crew cabin of the Space Shuttle orbiter when the solid rocket boosters ignited at Kennedy Space Center.

Fear took over. I panicked. "Lawrence, make it stop!"

"We *can't* turn back."

In the time I'd known Lawrence, he'd never waffled on anything. Now seemed like a good moment for him to change his mind, maybe for the first time ever.

I didn't mince words with my reply. "We *can't* turn back—or you *won't*?"

Lawrence countered my accusation without warning. In one sweeping motion, he released his left hand from the steering wheel and cracked me across the face. I was too stunned to speak. Lawrence wasn't.

"I got us into this mess," he said. "If we turn back now, I can't get us out of it."

The side of my face was sizzling. Sweat poured down my head. My leg muscles tightened, the way they would on a basketball court whenever our team lost the ball and I needed to reverse thrusters on defense to thwart an enemy fast break. Only this time, I had nowhere to run because I was trapped inside a vessel powered by a supernatural force I couldn't comprehend, heading into a cosmic structure not of this Earth.

"So what you're saying is you could stop this thing if you wanted to?"

"I need to fix this mess. It's what friends do."

Lawrence had only two friends. The other was Nathan, my often-enraged chess-master boss at Chip's.

In my short time on this planet, I'd learned that when something you cherish is in short supply, the risk of losing it makes it inherently more valuable.

I figured Lawrence had the ability to abort the mission, but my faith in his deep connection to the 7th Dimension was stronger than my instinct to play it safe and run for higher ground. I needed to ride it out, if not for the legacy of James Naismith, then for my friendship with the math nerd.

I realized that the flickering light must represent days and nights passing at hyper speed—in reverse order, I assumed, since we were supposed to be traveling *back* in time. The oscillating light and dark soon blended into a shimmering gray that bathed the truck cab's interior, flicker-free. It also illuminated what appeared to be the inner walls of a tunnel outside the truck cab. We seemed to be blasting our way through a narrow, winding tube.

"How much longer till we get there?"

Lawrence didn't answer, instead holding up a hand to silence me. He cocked his head to one side as if to sharpen his senses.

"What is it?" I asked.

"Did you feel that?"

"Feel what?" All at once, my intestines lurched into my throat as our craft nosed forward into what I knew must be a hypersonic death plunge.

"That."

Lawrence mashed the clutch to the floorboard and downshifted into second gear, but the maneuver had little effect on our rate of descent. He gripped the wheel with white knuckles and tried to guide us out of the dive but was unsuccessful.

"Uh-oh."

"What does that mean?" I said.

"Here, take the wheel."

"What?"

"Just do it. Don't make me smack you again."

I unbuckled my seatbelt, leaned across, and grabbed hold of the steering wheel. The familiar feel of basketball leather offered temporary relief from the dread of impending doom. As soon I had gripped on, Lawrence let go. When he did, the truck cab went into a barrel roll, my head banging off the thin headliner and steel roof above it.

"That's gonna leave a mark, bro," Lawrence said once again as he wrestled the dual-heptagon antenna from the windshield. He held the device to his ear and shook it. Then he extracted a wad of bubblegum from his mouth and jammed it onto the device where a pencil joint appeared to have shaken loose.

He stuck the pencil antenna back onto the windshield. The truck cab pulled out of its dive and stabilized.

Then a flash of light transformed all six of the cab's windows into a wraparound grid of flashing numbers, letters, intersecting lines, and math symbols. It appeared to be some sort of aeronautical navigation chart.

"I need to make a course correction," Lawrence said as he tinkered with the dashboard's knobs and controls until he seemed satisfied with his adjustments.

Lawrence took back the wheel. "Cover me, I'm going in."

He shifted the Chevy back into third gear. That made the truck cab feel like it was floating back down to Earth. I had no idea whether any of this was real, but I had a feeling I would soon find out.

"How much longer?" I needed it to stop.

"Buckle up, bucko."

I fastened my seatbelt and cinched it tight.

Sherman Tuckerman was *in the zone.*

He downshifted back into second gear. When he did, the navigational grid faded from view and was replaced by the now-familiar radiant gray light. Then he pounded down on the clutch and threw the truck into first. That steadily slowed the pulse of the flashing light until it was clear that the outside world was alternating between broad daylight and dead of night.

At least I had got that right.

Lawrence made final adjustments to the knobs and controls. The narrow tunnel spit us back onto the ground. The Chevy thumped and skidded before coming to a stop. When it did, I noticed that the staticky hum and leathery aroma were gone.

We were surrounded by blackness and silence.

We were alive.

23

I'll Stay Here and Guard Our Stuff

It was so dark, I couldn't see my hand in front of my face. "Where are we?"

"Abandoned warehouse," Lawrence said, "seven blocks from the International YMCA Training School, Winchester Square, corner of State and Sherman streets. Do you think they named that street after me?"

"A century before you were born? Very funny. No."

"Yeah, you're probably right. Anyway, we made it to Springfield, Massachusetts, just as you requested. It's December 21, 1891—daybreak, to be exact."

I heard Lawrence poking around inside his metal lunch crate. There was a *click!*—and we had light inside the truck cab. Lawrence had brought along a flashlight for the journey.

He returned to his food storage suitcase and fished out a pocket compass.

That oversized lunchbox of his had more going on inside it than I'd realized.

Lawrence studied the compass. "I stuck the landing. You need to walk that way," he said, pointing dead center toward the windshield. Then he got out and used the flashlight to inspect the exterior of the truck cab's metal hull.

"What are you doing?"

"Surveying for reentry damage."

That shot a ripple of fear across the lining of my breadbasket. "How's it look?"

"A little scraped up, but otherwise shipshape."

That was a relief, one less thing to worry about on a list of a gazillion details that could possibly go wrong. I turned my focus to the task at hand and soon realized I had no plan beyond showing up unannounced at the training school's main entrance.

"What do I need to know?"

"Why are you asking me?" Lawrence said as he rocked side to side, arms flapping. "You're the basketball expert."

Maybe, but I knew there had to be more to it than that. If I were going to single-handedly correct the course of basketball history, I needed to know what I'd be up against once I stepped outside the warehouse.

"C'mon, Lawrence."

"How about this? People will instantly become suspicious when they see what you're wearing."

I hadn't considered that. I had on a pair of black Converse high-tops, khaki pants, and a Chip's Sporting Goods short-sleeved polo shirt with my name tag pinned to the pocket. I needed to find a change of clothes, and fast.

"I'd leave on the name tag," Lawrence said. "The YMCA could probably use an experienced part-time sales clerk."

"That's less than helpful."

Lawrence focused on the balance of relevant details.

"According to my calculations, we need to fire up the Chevy to return home within seven hours and seven minutes of our arrival here. After that, the wormhole will terminate, and our next window of opportunity to travel through it won't come around for another seventy-seven years."

It would've been nice to know that minor detail before I let Lawrence talk me into fixing everything. The prospect of not playing three-on-three with Curtis and Stretch again until I was in my late nineties was daunting. And I didn't even want to think about losing my chance to walk on at KU.

"That's a lot of sevens."

Lawrence shrugged off my observation. "The 7th Dimension has a certain way of doing things. I don't question it."

Lawrence said he had calculated our arrival to occur thirty minutes prior to what he estimated was Phineas Bartholomew Decker's mysterious appearance at the training school. That meant I had no time to waste in convincing James Naismith to take his idea for the new game to Dr. Gulick before Brock's convicted-criminal relative could get to him first.

I glanced at my wristwatch. It was 7:30 a.m. I did the math in my head and made a mental note of the 2:37 p.m. deadline for our wormhole return-trip throttle up, while also realizing that I needed to keep my twenty-first-century watch hidden from view.

"Anything else?"

"Yeah. I did the research," Lawrence said. "The temperature outside is below zero."

"How much below?"

"Better step on it."

I exited the truck and took stock of the task at hand. I felt a sudden longing to be back home in the kitchen, talking with my mom about her day at the hospital.

I offered my fist for the symbolic bump friends do at times like this. Lawrence stared at it.

"C'mon, bud, don't leave me hanging."

"Don't be late. And you have to be careful not to say or do anything that could alter the course of history—the 7th Dimension made that *very* clear. Your words and your actions will determine your fate—and the world's."

I wondered why Lawrence had waited so long to tell me that. "Gee, I'm glad you mentioned it."

"I'll stay here and guard our stuff. Maybe we can bump fists after you've successfully completed the mission."

There was no time to lose. Lawrence used the beam of his flashlight to lead the way to the warehouse door. I turned around and took one last look at Lawrence standing along-side what used to be my big brother's most prized possession. I wondered whether Wade had ever dreamed it would end up like this—carved up and then dispatched to another century.

I opened the warehouse door and stepped outside. Egad, it was cold. I closed the door behind me.

I was supposed to be packing my bags and saying farewell to family and friends before hitting the open road in my vintage pickup truck bound for the Midwest. How did I end up *here*?

I took a deep breath. My nose hairs froze.

24

Sitting at a Wooden Desk Was the Future Inventor of Basketball

The ground was covered in a blanket of snow that glistened beneath the rising sun as it parted the clouds. I understood at a primal level that if I didn't start moving right away, I would be frozen solid where I stood.

I also knew from the American history class I had taken at Jefferson that the first successful gasoline automobile was designed by bicycle mechanic brothers Charles and James Duryea, in of all places, Springfield, Massachusetts. But that wasn't until September 1893, nearly two years after the invention of basketball.

That meant there would be no cars on the road, just horse-driven carriages and folks riding funny-looking bicycles, some with huge front wheels—if a person could even ride those things in snow.

I scooted along the sidewalk past ancient-looking brick buildings in the direction Lawrence had pointed me. Many of the storefronts had awnings that were bulging downward from the weight of freshly fallen snow. Planters along the ground contained brown sticks that might have been colorful flowers just weeks earlier.

I was trying to keep a low profile in the hopes that no one would notice the strange visitor from another world who was wearing a polyester polo shirt fifty years before the invention of polyester.

I lost concentration for a brief moment when I stepped off the sidewalk to cross the street. My mind drifted to a happier time a couple of years before when I was sitting on a blanket close to Rebecca, our bare feet warmed by the Zuma Beach sand as we watched Curtis riding the nose of his longboard atop a cresting wave.

Just then, I was brought back to reality by the sound of heavy wheels slosh-skidding toward me across the ice. I looked up to find a pair of hooves descending on me as a horse pulling a delivery wagon neighed and whinnied.

I dove for safety and narrowly escaped being crushed by the massive animal.

"Watch where you're going, or cold coffee awaits you!" yelled the man on the wagon as he hauled back on the reins.

"Sorry, sir."

I got up and brushed the snow from my clothing. With my heart rate now tripled, I was a shivering human icicle by the time I arrived at a pair of road signs that confirmed I was standing at the intersection of State and Sherman streets.

The building on the northeast corner had a brass sign with the words ARMORY HILL YOUNG MEN'S CHRISTIAN ASSOCIATION mounted on the wall under an alcove to the right of the entrance.

I knew from a photograph I'd seen in the sports history book that the brick building was the hallowed ground on which basketball was invented. But more to the immediate point, it was the place where Deckerball would soon be conceived if I didn't work my way inside and try to intervene.

I turned the doorknob. It was unlocked. I slipped inside the building. The warm air felt thick and welcoming against my skin.

There was no one around. I spotted a coat stand in the corner of the foyer with numerous overcoats hooked onto it. I pulled one off and slipped it on. The heavy wool coat covered my polo shirt and khakis well enough, but my space-age high-tops remained in full view.

I saw several boots lined up against the wall. I searched for a pair that matched and might also be my size, and I slipped them on. The boots were waterlogged and my toes were cramped, but I thought it best not to press my luck.

I was careful to hide my high-tops from view behind a club chair in the lobby. I was hoping they'd still be there when it was time to return to the mothership.

The directory on the foyer wall said the building housed dormitory rooms, a parlor, classrooms, a reading room, a recitation room, an amusement room, a gymnasium, a locker room, and offices for faculty and staff.

The directory indicated that the faculty and staff offices were upstairs on the second floor.

I took a moment to get my bearings. If Curtis had accompanied me on that fateful adventure, he would have speed-shuffled straight to the gymnasium. Stretch would have hit up the parlor in search of snack items.

It reminded me that I had plans to get together with Curtis and Stretch for pizza that evening before taking off for KU the next morning—providing that Lawrence and I could make it back to Biffmann's in one piece.

If Lawrence were with me at the YMCA building, he would have selected the reading room. With Brock, the smart money would have been on the amusement room.

I set my sights on the faculty and staff offices, as that seemed the likely place to find James Naismith. I climbed the narrow granite-and-brick stairway to the second floor.

The hallway walls were lined with black-and-white photos of YMCA officials, past and present. I tiptoed past several rooms until I found a door with a sign on it that read PHYSICAL DEPARTMENT. Next to it on the wall were several placards. I scanned them and instantly recognized two names:

Dr. Luther Gulick—Dean of Physical Education
James Naismith—Faculty Member

I noticed that Naismith didn't have the Dr. designation in front of his name. I remembered from the sports history book—the version of the book *before* history had been altered—that Naismith didn't earn his medical degree until 1898, after he left Springfield to attend Gross Medical College in Denver.

The door was ajar. I heard voices inside. I moved closer to eavesdrop on the conversation.

"These two weeks have passed by rather quickly indeed, Jim, and the deadline is now hard upon us. How are you coming along with my challenge?"

That had to be Dr. Gulick's voice. Gulick had tasked Naismith with creating a new winter game that YMCA students could play indoors with minimal risk of injury. Gulick had mandated that the game be easy to learn and accessible to many.

"Luther, I have tried to modify our traditional out-of-doors games, beginning with football, but even when I implemented an altered form of tackling, it proved to be too perilous when practiced indoors, even for the most agile and stalwart of young men." That voice belonged to James Naismith, I just knew it. "The same held true in various ways for soccer, rugby, and lacrosse, I am afraid to say."

"None of that, sir, sounds encouraging."

"Oh, but there is reason for optimism. Just last night, I dreamt that roughhousing might be greatly reduced if we removed tackling and similar maneuvers from the equation entirely. And the way to accomplish that is to forbid participants from running while in any way carrying or kicking the ball along."

"This is all well and good," Dr. Gulick said, "but the greater danger in connection with athletic sports is not that the young men will get hurt. Rather, it is that in the excitement of the game and spurred on by their great desire for victory, the men, especially the incorrigible ones, might do things that are ungentlemanly and discourteous, and which they would be ashamed of in their calmer moments."

Hmmm. So safety was not the main point of Gulick's challenge after all.

"I will concede that point, Luther." I thought I detected a flash of frustration in Naismith's voice. "Consequently, my challenge is not only to devise a game with safety as a cornerstone, but to incorporate thoughtful governance in the form of rules that may ensure good order and discipline amongst all participants."

"Well, then, Jim, I will leave you to your work."

Witnessing that conversation was the most surreal moment I had ever experienced in my life. Which is saying something, because ever since I had gotten to know Lawrence, the surreality quotient in my life had risen relentlessly.

I heard footsteps approaching from inside the office. The door swung open, and out stepped Dr. Gulick. He was formally dressed in a neatly pressed, double-breasted herringbone suit with a pocket square, as a man in charge would be in 1891. I tried to look as innocent as the circumstances would allow.

"Good morning, young man. If you are looking for the gymnasium, it is downstairs in the basement."

"Thank you, sir."

With a sense of purpose, Dr. Gulick descended the staircase.

I peeked inside the office. There were stacks of files and papers everywhere and a potted plant in the corner that looked as though it was in desperate need of sunlight. A banner sporting the YMCA's insignia was tacked onto the wall beside an empty hatrack.

Sitting at a wooden desk was the future inventor of basketball—or at least he would be if I could get to him before Phineas Bartholomew Decker could commandeer Dr. Gulick.

Naismith was slumped down in his chair. He seemed dejected and disheartened. He had his elbows resting on his desk, head in hands. The sleeves of his white shirt were rolled up, his necktie loosened. His desk was littered with eight crumpled-up pieces of paper. Yes, I counted them. Had there been seven, I might have panicked.

This was my chance.

I stepped inside the office.

25

I Hadn't Called Bank, but Naismith Didn't Make an Issue of It

I startled Naismith when I cleared my throat to announce my presence.

"Young sir," he said with a mild degree of irritation as he adjusted his round spectacles, "the gymnasium is two floors beneath us, in the basement."

I fumbled for a response. "Yes, thank you, Mr. Naismith, sir. Dr. Gulick was just pointing that out to me."

"Then is there something else I can help you with?"

I had a gut feeling that Phineas Bartholomew Decker's arrival at the training school was imminent, at least based on the timetable Lawrence had outlined for me when we touched down, but I couldn't double-check it against my modern-day watch because I needed to keep it hidden from view.

My mind started spinning around like the wheels of a slot machine. Based on Naismith's conversation with Dr. Gulick, combined with what I had read in the sports history book about Naismith's thought process during the two-week incubation period of basketball's invention, I knew he was on the verge of his breakthrough.

When Naismith was a teenager, I had learned, he'd spent time with friends at Bennie's Corners, a small town near his birthplace of Almonte, in northern Ontario, Canada.

The boys created a game they called Duck on the Rock. The game coupled elements of tag with the skill needed to throw a small stone at a large rock with great accuracy. Naismith had said he enjoyed the game because it combined alertness, good timing, and dodging ability—all essential skills on a basketball court.

Naismith's new creation up to that point was nothing more than an advanced form of Keep Away. The crucial next step, creating an objective for the players, had him flummoxed.

"Young sir, did you hear what I said? Is there some other way I can assist you?"

Technically, what I was about to say was true, but just in case, I shifted my nonshooting hand behind my back and crossed my fingers.

"This is my first day here, sir. I stopped by to find out what time the cafeteria serves breakfast."

"Promptly at eight o'clock. The kitchen and dining room are located inside the chapel of Hope Church. It is the building adjacent to this one. I might add that the oatmeal is the superior choice."

That had bought me a little time, but I still had to find a way to accelerate Naismith's thought process about the new game without his knowledge and without altering the nature of its development. I was mindful of Lawrence's mandate to say or do nothing that would change the course of history, only correct it.

That led me to say something so off the wall, it seemed to stun Naismith where he sat.

"Sir, if you don't mind my saying so, I've heard it's bad luck to have *eight* soon-to-be-discarded pieces of paper on one's desk simultaneously."

Naismith's forehead wrinkled softly as he drew his eyebrows together. His angular jaw inched downward.

Before he could respond, I picked up one of those crumpled wads of paper and pivoted on one boot heel toward the wooden waste bin at the opposite corner of the office, fifteen feet away.

Then in what Wade would have acknowledged was perfect shooting form—knee, elbow, and wrist, all moving in alignment and harmony—I floated that paper ball spinning in a high arc toward the waste bin. It banked off the bin's lip at the rear, but the backspin I had applied caused the ersatz basketball to bounce backward before finding the center of its target, on top of a pile of similarly crumpled-up sheets of paper.

I hadn't called bank, but Naismith didn't make an issue of it.

"Seven. That's better," I said as I darted from the office and sped toward the stairway.

Before I hit the first step, I heard the faint sound of a finger snap, that kind of deliberate clicking noise that happens when the pad of your middle finger slaps down against the ball of your thumb.

"I've got it!"

What I heard in Naismith's voice was pure joy.

26

I Understand the Oatmeal Here Is Sensational

I arrived at the first floor and bowed my head as a wave of relief flashed over me. I was secure in the knowledge that the first phase of my covert basketball rescue mission was complete.

I had no idea what phase two would look like, but I took a brief moment to ponder the what-ifs. That's when I felt my legs wobble. Then there was this awful pressure squeezing my temples and forehead, like someone was turning the tommy bar of a C-clamp on the inside of my skull.

It was my body's way of reminding my brain that I hadn't eaten anything since breakfast at the apartment. And that seemed like more than a century ago. Although it actually wouldn't happen until more than a century *later*.

I stepped back outside and was jolted by what must have been a seventy-five-degree drop in temperature. If Hope Church was farther away than the length of a basketball court, I was doomed.

Luckily, I spotted the church right away on the other side of the street. I hustled inside and found a sign that pointed to the kitchen and dining room. I made my way there and tugged on the handle. The door was locked.

I looked at my watch. Great, 7:50 a.m. The dining room wouldn't open for another ten minutes. That's when I remembered that I was still wearing someone else's boots and wool overcoat over my clothes from the future. I figured the best place to borrow a change of clothes so I could blend in would be the locker room back at the training school building.

I was about to exit Hope Church when someone confronted me from behind.

"Pardon me." I turned around. It was a young fellow about my age, maybe a bit older. I wondered whether he was the Hope Church staff constable patrolling the grounds for intruders. "May I help you?"

I took a closer look and determined from the stack of books he was carrying that he might be a student.

"I'm new here. I'm trying to find the locker room."

"Follow me," he said. "I was just going there myself."

The kind stranger led me back inside the training school and down several corridors until we arrived at the entrance to the locker room.

"I'm William R. Chase, but my friends call me Will." The name sounded familiar, but my head was so foggy, I couldn't place it.

William R. Chase extended his hand. I met it and offered my best Chip Spears–sanctioned handshake—three pumps over three seconds, with friendly sincerity and a smile. In some strange way, Will reminded me of Curtis—they both had the same innate confidence and easy-going persona.

I sensed that Will had expected me to reveal my name. Then I remembered Lawrence warning me not to say or do anything that could alter the delicate thread of history. But I was in so deep by then, I decided to take a leap of faith in the hope it would somehow all work out.

"I'm Ezekiel Archer, but my friends call me Zeke."

"Well, Zeke, it is a pleasure to make your acquaintance. Where are your bags?"

The biceps muscle of my left arm was already fatigued from the behind-the-back finger-crossing I'd done in the presence of James Naismith. I was reluctant to test it a second time, but had little choice.

"That's an excellent question," I said.

"Has the janitor assigned you a locker?"

"Not yet."

"I think it would be all right if you used Lyman Archibald's locker until then. Lyman was called away yesterday on family business in Boston and won't be back until tomorrow. That should give you ample time to settle in and arrange your affairs."

Will took me to a steel locker that had Lyman Archibald's name etched onto its brass nameplate. Along the same row were three other names I recognized from the sports history book.

The first two were Eugene S. Libby and T. Duncan Patton. Naismith had named them as team captains when it came time to choose sides prior to the start of the first-ever basketball game.

The third was Frank Mahan, a member of the YMCA's football team, who Naismith described as a burly, impatient Irishman from North Carolina. Naismith had further characterized Mahan as someone who held a psychological influence over his YMCA classmates that was proportionate to his physical strength, which was considerable.

Standing there in that fleeting, privileged moment, I had an overwhelming sense that I would soon witness history in the making, regardless of what the game would ultimately be called.

"I'll meet you back at the dining room," Will said.

I waved goodbye and turned my attention to Lyman Archibald's locker. I gripped onto the metal handle and swung open the door. Hanging up inside were a pair of long gray trousers with a belt slung through the belt loops, a short-sleeved wool jersey with the number 7 stitched onto the back, and a couple of well-worn black leather athletic shoes. I recognized the soft-soled low boots, with their brown cowhide laces spiraling through a dozen metal eyelets, as the precursors to the modern-day high-tops that Nathan and I sold at

Chip's. Gullyfluff of the era lay strewn about at the bottom of Lyman Archibald's locker.

By then, more students had filtered into the locker room. I greeted each who walked past while I waited for the coast to clear. Once I was alone again, I stripped down to my boxers and removed my watch. Then I pulled out all of Lyman's gym clothes, stuffed my own gear into the locker, and softly closed the door.

I wasted no time putting on Lyman's clothes. Someone must have been looking after me, I thought—everything fit perfectly.

I made the frozen-tundra trek back to the church dining room and caught a glimpse of Will waving me over to his table. Then I spotted James Naismith sitting by himself with a scratch pad, a bowl of oatmeal, and a cup of coffee. He hadn't touched the oatmeal, but he was writing vigorously on that pad of paper.

I glanced down at Naismith's notes as I approached on my way to Will's table. Luckily, Naismith was too preoccupied to look up.

He was using a pencil to draft some sort of numbered list. He had already written the text for one through four and was working on number five as I passed by.

Wait a minute. He had to be drafting the Original 13 Rules of Basketball. That meant the stunt I'd pulled upstairs in Naismith's office must have worked. And there was still no sign of Phineas Bartholomew Decker, so I felt a renewed sense of hope that my peculiar actions might have restored order and ensured the course of basketball history.

I joined Will at his table, choosing a seat that afforded me a view of Naismith, who was still doing a whole lot of writing, but not much eating.

Will, on the other hand, had piled his plate high with pancakes, scrambled eggs, biscuits, and bacon—and was making quick work of it. I wished there'd been a cafeteria like this one in the public library back in Los Angeles when I passed out on the floor there.

"I understand the oatmeal here is sensational," I said.

"Where's the fun in that?" Will said as he slathered a layer of maple syrup over everything on his plate.

I excused myself to go snag a well-worn wooden tray and take my place in the food line. By the time I had loaded up my plate, three other guys had joined Will at the table. When I went back to reclaim my seat, Will introduced me.

"Zeke, these are my friends Gene Libby and T. D. Patton. This other fellow is Frank Mahan, who may be somewhat less of a friend, according to how much food the beast leaves in the kitchen for the rest of us on any given morning."

That description of Frank Mahan made me think of Stretch. For a brief moment, I felt sadness for my friend having to give up on his dream of becoming a private eye.

Mahan wasn't nearly as tall as Stretch, but they apparently shared an ardent fondness for eating.

There were good-natured laughs all the way around as I shook hands with three more of the men who, according to the sports history book, were among the eighteen fortunate souls to have taken part in the first basketball game of all time.

I was surprised by how *real* the pancakes, eggs, and toast tasted. That heavenly breakfast was hands-down better than any processed food I had eaten in a restaurant or even at—sorry, Mom—my own breakfast table at home.

The question of whether the game would eventually be named basketball or Deckerball would have to wait because trouble had just strolled in through the dining room door.

27

Not on My Watch

A young woman with a full head of steam bounded into the cafeteria.

She was headed straight for Naismith's table. I was sitting close enough to pick up their conversation.

"You must be psychic, Miss Lyons," Naismith said. "I was just finishing up here and getting ready to find you upstairs."

I knew that name! Miss Lyons was the YMCA training school stenographer. More importantly, she was the person who Naismith had tasked with typing up his original handwritten rules. He eventually posted those thirteen rules at the entrance to the gymnasium, under the belief that the men's actions on the court would benefit from some carefully crafted framework.

Everything was in motion to reclaim basketball history.

"Mr. Naismith, there's a gentleman in the front lobby, a Mr. Phineas Bartholomew Decker," Miss Lyons said. "He is insisting on meeting with Dr. Gulick at once, on a matter of vital import."

That caused my heart to thump up against my ribcage.

"Where is Dr. Gulick?" Naismith asked.

"I'm afraid he's up the street at City Hall for his weekly conference with local government officials and won't be back until noon." Oh, great. That's when the historic first basketball game was known to have tipped off. "That man is shivering, and he appears to be disoriented. I think he is in need of immediate assistance."

"Very well. I will attend to him," Naismith said as he abandoned his breakfast and scratch pad and disappeared through the door.

Oh, well. The momentum to reclaim the game had felt nice while it lasted.

I knew that Phineas Bartholomew Decker was a grifter, a braggart, and a bunco artist. But above all, he was a Decker. That meant he possessed familial traits that were handed down to future generations of Deckers through the bloodline—apparently including an inherent knack for being where he was least wanted, and at precisely the wrong time.

Frank Mahan interrupted my concentration when he returned to our table carrying a tray with enough food on it to feed ten men.

"I've heard a rumor that James Naismith is planning to experiment with another one of his newfangled winter games," Mahan said between sizable bites of French toast, "and we've been selected as his laboratory guinea pigs—again."

THIS WAS ALWAYS ABOUT BASKETBALL

Naismith returned to the dining room moments later with a man wrapped in a woolen blanket. There was no mistaking the resemblance. Phineas Bartholomew Decker's head looked like a cement block adorned with woolly sideburns and a walrus mustache. It was as if someone had given Brock a dated haircut before transporting him back in time to serve as my nineteenth-century archnemesis.

Naismith went to pour the fraudulent inventor of "Decker-ball" a cup of hot coffee. I watched as Phineas Decker craned his neck to catch a glimpse of what was on the scratch pad.

Naismith delivered the beverage to Decker, who took a long sip as he pointed toward Naismith's notes. The two men then engaged in spirited conversation. I tried to listen in, but with the boisterous Frank Mahan drawing the long bow between copious gulps of his second helpings, it was impossible.

To my surprise, Naismith got up from his table and led Decker to where I was sitting with my new friends. "Gentlemen, this is Phineas Bartholomew Decker. Would it be possible for you to look after him for a little while?"

"We can do that," Mahan said.

"I appreciate it, Mr. Mahan. Mr. Decker says he has an urgent and private matter to take up with Dr. Gulick, so I must walk over to City Hall to secure his release from bureaucrats who are no doubt intent on holding him against his will."

I noticed a twinkle in Naismith's eye when he said that. He seemed to know that Dr. Gulick's heart belonged to the training school, where he worked tirelessly to promote the spiritual and physical development of its students and prepare them to work and teach at distant YMCA outposts, as well as in schools, churches, and youth organizations all over North America.

"Well, Mr. Decker, how about some breakfast, then?" Mahan said.

"Is it free?" Decker replied.

"Yes, it is, Mr. Decker," Will said, "and that is a brilliant idea, Mahan, providing you've left behind enough crumbs for us mere mortals." Will seemed to enjoy challenging Mahan at every turn.

The four friends were exchanging goodhearted barbs while Decker and I watched Naismith return to his table and slide his pad into the back pocket of his trousers. Naismith stepped toward the door, but before he exited, the pad wiggled loose from his pocket and fell to the floor.

Decker and I looked at each other and soon realized that we had both witnessed what had just happened. He got up from his chair and made a move for those history-making notes, but I was quicker, circling around and boxing him out as I snatched up the pad and jammed it into my pocket.

It was only the second time I had outmaneuvered a member of the Decker family. The first was on the final play of the three-on-three tournament title game in Los Angeles a couple of years earlier, when I ran Brock into a screen set by Stretch before I banked home the game winner on a bounce pass from Curtis in the lane.

"Give it," said an agitated Phineas Decker.

Not on my watch. "Make me."

It wasn't much of a standoff. Decker gave up and returned to the table for a warm meal with his newfound acquaintances. He glared at me between bites while I pondered whether he would get the chance to bend Dr. Gulick's ear before Naismith could ever get his notes to Miss Lyons.

All the while, the new game's destiny hung in the balance.

28

I Do Not Believe
I Know Your Name

About twenty minutes had passed since James Naismith took off for City Hall in search of Dr. Gulick. I sipped my coffee as I kept a sharp eye on Phineas Decker.

The Hope Church dining room door swung open. In walked Naismith, with Dr. Gulick in tow. Naismith made the introductions.

"Phineas Bartholomew Decker, this is Dr. Luther Halsey Gulick, Jr."

"No need to be quite so formal, Jim. Mr. Decker can simply call me Dr. Gulick."

"You're a difficult man to get hold of, doc," Decker said, with a bug-eyed smirk.

I was hoping the formalities wouldn't take much longer. It was a long way home, and I would hate to miss my ride.

"I understand you asked to meet with me on a matter of considerable gravity," Dr. Gulick said.

"Is there somewhere we might talk in private?" Phineas Decker made it clear he didn't want anyone else to know what was on his mind. It was a textbook Decker move. A century later, the cement apple had not plummeted far from the tree.

"Let's go to my office. We can speak privately there."

Naismith returned to his cold oatmeal, and the race against time was underway. He tugged on the miniature gold chain looped through a buttonhole in his waistcoat and removed a pocket watch from one of its pockets. Naismith flipped open the round metal cover with his thumb as I gazed at the wall clock behind him. It was 9:00 a.m.

Decker and an unsuspecting Dr. Gulick were likely deep in conversation in Dr. Gulick's office by then, and Naismith hadn't yet noticed his notes were MIA. To make matters worse, Miss Lyons was nowhere to be found.

I felt like I had to say something to Naismith, but Lawrence's directive had taken up residence inside my head. He made it clear I shouldn't say or do anything that might fray history's fragile ribbon.

Naismith reached for his back pocket and realized his scratch pad wasn't where he had left it. He patted down all his other pockets. No luck—I knew he wouldn't have any.

Deep in thought, Naismith slumped down into his chair and ran his fingers impatiently through his hair.

Lawrence's mantra from our road trip to Kansas two years earlier drifted into my mind: *"It's always time to take action when there's danger."*

I needed to do something.

"Cover me, I'm going in . . . for seconds," I announced to the guys at the table.

"Saw your timber, then, good fellow," Mahan said, "I don't believe I've left you much."

I picked up my tray and took the long way to the food line. As I passed behind where Naismith was seated, I pulled the scratch pad from my back pocket and slid it under his chair.

"Sir, did you drop something?" I said as I pointed toward the errant pad.

Naismith reached under his chair and surfaced with what I had hoped would soon be the future rules of basketball.

"Thank you, young sir." Naismith seemed to break his concentration long enough to take a closer look at my face, no doubt recognizing me from our momentary chance encounter in his office. "I do not believe I know your name."

There I was, standing at the crossroads. Again. I decided to play it safe by sticking with the game plan I had established when I met William R. Chase.

"I'm Ezekiel Archer, sir, but my friends call me Zeke."

"Ezekiel, is it? If I am not mistaken, that is Hebrew for 'God gives strength.'"

"Yes, sir." I remembered my dad telling me that a long time ago when I confessed that some kids at school were making fun of my name. He said that he wanted me to know its origin, and that a man needed to know where he came from in order to figure out where he was going. I wasn't exactly a man back then, but the lesson had taken root.

The longer I stood there speaking with James Naismith, the higher the likelihood I'd somehow screw up the history of the game. I turned toward the food line, but I didn't get far.

"Ezekiel, do you have a moment to converse? I have been working on a new project these past two weeks and could use the benefit of a fresh and impartial point of view."

I stopped breathing long enough for my stomach to make its way to my throat, where it took up temporary residency. I managed to choke out a reply.

"Yes, sir."

29

Naismith Seemed to Sense My Confusion

I took a seat at Naismith's table and wondered what would happen next. Over his shoulder, I could see Mahan and the others pointing at me and snickering.

If Lawrence had been at my side, he might have asked Naismith if he could borrow his scratch pad to calculate an inverse-ratio formula showing that the number of available flapjacks would decrease in proportion to the number of minutes it took Naismith to disclose to me the details of his new game.

"Sir, how can I help?" I asked, hoping it was all I would have to say.

"I will not burden you with the minutiae of why I am developing a new activity for the training school. Suffice it to say that men such as Frank Mahan could benefit from an indoor wintertime endeavor in which surplus energy might be expended in a gentlemanly manner."

Naismith explained that he was seeking to combine elements of physical conditioning, teamwork, perseverance, leadership, courage, self-sacrifice, and integrity.

"Those are the seven tenets which I feel are intrinsic to developing men through sport."

Seven. There was that number again. "Yes, sir."

"I have spent the past fourteen days experimenting endlessly with creative modifications to the rules of football, soccer, lacrosse, and then rugby, not to mention baseball and even cricket. It has led to instructional opportunities in the practical application of first aid, but little else."

Naismith went on to explain that he made a breakthrough after I had left his office. I was relieved to learn that he didn't attribute his discovery to the moment when he'd watched me can a free throw.

"It is all well and good that I have established the physical manifestation for how points may best be tallied, but as you might imagine, a game needs its rules. That is a universal truth."

"I understand, sir."

Naismith peeled off the top two sheets of paper from his scratch pad and handed them to me.

"Ezekiel, please give me your thoughts on these rules."

Before I looked at them, I weighed the gravity of Naismith's words, and of the moment. I felt honored to witness the conception of what would be the most important aspect of my life—regardless of what it might be called. At the same time, I felt mortal fear that Naismith might never be credited with basketball's invention because his decision to discuss his new rules with me was giving Phineas Decker all the time he'd need to steal away the game.

Naismith's words were written in an elegant old-fashioned cursive that was surprisingly easy to decipher. As I expected, there were thirteen rules in all, each one remarkably true to those of the modern game I'd spent my entire life trying to master. As I took in each rule, I could sense Naismith's eyes examining mine, almost as if he were applying a similar code of conduct to examine the depths of my soul.

"These all look good to me, sir."

"Do you have any idea which of the rules is most essential to the game's success?"

I wasn't sure if that was a trick question. I was intimately familiar with rule number five, which disqualifies a player for the rest of the game if he exhibits evident intent to injure another person.

I had violated that rule in the city finals during my senior year at Southland Central High, and I paid a high price as a result. My team was forced to forfeit the game. Days later, the University of Kansas rescinded my athletic scholarship, and I had been trying to get my life back on course ever since.

"They're all important, sir, but if you pressed me, I'd probably go with rule number five." I wasn't worried that my answer to Naismith's question would affect the new game in any measurable way because I already knew how he felt about that particular rule.

"I am inclined to agree," Naismith said. "One need look no further than Frank Mahan tackling an unsuspecting opponent on the football field to understand that an indoor activity carried out on a wooden floor requires such a rule."

Will Chase, I thought, would have enjoyed hearing Naismith make an example of Mahan as the reason why a rule limiting physical contact was integral to the new game.

"But there is more," Naismith said.

Naismith told me that earlier in the year, the International YMCA Training School had adopted Dr. Gulick's inverted equilateral triangle logo as its emblem, with the triangle's three sides representing man's spirit, mind, and body.

"The triangle's strength transcends its three separate sides," Naismith said. "This is because man is surely not comprised of three wholly independent elements. Rather, he is a wondrous outcome of their union, with each side dependent on the other two."

Now *that* sounded like Sacred Geometry to me—I wondered what Lawrence would think. I understood on a conceptual level what Naismith had said, but I was unsure as to how rule number five, with its punishment for unequivocal intent to injure another, was connected to the three sides of the triangle.

Naismith seemed to sense my confusion.

"Rule number five came about through my expanded interpretation of Dr. Gulick's philosophy. In examining his teachings, I concluded that acts of violence run contrary to the union of the triangle's three sides. More to the point, however, I wanted the students to consider the basic philosophy that violence as a means of resolving conflict is ineffectual."

I nodded my head in agreement.

"It seems you understand all too well the necessity of rule number five," he said.

In that moment, Naismith dispelled any doubt as to whether he had taken a detailed inventory of the dark, secret places within me.

30

Mr. Libby,
Call It in the Air

I slid the rules back across the table to Naismith, who scanned the two sheets of paper while I waited for whatever would happen next.

"I think we are about ready to find out what the students might think," he said.

Naismith's attention was momentarily diverted by someone cutting a path across the dining room.

It was Miss Lyons again.

"Mr. Naismith, I thought I would find you here. Dr. Gulick is inquiring as to when you might be available to meet with him and this Phineas Decker fellow."

Naismith rose from his seat and handed Miss Lyons the rules.

"Miss Lyons, would you mind typing this up for me? I will need it for the eleven thirty a.m. exercise class in the gymnasium." Naismith then took a moment to savor the last of his coffee.

"When can I tell Dr. Gulick that you'll be free for a discussion?"

"Please ask Luther if he and Mr. Decker might meet me in the gymnasium sometime during the eleven o'clock hour."

"Very well, Mr. Naismith."

Naismith walked to the far end of the dining room to turn in his cup and bowl to the kitchen staff. He returned to gather his pencil and scratch pad.

The wall clock said 9:30. I had no idea how I would occupy my time for the next ninety minutes before I could attempt to be a fly on the wall at the gym for a conversation that could change the course of sports history. I wondered how Lawrence was passing his time in the truck cab, given he had a dwindling supply of bubblegum and no more paper.

"Are you free to accompany me to the gymnasium? I must set things into motion with the superintendent of buildings."

I knew from the sports history book that Naismith was referring to Pop Stebbins, the man responsible for helping to set up the equipment for the first game.

"I think so." I felt the blood drain from my face. I was totally petrified that I might risk altering history by my mere presence in the gym.

"So, that is a yes?"

"Yes, sir." There was no turning back now.

The bitter-cold wind stung my face as Naismith and I trudged across a thick layer of ice and snow on our way back inside the training school.

I followed him downstairs to the gymnasium entrance at the rear of the building. We walked inside. There was that familiar scent of sweat, floor wax, and possibilities. A man in blue denim overalls was on a ladder taking a hammer to the metal railing that served as a protective barrier for the gallery and the elevated running track that encircled the gym. The metallic bashing sound echoed off the walls.

"May I speak with you when you have a spare moment!" Naismith said to the man, his voice rising above the racket.

"I'll be down in a minute, Jim."

Naismith used the opportunity to inspect the planks of the gymnasium's wooden floor. He used the heel of his boot to tamp down into place the ones that had popped up.

The man on the ladder climbed down, tossed his hammer into a toolbox, and wiped his hands with a cloth.

"Ezekiel, this is James W. Stebbins, but those of us here at the YMCA call him Pop." Naismith seemed to enjoy a favorable relationship with Stebbins. "Pop, this is Ezekiel's first day with us, and I would venture to say it might be an eventful one, as well."

Pop Stebbins extended a calloused and muscular hand, one belonging to a man who relied on tools and elbow grease to solve problems. I gave Stebbins an even firmer handshake than my go-to regulation Chip Spears.

"That's a right fine grip you've got there, Ezekiel. What can I do for you two noblemen?"

Naismith was the one who needed help from Stebbins. I was just hanging around secretly running interference for the possible future inventor of basketball in the hopes I could help restore his legacy.

Naismith asked Stebbins if he had two boxes about eighteen inches square.

"No, but I do have two old peach baskets down in the store room, if they will do you any good."

Naismith asked Stebbins to bring them up. A few minutes later, Stebbins reappeared with the baskets tucked under his arm. The baskets were round and somewhat larger at the top than the bottom.

"Those are dandy, Pop," Naismith said. "If you have some square nails with you, I could use your help tacking the baskets to the lower railing of the gallery."

A smile creased Stebbins's face as he retrieved his hammer and dug a fistful of nails from one of his front patch pockets. He set up his ladder at the far side of the gym. Then he unclipped an old-school brass tape measure from his toolbelt and ran the cloth tape from the lower rail down to the parquet floor below.

"Looks to be exactly ten feet, Jim. Will that work?"

"If that is the height of the track, then I suppose it will do just fine," Naismith replied. "Can you come down from there and spot me?"

Naismith scaled the ladder and nailed a peach basket to the wooden railing before repeating the process at the other end of the gym.

And just like that, the first basketball court was born.

THIS WAS ALWAYS ABOUT BASKETBALL

"Leave the stepladder, Pop, we might need you to retrieve the ball later."

When Naismith issued that instruction, it occurred to me that he had not yet selected the type of ball he would use for his new game. He walked over to a metal equipment rack in the corner of the gym and picked up both a rugby ball and a soccer ball.

"Which of the thirteen rules prohibits a player from running with the ball?" Naismith asked me.

"I believe that's rule number three, sir."

"It seems you were paying attention, Ezekiel. If running with the ball is not allowed, and a rugby ball is designed to be carried, which of these do you think would be the superior choice?"

"I'd go with the soccer ball," I said, noticing how weird 1891 soccer balls were: they had laces.

"Then the soccer ball it shall be."

The clock on the gym wall was approaching 11:00 a.m. I was afraid of a heated confrontation should Phineas Decker and Dr. Gulick arrive before Miss Lyons could hand over the typewritten rules to the real inventor of basketball.

Naismith and I heard footsteps approaching the gymnasium entrance. A wave of nausea swept across my stomach and aimed itself up toward my throat. I instinctively searched for the nearest exit.

In walked Frank Mahan.

When I'd met Mahan in the dining room, he mentioned that there had been gossip circulating of Naismith's plans to foist an experimental activity on the 11:30 a.m. exercise class.

It appeared that Mahan, a man who Naismith had earlier described as the ringleader of the group, had arrived at the gym in advance of the others so he could see for himself what Naismith might have up his sleeve. I believed that Naismith knew enough about human nature to understand that if Mahan approved of the new game, then it would be readily accepted by the rest of the class.

Mahan saw the soccer ball in Naismith's hand. His eyes met Naismith's. Then Mahan looked up at one end of the gym and noticed the peach basket hanging from the railing. He swiveled his head and saw a basket at the other end.

He looked back at Naismith.

"Huh, another new game!" Mahan said.

Naismith seemed amused, but there was neither doubt nor concern on his face. Actually, I sensed an air of confidence in how his new activity might turn out.

It caused me to wonder whether Mahan and the others had any idea that their discontent with the gym class up to that point had been a contributing factor in the creation of Naismith's soon-to-be world-renowned game.

A moment later, more footsteps approached, but they sounded lighter and shorter. It was Miss Lyons.

"Here you are, Mr. Naismith," she said as she handed him two sheets of paper. "Will there be anything else?"

"Thank you kindly, Miss Lyons," he said as he inspected the documents. "These will do just fine."

Miss Lyons exited as Naismith stepped to the bulletin board inside the gym adjacent to the door. He removed four unused thumbtacks and fastened the rules to the board.

| 154 |

Mahan parked himself in front of the new rules as more members of the class filed into the gym. Soon there was a humming beehive of activity surrounding Mahan and the bulletin board as the other men jockeyed for position to get a look.

At precisely 11:30 a.m., Naismith blew a brass whistle and waved the men to the center of the court. Pop Stebbins stood at the ready next to his ladder on the off-chance someone might bury one from downtown. Or uptown, even.

Naismith began the class by taking attendance. He did so alphabetically. Lyman Archibald's name was called first. There was no reply.

Will Chase stepped forward. "Lyman went to Boston to handle a family affair, I'm afraid to say. He won't be with us today."

Naismith continued down the list until he had called the rest of the names on the exercise class roster. With the exception of Archibald, each of the other seventeen men was present.

With the formality of roll call behind him, Naismith answered a round of questions from his students as I slid into a chair by the door. Once Naismith seemed satisfied that his students were all on the same page, he announced what would happen next.

"I would like Mr. Libby and Mr. Patton to serve as team captains and choose sides."

Naismith told his students that he had designed the game to accommodate all eighteen members of the exercise class, and that the teams should start the game with an equal number of players on the court.

"After you have split into two groups," he said, "the team with nine players must designate one man to the sideline as an alternate so that the teams will each have eight players on the court. Fair play, as you know, is one of our cornerstones."

Naismith reached into his pocket and emerged with a silver dollar.

Just then, Dr. Gulick and Phineas Decker entered the gym a few feet from where I was sitting. I watched as Dr. Gulick's eyes studied the two pages of typewritten rules that were pinned to the bulletin board. Then he gazed up at the peach baskets hanging at either end of the gallery's railing.

"Mr. Libby, call it in the air," Naismith said as he used his thumb to flick the shiny coin skyward.

Naismith squeezed the coin into the palm of his hand as it landed, but before Eugene Libby could render his decision, Dr. Gulick broke the silence.

"Mr. Naismith, I'm very sorry to interrupt the class. Might I confer with you over here for a moment? It is a matter of some urgency."

31

Maybe Naismith Hadn't Heard Dr. Gulick Correctly

Naismith pushed the coin back into his pocket.

"Please excuse me for a moment," he told the class as he walked over to Dr. Gulick and Phineas Decker.

On his way there, he rolled the soccer ball along the court's wooden floor right to where I was sitting. I scooped up the ball with my foot and squeezed it with both hands. I figured Naismith had given it to me for safekeeping because he didn't want his students to venture off into the winter-game unknown without his supervision.

The gym fell silent. I knew for certain that the future of the new game would soon be determined. I leaned forward and cupped my hand to my ear.

"Jim, since you two have already become acquainted, I will dispense with the formalities." I had a sense that Dr. Gulick was laying the groundwork for an arbitration between Naismith and Decker that I hoped wouldn't degenerate into a full-blown confrontation—or worse, since it involved a member of the Decker family.

Naismith bowed his head and extended his hand to Decker. Decker took it and offered but a single, terse shake before the release. Chip Spears would no doubt have expressed a strong opinion about Decker's ungentlemanly conduct.

Dr. Gulick, as the training school's dean of physical education, had a responsibility to hold court in matters involving integrity and principle.

"Jim, I had a most fruitful discourse with Mr. Decker. Strange as it might seem, you were both on similar paths with regard to the creation of a new wintertime exercise activity for our students."

Naismith's only reaction to Dr. Gulick's unexpected news was a gentle smile.

"In fact," Dr. Gulick said, "the only discernible difference between your two concepts is quite simply rule number five. Mr. Decker apparently envisioned a more robust contest between the men. Consequently, he didn't see fit to include the kind of strident wording in his version of rule number five that might curtail roughhousing or evident intent to injure an opponent."

Once a Decker, always a Decker, I thought. It was clear that nothing had been lost in translation when Brock dropped in on his rule-breaking nineteenth-century ancestor to rewrite history.

Dr. Gulick and Phineas Decker stood and waited for Naismith's reaction to the news that his invention had been unjustly co-opted.

"This is a wonderful development," Naismith said.

Wait, what? Maybe Naismith hadn't heard Dr. Gulick correctly. It was all I could do to keep from walking up to Decker and poking an accusatory finger into his chest—or worse.

Naismith continued: "I never intended to possess sole ownership of the idea, as that would not honor the training school's philosophy. This new game shall, by all rights, belong to all who participate in it."

Naismith's gesture seemed as misguided as it was honorable. Once I recovered from the shock of it, I concluded that my decision to travel back in time in an attempt to restore Naismith's rightful credit as basketball's inventor was heading for complete and total failure.

32

Who Knows,
Maybe We'll Make History

I stared at the wall clock on the other side of the gym. Lawrence's firm deadline to depart Springfield for the return trip to Biffmann Self-Storage—2:37 p.m. on Monday, December 21, 1891—was less than three hours away.

The penalty for missing the cutoff due to wormhole termination was a stiff one—we wouldn't be able to attempt another return home until 1968. That meant I'd never know if I could have made the team at the University of Kansas as a walk-on.

As for Lawrence, he would miss his opportunity to travel to Mars on NASA's first manned expedition to the Red Planet. But with a little luck, he might get to watch two American astronauts on TV as they landed on the moon for the first time in 1969.

I racked my brain for some way to influence the restoration of Naismith's legacy, but came up empty. Maybe there was nothing left to do but brave the bitter-cold winter weather and hike back to the warehouse to find out if Lawrence could get the Chevy running again. I thought I should get there early, just in case my gum-chewing, nerdy wingman ran into a jam. Not that I was likely to be able to help much with wormhole travel.

Dr. Gulick and Decker exchanged parting words with Naismith and disappeared, but Dr. Gulick returned a moment later to share some private thoughts with the almost-inventor of basketball. He set his hand on Naismith's shoulder.

"Jim, Mr. Decker was paroled from the Massachusetts Reformatory just last week. I have never met a more lost soul than he. If you will agree, I would like to offer him a dormitory room, three squares a day, and a maintenance job until he can figure things out."

I was mindful that Phineas Bartholomew Decker was, at his core, a Decker, so I hoped Dr. Gulick might know what he was getting himself into.

"Splendid idea," Naismith said. "I am certain Pop could use the extra set of hands."

The two men shook on it, and Dr. Gulick departed for the second time as Naismith stepped toward midcourt to reflip the coin. I tried to get Naismith's attention, but he walked right past me. I chose not to interrupt him or delay the start of the game, so I sat in silence and waited for my opportunity to make a graceful exit. In doing so, I was honoring Wade, who had taught me the importance of respecting the game and putting the needs of other players above my own.

"Mr. Libby, please call it in the air."

Eugene Libby called heads, and heads it was, so Libby had the honor of making the first selection.

"I'll take Frank Mahan."

The other students howled in laughter. Even Naismith chortled.

"Clearly, a selection motivated by self-preservation," T. D. Patton said.

I took it to mean that Libby chose to align himself with Mahan because he doubted the notorious gridiron bruiser would in any way observe rule number five.

T. D. Patton's first pick was Will Chase. After that, the two captains made their choices until the rest of the students were spoken for.

"Mr. Libby, you will have to designate your alternate so that we will have two equal teams of eight players," Naismith said.

Eugene Libby sized up his teammates. "Our alternate will be—"

"I have an idea!" Will Chase interrupted Libby before whispering something to his team captain, T. D. Patton.

Patton pointed at me. "We'll take Zeke. That will give both teams nine players."

"Then it is settled," Naismith said.

That sent an eerie chill ricocheting through my body. T. D. Patton had offered me the privilege of playing in the first-ever basketball game—the purest and rawest evidence of Naismith's invention there ever would be.

Lawrence had warned me not to say or do anything that could alter history's predetermined pathway. He'd made that crystal clear. Obviously, that meant I couldn't call out picks on defense or throw any no-look passes. But how could I possibly be on the court at all for the first game ever played without influencing its outcome in some way? All my words and actions would have to be somehow undetectable to the future—I mean, the future from the point of view of 1891.

"Nah, that's okay. I think I'll sit this one out."

"Where's the fun in that?" Will said. "Let's give it a go. Who knows, maybe we'll make history today."

(33)

Nothing but Wood

William Chase was right.

The chance to be a part of history by participating in the first game, regardless of what that game would ultimately be called, was too good to pass up. I figured all I had to do was stay out of everyone's way and avoid scoring a basket. And because of the simplicity of the Original 13 Rules—no three-seconds-in-the-paint violations, for example, because there *was* no paint—I thought I must be very unlikely to do anything memorable, recordable, or even describable.

Simple enough.

We were all wearing regular gym clothes, not uniforms, since we were taking part in a basic exercise class, and basketball hadn't yet been invented.

The court was quite a bit smaller than the ones I had normally played on, even in the early days when I competed in park league. Of course, there were no markings or boundaries taped or painted onto the court's wooden playing surface. The gymnasium lights were dim by Jefferson Community College standards.

Naismith took a moment to go over the rules and offer a last-minute pledge to his students. "If the game is not a success," he said, "then I will not burden you with any additional experiments."

If he only knew.

Naismith positioned all of us in lacrosse formation, with each team consisting of three forwards, three centers, and three backs. The backs, I presumed, would later evolve into the modern-day guard positions I was most familiar with.

The original rules called for a referee and an umpire to maintain good order on the court. However, on that momentous day, Naismith would serve as the sole official. I wondered whether the first-ever game might require assessment of more penalties than any one man could fairly and reasonably handle.

Naismith moved to the sideline, blew his whistle, and tossed the ball in the air toward midcourt. Two of the centers jumped for it, and the new game was born.

It was utter chaos. Players darted around the court in all directions trying to figure out what to do when they didn't have the ball. With nine on each side and the tiny court, the play was insanely crowded. It must have seemed comical to the handful of curious onlookers in the gallery area above.

The act of dribbling the ball was not covered in Naismith's original rules. However, when players were closely guarded, they would often voluntarily lose possession of the ball in such a way that would enable them to recover it—a defensive measure that I interpreted as the forerunner of the dribble. It was amazing to watch this fundamental part of the game being invented right in front of me.

Several minutes into the game, a teammate finally passed me the ball. I was not about to test fate by putting the ball on the court, but before I could get rid of it, I was blindsided by someone who slammed me to the floor. I landed with an audible thud, the offender's full weight crushing my skull.

I was seeing stars, but the shrill sound of a whistle screeching across my eardrums brought me to my senses.

I blinked a couple of times and opened my eyes. There was a muscular hand in front of my face. I grabbed hold of it. The hand's hulking owner lifted me to my feet. I was woozy and wobbly, but the hand kept me from toppling over. There was a strange metallic taste in my mouth. I soon realized it was my own blood.

"That was a foul, Mr. Mahan!" Naismith was intent on restoring order before the game got out of hand. "A flagrant infringement of rule number five."

"Sorry, Zeke," Mahan said as he released my hand. "Old habits, I'm afraid."

If it were Stretch instead of Mahan who had cold-cocked me, he would have suggested that I rub some dirt on my bruises and walk it off. Of course, Stretch would never have crashed into me except by accident.

Naismith squared his shoulders and jogged to the bulletin board. He removed the thumbtacks from page one of the rules and brought the sheet of paper to center court.

"I would like to take this moment to review with you rule number five—in its entirety. I genuinely feel, and I think you might agree with me, Mr. Mahan, that rule number five may well be the most consequential of the thirteen rules."

"Yes, sir," Mahan said. Despite Frank Mahan's reputation as an instigator of mischief, I could tell he had great respect for Naismith.

Naismith cleared his throat loudly enough for it to be heard in the dining room at Hope Church. After that, the only sound in the gym was the knocking of condensed steam trapped inside the building's network of radiator pipes.

Naismith read from page one, enunciating each word as if they all carried equal weight: "No shouldering, holding, pushing, tripping, or striking, in any way the person of an opponent shall be allowed. The first infringement of this rule by any person shall count as a foul, the second shall disqualify him until the next goal is made, or if there was evident intent to injure the person, for the whole of the game, no substitute allowed."

Rule number five had never been clearer to me than when its creator read it aloud.

Frank Mahan raised his hand.

"Yes, Mr. Mahan?"

"Am I to assume you're assessing me with a foul?"

"That is correct," Naismith said, "and a similar, subsequent infraction would put you on the sideline until a goal is scored."

I must have been groggy because when Naismith stepped away to pin page one back onto the bulletin board, I leaned over and issued instructions into Will's ear.

"T. D. and I are gonna work the ball deep into the paint," I whispered. "Once the defense collapses, I'll kick it out to you on the wing for an open look. Bury it."

"Beg your pardon?" Will's look of confusion snapped me back to reality, or at least to the 1891 version of it.

All I could do was feign a weak smile. "Mahan must've hit me harder than I thought."

After that, we all made a great effort to avoid contact with our opponents. I did my level best not to exhibit discernible skill beyond crisp passing and random pick-setting.

There was not much teamwork at first, mostly forwards tossing up wild shots at the peach baskets while backs advanced the ball to their forwards and worked to keep opponents from getting in the way.

All eighteen of us fell into a chaotic, blissful rhythm as the game progressed. The number of spectators in the gallery increased, perhaps drawn in by voices that grew more boisterous as the level of competition heightened, or simply by the sound of so many athletic shoes squeaking across the court. It wasn't the kind of crowd that Curtis and Stretch and I had enjoyed at Jefferson's arena during our successful run for the Southern California Regional title. Nevertheless, I knew it was a sign of things to come for the new game.

So far, I had done my best to avoid being the center of attention. Then, as fate would have it, instinct took over.

T. D. Patton noticed I was wide open in the corner and rifled the ball to me. It was already late in the game in a scoreless tie, and activity on the court was at a frenzied pace.

Three opponents descended on me and tried to swat the ball away in what was no doubt the first known usage of the trap defense. I threw a head fake to create a sliver of daylight before jetting forward with an Archie Clark stutter-step move as I took advantage of the dribble, which had been invented about ten minutes before, by putting the ball on the court to lose my defenders.

When they caught up to me, I threw a left-handed wrap-around bounce pass to Will Chase. The ball caromed off the wooden planks and landed right in his mittens, chest high. Even the ball's laces came to rest under his thumbs.

My precision pass momentarily stunned Will, but he recovered long enough to take aim at the basket from near midcourt and chuck up a twenty-five-foot frozen rope.

Nothing but wood.

34

I Breathed a Secret
Sigh of Relief

Will's bucket led to pandemonium. There wasn't the high-fiving or dog-piling I was used to in my present-day world back in Los Angeles. It was mostly celebratory shouting and shoving.

Luckily, the mayhem drew attention away from the flashiest basketball assist completed to date. Naismith, possibly stunned by my precision move and unsure as to whether it may have violated any of the Original 13 Rules, swallowed his whistle on the play.

Stebbins knew his role in that history-making game. He climbed the ladder and retrieved the ball. The game ended soon after—a 1–0 victory for my team—because it was time for the students to move on to their next class.

Naismith seemed relieved that his new game had been broadly accepted by the group. I watched him return the soccer ball to the equipment rack while the students filed out for their next class. He put his hands on his hips and took one last look around the gymnasium. I could only guess that he was basking in the warm glow of having met Dr. Gulick's unique and necessary challenge. Naismith and I headed for the exit at the same time.

I focused on plotting my return to the warehouse for a rendezvous with Lawrence. My mind jumped to the possibility that Lawrence might be unable to fire up the time machine, a.k.a. Wade's dismantled Chevy. And if the problem was a dead 9-volt battery, and if Lawrence didn't have a replacement for it secretly squirreled away in his metal crate—well, we were sixty-five years away from the battery's invention.

Naismith stopped at the bulletin board to collect the two pages of rules, but they were gone. I joined him in his search of the immediate area around the gymnasium entrance, without success. The rules had vanished.

Naismith shrugged his shoulders and shook his head. "It appears that I will have to inconvenience Miss Lyons for a second time today."

Just then, Frank Mahan reappeared, a sheepish look on his face. Mahan reached into his satchel and pulled out Naismith's rules. It had me wondering whether Naismith should have included a fourteenth rule that assessed a foul for absconding with the only typewritten copy of the first thirteen.

Mahan offered a humble confession. "I'm sorry, sir. I know that this game will be a success, so I took them as a souvenir.

But I think you ought to have them." After that, Mahan seemed resigned to accepting his fate.

Naismith sized him up with a keen eye. I knew there was a lesson coming for Mahan, even if it would be one of compassion.

"Mr. Mahan, you seem certain of the game's chances for success, so I know you will share my opinion that this new activity may well require a name. Have you any thoughts in this regard?"

Mahan squinted his eyes and stared off into space for a moment. "How about Naismith ball?"

Naismith grinned in amusement. "Giving it a name like that would be a sure method of killing the game before it really got started."

"Well, we have a basket and we have a ball," Mahan said. "How about if you call it basket ball?"

"I think that sounds a lot better," Naismith said.

I breathed a secret sigh of relief. After all I'd been through to set basketball on its proper course, the game was now properly named and Naismith's legacy restored. Mission accomplished.

"On second thought," Naismith said, "perhaps a better name for the new game might be Decker ball."

Uh-oh.

Mahan seemed confused.

I was devastated.

"It appears that Phineas Decker and I have shared in the game's creation. I believe he is in greater need of redress and renewal than any of us here at the training school. It seems only fitting and proper."

THIS WAS ALWAYS ABOUT BASKETBALL

Mahan shrugged. "Whatever you say, sir."

"Ezekiel, what are your thoughts on the matter?"

I couldn't tell Naismith my actual thoughts because there was an odds-on chance they'd violate most of the principles of Dr. Gulick's inverted equilateral triangle philosophy. I also knew I couldn't say anything to Naismith that might change the course of history. Although, since Brock Decker had already altered history, I really only wanted to restore history to its original course. But beyond all that, it was his game to name, not mine.

I gulped hard. "It doesn't quite have the same rhythm and pizzazz as 'basketball,' sir, but if you think that's the way to go, I won't argue with you."

"Pizzazz?" asked Naismith, looking puzzled.

They must not have had that word in 1891. "Uh, I mean *zip, dash*—"

Naismith shook his head. "It is settled," he said. "The new game is to be called Decker ball, today and always."

| 173 |

35

Only Time Will Tell

Frank Mahan took off, leaving me standing there with the man who invented the game not called basketball.

I couldn't stick around any longer. I needed to get to the locker room to swap out Lyman Archibald's soggy gym clothes for my Chip's polo shirt and recover my black canvas high-tops from the lobby. There wasn't a moment to lose.

"Ezekiel, do you have a few moments to engage in conversation about the new game?"

I shot a quick glance over Naismith's shoulder to the wall clock. It was 1:15 p.m. I needed to be strapped inside the truck cab to give Lawrence the countdown in a little more than an hour. Sure, the man standing before me was James Naismith, but I really needed to get out of there. And the way things were going up to that point, it seemed risky to push my luck.

"Yes, sir."

I must be insane. There was no other explanation. I couldn't believe I had just agreed to let any more precious time slip away by sitting down to talk with Naismith, especially after learning from Lawrence that my words as much as my actions would determine my fate. Maybe it was my own subconscious mind taking over, telling me I'd never get another opportunity like the one in front of me.

"We can go upstairs to my office. I only have a couple of questions, and I promise not to take up too much of your time."

I was relieved that the delay would be brief. I took one last look around that tiny gymnasium in Springfield, Massachusetts, where it all started, trying to commit every detail to memory. I followed Naismith to his office, where he invited me to take a seat facing him across his desk.

"How can I help you, sir?"

"Ezekiel, I am not exactly sure how to say this."

The last person to utter those words was my mom a few months before, when she was searching for the right way to tell me that my dad had suffered a severe emotional breakdown while driving in from Denver for the regional title game at Jefferson.

And since Naismith hadn't put his thoughts in the form of a question, I was only required to nod in understanding of his predicament and wait for more words.

"It is most perplexing," he said.

Whatever Naismith was going to say, I was hoping he would just get on with it. "How about the direct approach, sir."

"Yes, of course. In watching you fill in today for Mr. Archibald, I could not help but think that this was not the

first time you have played Deckerball, as impossible as that
would be."

Argh, that name.

I measured my words carefully. "It was easy to catch on
because of how well you explained the rules, sir."

Nothing untruthful there. Naismith seemed amused. He
didn't press the issue.

"There is something else," he said. "I cannot help but feel
that we have met someplace else before."

Naismith was right about that. It had happened twice—
both times in the future, from the POV of 1891.

The first time was at Allen Fieldhouse at the University of
Kansas, when he mysteriously showed up in the dead of night
as the thirty-one-year-old arena janitor before revealing himself to me as a representative of the 7th Dimension.

The second was the following year at Parkway Fuel &
Food in Los Angeles, when he appeared as an elderly homeless beggar with a faint Canadian accent and an affinity for
peach-flavored iced tea. That time, Naismith had died in my
arms, but not before he explained to me that Wade's consciousness had survived his physical death on the battlefield
in Afghanistan.

So, yes, we had indeed met before. But without Lawrence
there to run the mathematical calculations, I had no way of
knowing how my traveling *back* in time would affect Naismith's memory of our *future* encounters—or if remembering
the future were even possible.

"My friend Stretch once told me that he saw my twin
walking down the street. I suppose that could explain it." I

felt it was a safe reply to Naismith's question, especially since my response was true. And I didn't think it would present a problem, which was a relief, since I was already facing more of those than I could count.

"Just one more question."

"Sir?"

"I make it a point never to ask a man where he has been. Instead, I prefer to inquire as to where he might be going. Where are you headed, Ezekiel?"

Naismith was only asking the good ones. This was the one question I never had an answer for because I was either spending my time trying to climb over self-imposed roadblocks or randomly headed in the wrong direction for no apparent reason—except on the court.

Maybe the best answer was the truthful one.

"I'm heading . . . into the future—my future. And home, sir. I'm going home."

"Godspeed, my young friend."

I got up and shook hands with the most influential person in my life—with the *possible* exceptions of my mother, my brother, my father, Coach Kincaid, rec center director Vernon Shields, and Chip Spears. Chett Biffmann had an impact on my life too, but a minor one, so his place on the influential-person ledger was a few spots below everyone else's.

As I was leaving, I asked a question of my own.

"Do you think your new game will have any kind of a future, sir?"

"I hope so," he said, beaming with pride. "Only time will tell."

36

You Had One Job

I flew down the stairs and made a beeline for the locker room.

I camped out in front of Lyman Archibald's locker and tried to look nonchalant until everyone around me had cleared out. Then I stripped out of Archibald's soggy gym clothes and hung them up where I'd found them. I was hoping for Archibald's sake that he'd feel inspired to launder the sweaty mess of fabric I was leaving behind before his next exercise class.

I got dressed and slipped into my borrowed overcoat to conceal the fact that I was a visitor from the future. I had fastened the last button when I heard footsteps advancing from behind.

"I hope you have been granted proper authorization to access that locker, young man."

My heart took its all-too-familiar place inside my throat. Was it the YMCA's afternoon watchman making his appointed rounds? Maybe Dr. Gulick was finally on to me after Phineas Decker somehow ratted me out as the on-again, off-again friend and teammate of his future great-great-grandson.

I turned around. It was William R. Chase.

"You startled me, Will."

"That might explain why your knees are rattling beneath that overcoat. Coincidentally, I've got one just like it."

I needed to keep the conversation short because I had no time to spare.

"Thanks for all your help today," I said. "I've put everything back inside the locker just the way I found it."

"I had hoped you would decide to enroll here at the training school."

If our conversation went on any longer, that would soon be my best option.

"Congratulations on scoring the winning goal," I said as I took a step toward the door.

"I've played my fair share of rugby matches. Football and lacrosse too. That move you made to convey me the ball today—it looked like something . . . from the future. Can you explain that?"

I knew I had to be careful how I responded. If I offered too much information, it might alter the course of the game, and of history. But not enough could prolong the conversation, and I was out of time. I opted for a classic Coach Kincaid move: I answered Will's question with one of my own.

"Wouldn't you say it is best, whenever possible, to size up your options and apply the best solution available to you?"

While those words didn't directly address Will's curiosity, they distracted him long enough for me to shake his hand and exit the locker room before he had a chance to ask a Darla Davenport–type follow-up question.

I worked my way to the front of the building and hung the overcoat, which might have been Will's, apparently, back onto the coat stand. I retrieved my high-tops from their hiding place and replaced my soggy borrowed boots where I had found them hours earlier. The clock in the foyer said it was just after two o'clock. The 2:37 p.m. deadline loomed like Stretch patrolling the boards in postseason play.

I opened the door and was reminded of how well the building's heating system had functioned during my brief stay.

I slushed my way across city blocks of slippery gray snow until I reached the abandoned warehouse. I turned the doorknob. It was locked.

"Lawrence, it's me," I hissed in a loud whisper. No response. I pounded on the metal door. It was so cold, my hand momentarily stuck to it in between the first and second thwacks.

"Lawrence!"

I thought I had heard a car door slam inside the warehouse. It was followed by a familiar voice on the warmer side of the warehouse door.

"What's the password?"

Good grief. "I know you're wearing your watch, so you

must be fully aware that we're almost out of time. Stop screwing around."

I heard the click of a lock a split second before Lawrence flung open the door. He slapped me across the face so hard that I almost fell over. Then he slammed the door shut and locked it again.

The pain was instantaneous, like a battalion of tiny frozen needles hopscotching themselves into my skin. I was hoping my eyes wouldn't start watering because it might cause my eyelids to become frozen shut.

The lock clicked again. The door flew open. I flinched. Thankfully, there was no open palm to greet me again. I stepped inside and closed the door behind me.

"What took you so long?" Lawrence said.

"Why did you slap me?"

"Your answering-a-question-with-a-question tactic won't work on me. I am impervious to the art of deception."

I knew there wasn't much time, but I also knew that Lawrence would stand there until I answered his question.

"There was a lot to do—breakfast, basketball, questions, answers. You have no idea. I did the best I could."

"I see."

"Why did you slap me?"

"It's my new password protection protocol. The penalties are stiffer."

There was no use trying to reason with Lawrence. It would only waste valuable time and lead to more red-hot frozen facial skin.

"C'mon, buddy, let's get this old Chevy back onto the interdimensional superhighway."

"Not so fast. How did it go? Were you able to undo the damage Brock caused when he tampered with basketball history?"

"No. Let's just go."

Lawrence popped a wedge of bubblegum into his mouth and shook his head in disgust. "You had one job."

37

It's What Friends Do

I had never felt so disappointed in myself as I did in that moment.

The last thing I needed to hear was that I had failed again. Knowing those words came from Lawrence, the nerdy whiz kid who looked to me to lead by example, made them all the more disheartening.

It was ten after two. That meant we had twenty-seven minutes of leeway before we'd be marooned in the nineteenth and twentieth centuries for most of our natural lives.

"Let's just go," I repeated as I climbed inside the truck cab.

Lawrence got in on the driver side and peeled the dual-heptagon antenna from the windshield. He unsnapped the device's 9-volt battery and touched the terminals to his tongue.

"*Yowch!* We've still got juice," he said.

It was a good thing because if that was our last 9-volt battery—as I suspected—then we would have been done for had it been exhausted by our outbound trip.

"Are you sure you don't want to go back to the YMCA and give it another shot? We've still got a few minutes."

"Don't be a wise guy. Please, just take us home."

"Aye-aye, captain."

"Maybe you can drop us off at Biffmann Self-Storage before Chett locks up the place. That way, we won't have to deal with ol' Gus."

Lawrence didn't respond, which at that point in our time-travel adventure, was a blessing. I wasn't in the mood for conversation either. I had a lot on my mind, starting with finding a way to reconcile Brock's newfound status as untrustworthy custodian of what used to be James Naismith's legacy.

Lawrence plastered the dual-heptagon antenna back onto the windshield.

"Ready for preflight check," he said as he tweaked the dashboard controls and clicked the radio's power knob to the on position. "Initiate the countdown sequence!"

By then, I knew the importance of my role and was ready to carry it out. "Ten. Nine. Eight. Seven. Six." It was probably no higher than fifteen degrees in that warehouse, but my forehead got sweaty as the stupid feeling gave way to abject fear. "Five. Four. Three. Two. One. *Liftoff!* Fire the rockets, commander!"

Lawrence released the emergency brake and pushed down on the clutch as he put the Chevy into first gear. Then he eased back on the clutch while simultaneously giving it gas.

"Going with throttle up, Houston."

The city of Houston, Texas, was home to NASA's Johnson Space Center, which had absolutely nothing to do with our mission, so I figured Lawrence was practicing again for his future expedition to Mars.

He gripped onto the steering wheel as that leathery basketball aroma drifted into the truck cab through the air vents again. The humming sound returned. The ground vibrated so much that the bottom of the truck cab was scraping against the concrete floor. I felt calm, then woozy, just like the first time.

"Hold on, Zeke! I've identified the wormhole."

The rocking and humming eased, to be replaced by the warehouse flashing bright white and pitch-black faster and faster until the surrounding structure dissolved into a pulsating gray dimness as before.

Lawrence's hands were locked onto the steering wheel. He was the picture of focus and determination as he upshifted into second gear and then into third. I felt the sensation of the truck cab rising off the ground and accelerating. The extraordinary speed caused the G-force pressure to squish my body back against the bench seat. I thought my brain was going to be squeezed out through my ears.

Unlike our maiden voyage to Springfield circa 1891, the return trip through the wormhole tunnel was smooth sailing. I was hoping that the sheer act of thinking everything was going to be okay wouldn't jinx it for us.

A bright flash of light converted the Chevy's array of windows into the familiar cosmological navigation graph.

"I'm making a slight course correction," Lawrence said as he adjusted the knobs and controls. I didn't ask why he needed to fine-tune the coordinates because I had supreme faith in his knowledge and abilities. He downshifted into second. A shimmering gray light blotted out the navigational graph. Lawrence threw the pickup into first gear, which gradually slowed the sequence of flashing light.

The Chevy banged off the ground a couple of times before skidding to a hard stop. It was so dark, I couldn't see a thing.

Lawrence unfastened his seat belt and fished the flashlight from his lunch suitcase. He clicked it on. It looked like we had landed inside space 1046, but the Chevy's chassis and the rest of the parts weren't there.

"Where are we?" I asked.

"We're back in Los Angeles."

I let out a huge breath with that news. "Where's the rest of the pickup truck?"

"It's still at Biffmann Self-Storage."

"I don't understand."

Lawrence ignored me, choosing instead to put the truck cab through a series of postflight cool-down procedures.

"Lawrence, you'd better answer me. Where are we?"

"In an equipment storage room."

"I can see that. But where?"

"Jefferson Community College."

I was confused. "Why are we at Jefferson? Did something go wrong?"

"Nope. Everything went according to plan."

"Level with me, Lawrence. What's going on?"

"We're in the equipment shed behind the Jefferson gym. We almost made it all the way back, but we came up a little short."

"How short?"

"About two-and-a-half years—February 26, to be exact."

I knew that date. It was when Curtis and Stretch and I had been thrown out of Southland Central after the brawl I started at the city finals. Our opponent was Brock Decker's team, Mid-City Prep. Brock had been expelled from his school too.

The game had been held at Jefferson.

I noticed I was still wearing my black canvas high-tops, but instead of a pair of khaki pants and a Chip's Sporting Goods polo shirt, I had on my high school basketball uniform. My old number, 23, was stitched onto the front of my jersey.

How had Lawrence done that?

Panic set in. Nausea too. I felt like I was going to throw up.

"What's going on, Lawrence?" I clamped down hard on my stomach muscles, trying to prevent the unpreventable. "Why am I wearing my old high school uniform?"

"The 7th Dimension works in strange and mysterious ways," he said. "You're wearing that uniform because I arranged for you to have another chance. It's what friends do."

"Another chance at what?"

"Undoing the mistake you made at the city finals. You know, the one that caused the University of Kansas to take away your scholarship."

38

Prepare to Get Torched, Cement Head

"C'mon, Lawrence, you're supposed to be taking us home!" I said in protest. No response. "Get us out of here. I've already gotten past it. I've moved on."

"Then why are you always talking about what happened in that game?"

My guts were really churning now. "I'm not." I said those words, but I knew Lawrence was right.

"Really? Why don't you ask Curtis and Stretch, or even Brock or Rebecca? How many times can they listen to you say how different your life would've been if you hadn't thrown that punch?"

If Curtis and Stretch were tired of hearing about it, they'd never say anything to me because they wouldn't want to hurt my feelings. And I almost never talked to Brock anymore, except for those times at the rec center when he would corner me and yammer on about knocking down the winning shot in the regional finals.

As for Rebecca, my days of talking to her about my feelings ended abruptly when she broke up with me and moved to Kansas. Which was only a first step, it had turned out, on her way to Senegal.

"How is it that I'm wearing my old high school uniform?"

Lawrence ignored my question. "It's halftime," he said. "You're supposed to be in the bathroom."

"How do you know that?"

"I went to all your games."

He *what?* I was hoping Lawrence would give me a pass for being unaware of that. My level of intensity during games didn't allow me to scan the crowd, especially the top row of the bleachers, where Lawrence was known to routinely set up shop and calculate shooting percentages and free-throw probabilities.

"Every time your team is down at halftime, you run into the bathroom to drive the porcelain bus."

I remembered trailing Mid-City Prep in the city finals by thirty-two at the break.

"I feel like I have to barf."

"Want some gum?"

"No."

"If you think you're going to spew chunks inside this truck cab, think again." Lawrence sounded serious. "You'd better get in there."

I knew there was a door in the equipment storage room that opened into a hallway near the gymnasium's bathrooms. I felt so sick, I didn't know if I could make it to the toilet in time. Then I had a weird thought.

"What if I run inside the bathroom, and I'm already in there puking when I arrive?"

"You mean, would there be two of you in there hurling in stereo?"

"Yeah," I said, attempting to stifle the inevitable.

"The 7th Dimension has arranged for you to be *you* in this case, so to speak. Unless you want to get slapped again, you'd better make a run for it."

I unbuckled my seat belt and bolted for the storage room door. I was grateful that the basketball gods—or the 7th Dimension—had arranged for that door to be unlocked.

"Your words and your actions will determine your fate— and the world's."

I could hear Lawrence's pronouncement bouncing around inside my skull as I sprinted down the hallway and past the trophy case to the men's restroom. I yanked open the door. There were kids everywhere, but I didn't care. I kicked open the only available stall, latched the door behind me, and dropped to my knees.

I won't go into elaborate detail about what happened next, except to say that I cleared out the entire bathroom in a matter of seconds. Not a single, solitary soul had enough guts to stick around.

I flushed. Then for good measure, I flushed again. Trailing at halftime never did sit well with me. The self-imposed pressure of finding a way to get our team back in a ballgame always exacted a hefty toll.

I needed to sneak back to the truck cab undetected so that Lawrence could take us the rest of the way home. I heard the restroom door creak open. It was followed by the sound of feet shuffling toward my stall. I flushed for a third time to announce that my bathroom cubicle was occupied.

"Dude, are you all right?" Oh, great. It was Curtis. There was a lightness of being in his tone, the way he used to speak before his mortal fear of the ocean led to his walking away from surfing. I wondered whether he would ever return to that joyous state of mind.

"I'm good. You know the routine."

"Thirty-two is a lotta points, bro," Curtis said. "I figured you might be in there awhile."

"Get out of the way and let me talk to him." I knew that pushy voice anywhere. It was Stretch. "It smells unusually bad in here. Know anything about that, Zeke-ster?"

"I'm almost done."

"You'd better be, mister all-league future Jayhawk," Stretch said. "We've still got two quarters of Deckerball left to play."

Stretch's confirmation of my failed attempt to restore Dr. Naismith's legacy caused my heart to shrink inside my chest. I needed to throw up again, but I had nothing left inside to give.

I flushed for an unprecedented fourth time and rose to my feet. I was lightheaded but otherwise felt well enough to take the court, even though I didn't want to.

"On a scale of zero to slightly above zero," Stretch said, "what are our chances of pulling this game out of the fire?"

I took a deep breath and gathered my wits. I knew there was no turning back. No way could I abandon my friends by slinking off to time-travel back to the present day without playing out the rest of the title game. I had a chance to undo my awful decision and get my life back on course. I wasn't going to blow it a second time.

I gave in to the moment.

"It's you and me, big man," I said to Stretch, poking him in the chest for extra emphasis. "Let's pick-and-roll these guys out of the gym." Then I turned to Curtis. "Look for daylight in no man's land. I'll find you out there."

My best friends and I bumped fists and took off for the gym. As we hustled back inside, I remembered that capacity crowd and all-or-nothing vibe. The scoreboard confirmed the Southland Central Cougars' dire circumstances. We were trailing Mid-City Prep, 49–17.

Our coach, Coach Jackson, waved the team to the bench before giving those of us on the starting five our second-half assignments. Coach Jackson had been my coach for all four of my varsity seasons at Southland Central. In that time, we had developed a strong trust in each other.

"Rodrigo and Chen, I need you fellas to do the heavy lifting—call out the picks and play lockdown D," Coach Jackson said. "Curtis, get yourself free beyond the arc. Zeke, you and Stretch work the paint, but kick it out to Curtis when the defense clogs the middle."

"Got it, Coach," I said. "Let's go get us some hardware."

One of the referees blew his whistle to signal the start of the third quarter. All ten players converged onto the court. It was our ball out of bounds. Brock jogged over to guard me.

"Big lead, dweeb," Brock said. "I have a feeling I won't need to break a sweat in the second half against you losers."

I got in Brock's face, standing chin to chin. "Prepare to get torched, cement head."

Brock slammed me with a chest bump. I didn't give an inch and thumped him back.

The ref blasted his whistle and wagged an accusatory finger at both of us.

"Double technical foul!"

Curtis hustled over and slid in between Brock and me. "Easy, dudes. How about we settle this thing on the court like a couple of bros."

I shook it off and tried to shake Brock off too when the ref handed Rodrigo the ball so he could inbound it. Brock cut in front of me and intercepted the pass. I hounded him as he drove his teammates, Thatcher and Duncan, downcourt on a three-on-two fast break.

Instead of stopping at the free-throw line to explore all options the way they taught us in fast-break school, Brock pulled up at the top of the key and drained a three-pointer.

Only seven seconds had elapsed in the third quarter, and we were behind the eight ball to the tune of 52–17.

39

Brock Had Seen Enough

I was in a daze.

One moment, I was bearing witness to the invention of what I had hoped would be basketball. The next, I was standing on the court for the most consequential game—and moment—of my life to date.

There would be so much to deal with in the next sixteen minutes of play that I guess I had mentally checked out.

Brock lit me up, scoring the game's next dozen points on a series of long-range jumpers and teardrops in the lane. When he buried a trey from the hinterlands, Coach Jackson sprung from the bench and signaled for a timeout. Coach's look of disappointment was on full display as it cut across his wrinkled face.

We had fallen behind, 67–17.

"Earth to Zeke, come in." Whenever Coach had said those words to me over the course of four seasons, it was his way of telling me that I had lost my focus.

"I'm good, Coach," I said, even though clearly I wasn't. Curtis and Stretch stood silently on either side of me as I toweled the sweat from my face.

Coach Jackson ran his hand across his bald head and glanced at the scoreboard. "Fellas, I could tell you this is just another game, but it wouldn't be true. It's the dang city championship. You've worked your entire lives for this moment."

My teammates did a lot of foot shuffling, but nobody said a word. They didn't have to. We all knew we had dug a colossal hole for ourselves, and I was the one holding the shovel.

"Ten seconds, Coach." The ref was anxious to get the game back underway.

"This moment is not bigger than any of you," Coach Jackson said. "See that trophy on the scorer's table? You're not entitled to it. It will not sprout legs and trot across the court to your locker room. You have to go out there and take it."

The ref whistled for play to resume. Coach sent the guys back onto the court, but he motioned for me to hang back.

"This is your team, Zeke. You're the one in control of its destiny."

Coach was right. When I had stepped onto the court for the start of the second half, my brain was consumed with how painful the outcome had been the first time around. Now, thanks to Lawrence, I had a chance at a better conclusion to my high school career.

As the players took the court, I pondered the importance I had always placed on winning a high school championship. Every kid who ever went up against his big brother in a game of Horse in the driveway would tell you it was his dream.

I huddled the guys together at midcourt. "We're only down by fifty. Could be worse."

Curtis responded with a look of amusement. Stretch, usually the optimistic one of the group, except when glaring reality dictated otherwise, delivered a blank stare.

"I got this," I said. "Follow my lead."

Lead. Root syllable of the word *leadership*.

Then, with every passing moment, it all came back to me. Each decision I faced seemed eerily and uncannily familiar, until I was predicting the future in real time as if I were witnessing dominoes falling. Tossing a lob into Stretch for an alley-oop slam dunk. Finding Curtis wide open for a series of three-pointers from far-off ZIP codes. Forcing Brock to go to his weak side before stealing the ball and taking it coast-to-coast for an easy breakaway deuce.

Brock had seen enough—again. "Timeout!" We had trimmed Mid-City's lead to thirty-five points with four minutes left to play in the third. The momentum had shifted.

I caught my breath on the bench while Coach Jackson drew up a play on his clipboard. Over his shoulder, I spotted a girl at the media table standing up and shouting something in my direction.

"Hey, Zeke, I just checked. No one's ever come back from a fifty-point deficit in the third quarter of a city championship!"

I recognized the freckles, spiky red hair, and silky tone of voice. And I remembered those exact words. It was Darla Davenport, ace sports reporter for our school paper, the *Southland Central Sentinel*.

Darla's comment wasn't mean-spirited, like something Brock would have said to get under my skin. Instead, the subtext I understood was, *"Hey, team captain, wake up. This is a formidable challenge. Show me you're up for it."*

Temporary lack of sportswriter impartiality aside, Darla's words were exactly what I needed to hear. There was a part of me that wanted to check myself out of the game and keep stats for her at the media table, but I maintained my focus instead.

When play resumed, I put the team on my back, just as I had the first time around.

The ball felt like it was an extension of my right hand as I executed a series of steals, fast breaks, and assists that closed the gap to 74–56 when the horn signaled the end of the third quarter.

40

You Think You Can Stop Him?

Curtis and Stretch staggered to the bench drenched in sweat and completely gassed. Rodrigo and Chen weren't in much better shape.

I had pushed my teammates to the limit of their endurance in an effort to get us back in the game. The only roadblock standing in the way of a city title was Brock Decker's knack for screwing things up for me.

Mid-City Prep came out for the fourth quarter with a clock-management game plan. I figured Brock and his teammates would use stalling tactics to bend the math in their favor. Eighteen points were a lot to overcome in only eight minutes.

For the next several possessions, Brock dribbled around in the backcourt to run down the shot clock before forcing up brick after off-balance brick. He only made one of them, but it didn't much matter. With half of the fourth quarter in the books, Brock's team still enjoyed a comfortable twelve-point advantage.

Coach Jackson called a timeout. The reserves got up from the bench to make room for us. I recalled that Coach had rotated the second-stringers into the game in the first half to keep the starters fresh. So with just four minutes left to play and the city championship on the line, I remembered that the coach would keep his starters on the court.

Stretch downed the entire contents of a half-gallon container of water, discarded the empty under his seat, and motioned for our team manager to bring another bottle.

Curtis removed his sweatband, closed his eyes, and ran the fingers of his shooting hand through his sopping-wet hair. It was vintage Curtis Short. My friend was drawing his focus inward in preparation for the task ahead. The process was always the same, whether he was fending off a riptide at Zuma or sizing up a defender before launching a missile from downtown.

I kept to myself on the bench. My thoughts drifted to Wade and what he might have said to me in that moment, had he been in the gym instead of deployed to Afghanistan when the title game originally took place.

My shoulders drooped when I realized he was still alive back then—I mean, now. The only communication I still expected to receive from my brother was whether he would make good on the promise he'd alluded to in the letter he left behind. Wade had written that his vintage pickup should go to me if he didn't make it home alive, but the promise was to send me a sign when he got there, wherever *there* was.

"Zeke!" Coach Jackson must have sensed I had mentally stepped away to ponder a couple of what-ifs that had little to do with leading my team to victory.

Coach knelt in front of the starting five with his clipboard and drew up what appeared to be a desperation defensive strategy. "Looks like this Decker kid wants to do it all by himself. We're going to hit him with a box-and-one."

A box-and-one zone defense puts four players in a box-shaped zone around the key, with the team's top defender responsible for guarding the opposing team's best offensive player.

Coach Jackson set down his clipboard and gave me what players commonly refer to as the *coach's stare*. It lasted for what seemed like a week and revealed little about what might be going on inside his mind. "You think you can stop him?" Coach asked.

All eyes were on me. My teammates had followed me into battle all season long. They were looking to me for a sign that we could narrow the gap enough to have a chance in the closing minutes.

"Yes, sir. Every time down the court."

All I had to do was make good on my promise.

"Bring it in," the coach said.

"One, two, three—Cougars!"

41

Chance to Be a Hero

It's funny how an entire season can get condensed into a few fleeting moments in time. So much had happened to my teammates and me over the past four months, and now we were in a position to win it all.

We were down, 76–64, with just under four minutes to play. Mid-City's center inbounded the ball to Brock, who dribbled leisurely in the backcourt until I met him at the mid-court stripe. He tried a crossover dribble but forgot to take the ball with him. I grabbed it and took off downcourt with Brock in hot pursuit.

I lowered my head and dipped my right shoulder forward as if I were going in for a layup, causing Brock to commit. When he did, I flipped the ball over my shoulder to Stretch, who was charging down the court trailing the play. Stretch caught the ball in midflight and threw down a thunderous tomahawk dunk that electrified the crowd. The ball flew through the net and bonked off the top of Brock's designer haircut and the concrete skull beneath it.

Brock took a step toward me and snarled. "That pencil-neck geek is going to regret he did that."

The trash talk was underway.

"Pay attention, cement head. He just cut your lead to ten points."

And so it went as precious seconds ticked off the clock. Brock, as stubborn and blockheaded as ever, tried to go one-on-five as my teammates and I chipped away at Mid-City's lead. I hit a runner in the lane, Chen dropped in a pair of free throws, and Stretch floated home a twelve-foot skyhook from the corner.

A Curtis rainmaker brought us to within a single point at 76–75 with twenty-five seconds to go.

Both teams still had one timeout left. Mid-City's coach used theirs.

Coach Jackson waved us over to the bench and delivered a spirited pep talk that included words like *focus* and *destiny*.

With the thirty-second shot clock put to bed, I knew that Brock would try to run out the clock.

The ref blew his whistle for play to resume. Thatcher inbounded the ball to Brock. I crawled inside Brock's jersey and hit him with every defensive move in my arsenal as I looked for daylight and waited for him to make a mistake.

If he managed to run down the clock to ten seconds, I would foul him to put him on the line. If he made both free throws, I would try to get the ball to Curtis for a three-pointer to send the game into overtime.

At the twelve-second mark, I forced Brock hard to his left. He tried to fend me off by taking the dribble behind his back. I anticipated the move because I had seen him execute it against less-experienced players at the rec center for years. I overplayed the dribble near the top of the key and knocked the ball free.

I went horizontal and dove for the loose ball ahead of Brock's arrival. I gained control of it and dribbled out of traffic toward the basket.

I glanced at the clock. Seven seconds left.

I was running a classic, three-on-two fast break as Brock and Duncan backpedaled to protect their team's one-point lead. I faked a pass to Curtis on my right before delivering a wraparound to Stretch, who was steamrolling down the lane to my left. Stretch caught the ball in stride and went in for what I had hoped would be the winning bucket.

But Brock hooked my friend in the throat with his outstretched arm, just the way he had before Lawrence took me back in time for a chance at a redo.

Stretch fell awkwardly to the hardwood. The ball sailed out of bounds. The refs must have been watching the cheerleaders because they both missed it. They never called a foul.

I heard Darla's voice rising above the uproar. "HEY, REF, YOU'RE MISSING A GOOD GAME!"

One of the referees signaled that it was Southland Central's ball out of bounds. I checked the clock. Three seconds to go. There was still time to win it.

I pivoted my body around to search for open space. When I did, Brock was right there laughing in my face. I felt a familiar tidal wave of anger coursing through my body. It started in the pit of my stomach, moved north to my chest, then across my right arm to my fist.

Time seemed to stand still.

Every single basketball decision I had made up to that moment was supposed to translate into four seasons of running the point at the University of Kansas.

I shot a glance above Brock's shoulder to the bleachers. The entire crowd was on its feet—except for one person. I squinted and focused.

It was Lawrence. He was looking right at me.

Lawrence had done the unthinkable. He had left the truck cab unguarded. I guess he really needed to witness history— or the rewriting of it—for himself.

Three seconds left. Our ball. Chance to win.

Chance to save my scholarship.

Chance to comfortably ride out my high school days at my alma mater, Southland Central High.

Chance to be a hero.

Chance to live the dream.

42

Let's Go Home

I squeezed my fist into a steel cannonball, closed my eyes, and took a wild swing at Brock. He must have ducked. After my punch connected, Brock was still laughing, but one of the referees was lying on the court unconscious, blood gushing from his mouth.

Brock lunged and drove me to the ground with a flying body press. Curtis saw what had happened and jumped into the fracas. Then Stretch took on Thatcher and Duncan at the same time, and the melee was underway.

The coaching staffs and police finally restored order. After that, the referee I didn't wallop declared Mid-City Prep the winner by forfeit, and the police escorted me out of the gym and into the cold night air.

"Zeke, what happened on that last play?" It was Darla Davenport, sidling up to me. She was on the shortlist of people

I was hoping to avoid, even though the narrow gap between her two front teeth made her look cuter than usual, and she smelled good.

"Not now, Darla," I said, even though being in her presence made me feel instantly better about myself and the ignominious debacle I had set into motion in the Jefferson gym moments earlier.

"I'm on deadline. I'm not leaving here till you tell me what happened."

"Okay, here it is," I said. "When I saw Brock do that on purpose to one of my teammates, I just snapped."

"I'm not buying it," Darla said, as relentless as ever. "Three seconds is an eternity. You still had a chance to win the game. The readers want to know what *really* happened?"

"That's everything, Darla," I said as I walked away. "Put a period on it and file it."

I couldn't tell her what had really happened, that as the game went on, I came to realize that undoing the awful mistake I made at the city finals and saving my scholarship to KU weren't as important as getting tossed into McDerney Continuation.

McDerney was where I had met Lawrence. That's where we became friends. No way was I walking away from my nerdy amigo and into a future where I had never known him. If I did that, then all our adventures together, including the one we were having now, never would have happened. No college basketball scholarship was worth never having Lawrence's friendship and losing everything I had learned, and was still learning now, by being his friend.

There were policemen standing guard at the entrance to the gym. I knew they wouldn't let me back inside, so I waded through the exiting throng of spectators and made my way to the outside entrance of the equipment shed behind the Jefferson gym.

The door was locked. I called out Lawrence's name. No answer, so I knocked.

I heard the sound of a car door slamming. I was hoping it was Lawrence.

Did Lawrence know of no other way to close a door?

When I heard the click of the lock unlatching, I braced for the slap of fury, but it never arrived. Just Lawrence, who didn't make eye contact but seemed happy to see me just the same. He must have slipped back into the storage room using the shortcut near the bathrooms.

"How'd it go?"

"I don't want to talk about it."

"How'd it go?" Lawrence was more persistent than Darla.

"Knock it off," I said. "You know how it went."

"It's tough to turn back the hands of time, isn't it?"

"You got that right, bud."

"So I guess you're stuck with me." Lawrence's flash of insecurity caught me off guard.

"More like we're stuck with each other, friend."

My words put Lawrence at ease. His exhale was audible.

"I call shotgun," I said, evoking a rare smile from Lawrence. "Let's go home."

(43)

Brace for Impact!

I had left it all out on the court. Lawrence too. There were no more words to exchange. We climbed back into the truck cab for the return trip through the labyrinth of time.

I needed to get Lawrence safely home once we touched down at Biffmann's. After that, all I wanted to do was take a hot shower and meet up with Curtis and Stretch for dinner. And I still had to pack my stuff.

Lawrence put the Chevy through the customary preflight check, turned the necessary knobs and controls, and commanded me to once again initiate the countdown sequence. After I obliged, with the most genuine enthusiasm yet, he released the emergency brake and slipped the pickup into gear.

"Going with throttle up, Houston." There was an air of seriousness in Lawrence's tone. I knew he was hoping to say those words for real someday, strapped inside a rocket headed for Mars.

The familiar scents and sounds and sensations returned to the truck cab and my exhausted body. My butt felt the ground vibrating beneath us.

"Wormhole. Check."

For the first time since my interdimensional ride-alongs with Lawrence had begun, I felt totally at ease as he guided his time-travel express through a series of midflight maneuvers, complete with rhythmic flashing lights and navigational graphs.

I closed my eyes and drifted into the secluded recesses of my mind, daydreaming about hitting the interstate to Kansas and a chance to walk on as a Jayhawk.

I had mixed feelings about living so far away from my father after reuniting with him in Los Angeles. I knew his recovery would be a long one, and I was feeling guilty about leaving town just when it seemed like our relationship could get back on track.

I wondered how Curtis and Stretch would deal with their problems and whether I could do anything to help them before I checked out of L.A.

Then there was the issue of James Naismith's basketball legacy, which Brock had stolen away after coercing Lawrence into proving his theories on time travel. I had a feeling Lawrence might carry tremendous guilt over the outcome. For my part, I knew that my inability to reverse Brock's handiwork would haunt me for the rest of my days.

"Zeke, wake up!"

Lawrence startled me. "What is it?"

"Did you feel that?"

"Feel what?"

Just then, the truck cab bucked and shuddered before doing a double barrel roll.

"That." Lawrence's confidence faded fast.

My head slammed against the metal roof not once, but twice. I shook off the pain and looked over at Lawrence, whose hands were locked onto the steering wheel as if our lives depended on it. Then it occurred to me that maybe they did.

All at once, everything inside and out went black. Then the Chevy went into a steep dive. I felt my heart racing.

"MAYDAY! MAYDAY! MAYDAY!" There was pure panic in Lawrence's voice.

I knew those words as the distress signal a pilot would broadcast via radio communications in the event of a life-threatening emergency, usually aboard a ship or a plane. Lawrence was piloting a vehicle that was neither, but the sense of impending doom was no less real. My entire body was shaking. I couldn't control it.

It was way too dark to see what Lawrence was doing to get us out of that mess, but I sensed he was trying every trick he knew to level out the craft. It didn't matter, though. We were plunging straight down. I thought it was only a matter of time before I would join Wade on his journey to whatever realm his consciousness had transitioned to.

"Brace for impact!"

I had only one thought when Lawrence blurted out those three words: we were going to die.

44

Who's Going to Guard
Our Stuff?

"Lawrence, do something!" I screamed.

No response. None expected.

A faint glimmer of light appeared through the windshield. It enabled me to observe Lawrence's intense concentration as he worked the knobs and controls in an effort to pull us out of the dive.

He shoved the clutch to the floorboard and jammed the three-on-the-tree gearshift lever into second. That eased the angle of our descent, but I had a feeling we were a long way from wheels down at Biffmann Self-Storage. And the thought of Chett wheezing as he scraped us off the asphalt with a shovel and tossed our remnants into a spittoon gave me the heebie-jeebies.

Lawrence double-clutched and threw the Chevy into first gear. The truck cab wailed in defiance, but the maneuver pulled us out of the dive. I saw what looked like city lights flickering through the wall of the wormhole tunnel beneath us as we made our approach.

"We are cleared for visual, runway triple seven," Lawrence said as he guided the pickup back toward Earth. The truck cab made a squishy noise as it thumped off the ground. The sound was not as jarring as on the first two landings, when Lawrence had set us down on unforgiving concrete. This landing was softer.

We skidded to a stop. I peered out the passenger side window to discover that Lawrence had dropped us onto a plot of grass near a grove of trees. Biffmann Self-Storage was situated down the block from a city park where the guys and I used to shoot around. That meant Lawrence had missed the bullseye by about a 9-iron, but at least we were safe.

I was relieved to see that I was once again wearing my khakis and Chip's polo shirt, a positive development in a long day when those had been in short supply.

"You okay?" No answer. I watched as Lawrence ran the truck cab through a series of elaborate shutdown procedures, so I figured he was unhurt.

I took a closer look around outside. We definitely hadn't landed in the city park. The area looked familiar, but I couldn't place it.

"Where are we?" I asked.

"Some strange force took over the craft. I couldn't control it until the very end."

Lawrence had sidestepped my question, so I tried a different angle. "I have a feeling I've been here before. Any thoughts on that?"

"Just one, and you're not going to like it."

Things weren't adding up. An otherworldly presence commandeers the Chevy and throws it into a death dive before dropping us off at a familiar-looking grassy knoll?

"Give it to me straight, Lawrence. I can take it."

"See that grove of oak, sycamore, and pine trees over there?"

"Uh-huh."

"The intertwined root system beneath those trees is 7th Dimension world headquarters. I stuck the landing."

I shifted my body around and peered through the truck cab's rear window. There wasn't a soul around. My eyes followed a narrow concrete pathway to a rectangular stone-and-glass building.

It was Allen Fieldhouse, glistening under the cloudless, moonlit sky. I recognized the building because I'd been there twice before. The hairs on the back of my neck shimmied and swayed.

"What are we doing here?"

"There's only one way to find out," Lawrence said.

My hands were clammy. I was done with this adventure and scared out of my mind. I needed my life to get back to normal, even if the sport of basketball had been given a detestable new name and my lifelong hero had been stripped of his identity as the game's inventor. I wanted things to go back to the way they were, before all this 7th Dimension weirdness took over my life and dumped my neatly organized world on its ear.

"How about you just take us home."

"Can't."

"Why not?"

"You know how you're always doing stuff to help me face my fears?" Lawrence was dead serious.

"Yeah, I guess."

"I'm not stupid, you know. Just because I have autism doesn't mean I didn't understand the lessons. It's your turn now."

I had no idea what Lawrence was talking about. And I had *never* thought he was stupid. Maybe our interstellar road trip had been too much for him.

"It's my turn to do what exactly?" I said.

"Confront your fears. Live your own truth."

Lawrence had come a long way since the day we met in the McDerney cafeteria, when Brock the Bully threatened to beat Lawrence over the head with his own metal lunch suitcase. It was gratifying to witness my friend blossom into a wisecracking, know-it-all teenager, right before my eyes.

My gut instinct was telling me we couldn't go home until the final chapter of our crazy odyssey was written.

"I get it. You comin' with?"

"Who's going to guard our stuff?"

"I always have trouble remembering that," I said.

I unbuckled my seat belt and stepped out of the pickup. I marched to the driver side and motioned for Lawrence to crank down his window. When he did, I held out my fist. Lawrence waved me off.

"Don't leave me hanging, bro. Pound it."

The light outside the truck cab was dim, but there was no mistaking the tears cascading down Lawrence's cheeks.

Twice in one day. This was getting intense.

"Basketball, or Deckerball, or whatever it's called, it gives you a ton of options."

"I'm not sure I know what you mean?" I said.

"You can play, coach, referee, you can write about the game as a journalist. You can do all those things, and you can do them anywhere in the world that you want to."

"Yeah, I guess so." I had never thought about the sport in those terms. I didn't know where Lawrence was going with his line of thinking.

"There's only going to be one first-ever manned expedition to Mars. I need to be on that spacecraft. And even though my whole life depends on it, NASA will never pick me for the job."

It was no secret that the odds were long: no one knew whether or not Lawrence could meet the physical and mental criteria necessary to emerge as the top candidate for the mathematics flight specialist position. But there was no way I was going to let my friend throw in the towel on his dream.

"You cracked the communications code of an interdimensional energy being," I said. "Then when most scientists would've broken for lunch, you solved the mystery of time travel."

"So?" Lawrence wiped away his tears with his shirtsleeve again, but he didn't try to hide them as I almost always do. He wasn't ashamed of crying. Maybe Lawrence was braver than me.

"I'll spell it out for you: Your past is not your potential. But beyond that, your options are as infinite as your ability to think them up," I said. "You're Lawrence Tuckerman. You got this."

Lawrence's demeanor returned to its normal stoic state, so I seized the opportunity to complete the circuit. "Better pound it. Do not leave me hanging here."

"There can be no celebration until the mission is complete."

45

A Footbridge
Between Worlds

I worked my way across the concrete walkway to the main entrance of Allen Fieldhouse.

I had no idea what my mission was or what to expect when I got inside. All I knew was that fate, along with more than a little help from Lawrence, had somehow brought me back to the game's epicenter.

It was no secret that the sport was invented by James Naismith—and apparently Phineas Decker—at the International YMCA Training School in Springfield, Massachusetts. But the game took root at the University of Kansas under Naismith's tireless work as a physical education instructor, Presbyterian minister, and medical doctor. The game had been played at Allen Fieldhouse, the most hallowed of American basketball venues, since 1955.

I was strangely fearless as I approached the main door, even though the lights inside the arena were off.

I pulled the door handle. It was locked. No surprise there. I was no stranger to obstacles blocking my path.

I suppose if Chett Biffmann had accompanied me on what I had hoped would be the last leg of the journey, he would have banged on the door with his pudgy fist. Nathan, on the other hand, might have tried to kick it in. I simply knocked and waited.

A muffled voice with a distinctive accent appeared from the other side of the door.

"Go on, then, state your business," a man said.

That would've been easy to do if I knew what my actual business was.

"I think I'm supposed to be here. That's all I know."

There was no reply. I wondered if the man had left his post to flag down arena security to escort me off the premises. I knocked again.

"Go on, then, state your name."

I opted for the official version. "Ezekiel Archer."

All at once, the arena's windows lit up from the inside. Then the door cracked open, and a strange mist poured out and engulfed me.

"Pay heed, all who enter. Beware of the fog," said the voice inside.

Things then got a whole lot weirder because the door creaked open and out stepped William Webb Ellis. I recognized him from his leather boots, bow tie, and knickerbockers.

"All right, mate," William Webb Ellis said. "Jolly good to see you again."

My favorite sports history book credits William Webb Ellis with the invention of rugby in the small namesake town of Rugby, located in England's Midlands. According to the book, reputable historians believe that rugby's true origins had been lost in the mists of time. But it went on to suggest that one day during a public-school soccer match in 1823, William Webb Ellis picked up the ball and took off running with it, setting into motion the game's invention.

The first time I ever saw William Webb Ellis was at the Southern California Regional Championship in my freshman season at Jefferson. After that, he showed up unannounced at Wade's funeral, then in the rugby aisle at Chip's and hitchhiking in front of Parkway Fuel & Food.

The last time was at Allen Fieldhouse, when he explained that he was working in support of Dr. Naismith's basketball-related activities. That's when William Webb Ellis led me to Wade for our final conversation before Wade's consciousness crossed over to the other side.

It was not exactly the normal type of relationship acquaintances have, but I was happy to see William Webb Ellis just the same, mainly because I knew I was a step closer to finding out why Lawrence had dropped the truck cab on top of the 7th Dimension's command post.

William Webb Ellis pushed open the door. I stepped inside a swirling fog.

"Don't be alarmed," he said, "the fog is part of the charm of this old venue."

It was time to seek answers. "Why am I here?"

"In due time, mate. Follow me."

William Webb Ellis led me inside. We cut through the mist along a concrete walkway until we arrived at a concourse above the court.

That's when I heard the sound of a ball bouncing against the hardwood floor.

"This game you love so much? You will soon learn that it is a footbridge between worlds, best traversed wearing canvas high-tops." I had no idea what William Webb Ellis meant by that, but I had a feeling I would soon find out.

My feet felt the floor tremble when a thunderous *CLANK-THUNK!* circled the arena. Then I heard what sounded like heavy machinery roaring to life. I looked up as the foggy mist spiraled upward into huge intake vents mounted in the rafters. The air had cleared in a matter of seconds.

And William Webb Ellis was gone.

46

I Hope You Will Indulge Me While I Review Your Case

I had read in a national sports magazine that Allen Fieldhouse enjoyed a reputation as the loudest college basketball arena in the country.

The noise level of a typical game at Allen Fieldhouse gave new meaning to the term *home-court advantage*. But that sound would have been quite a contrast to the sound I was actually hearing as I stood wondering why I'd been summoned to that sacred basketball shrine.

Thump-thump-thump— Whoosh!

Other than that sweet sound, there was only dead silence inside the arena.

There was a man standing on the court wearing what appeared to be a janitorial uniform. He was holding a clipboard and talking to an older man who was planted at the line shooting free throws.

I'm a stickler for proper form at the free-throw line. Wade had instilled in me the importance of it. The old guy with the ball kept his knee, elbow, and wrist in perfect alignment with each shot he buried.

Thump-thump-thump— Whoosh!

Whether or not it was still called basketball, the game always seemed to draw me in, no matter what. So I stepped off the concourse and negotiated the narrow steps past rows of wooden seats all the way down to the court, with its pristine hardwood and enormous Jayhawks logo.

The janitor must have heard my footsteps. He whispered something to the guy at the line and turned toward me. The janitor appeared to be in his early thirties and was about my height.

When I noticed his rounded spectacles, aggressive jaw line, dark hair parted down the center, and orderly mustache, it didn't take me long to figure out who he was.

The man extended his hand to me. "It is good to see you again, Ezekiel. Thank you for coming."

It was James Naismith.

There was the faint flash of a Canadian accent in his voice. Except for the denim overalls and the name patch with JAMES stitched onto it, he was the identical James Naismith I had spent time with only hours—or was it decades?—earlier, when he invented the game at the International YMCA Training School in Springfield.

Chip Spears would have been proud of the handshake I offered in return, appropriately firm and resolute. Naismith finished his with an old-school, two-handed overclasp, executed to precision.

After my three pumps and release, I did a quick palm check. My swift analysis revealed my hands to be powder-dry, no hint of moisture to be found, which was a relief. Beyond sparing Naismith the need to wipe someone else's hand sweat onto the bib of his overalls, it was further evidence that I was not at all nervous about standing in his presence under such extraordinary circumstances.

Even so, I was at a loss for words—or at least ones that were intelligent. "Lawrence dropped me off. He's waiting for me in the car."

"Yes, I am aware of that."

The older gent at the free-throw line seemed oblivious to my conversation with the game's inventor. The man appeared to be in his late sixties or early seventies. He looked familiar to me, but I couldn't place him. I watched over Naismith's shoulder as he canned one fifteen-foot toss after another, nothing but net.

"Guy's got flawless form," I said. Geez, it felt like I was trying to make conversation. Naismith must have sensed it.

"I suppose you are wondering why I've brought you here."

"The thought had crossed my mind."

Naismith studied the notes on his clipboard long enough for me to feel uncomfortable about how much time he was spending studying it. I felt my jaw clench without first notify-ing me of its intent.

"I hope you will indulge me while I review your case."

"My case, sir?"

"Yes, your case. Did Lawrence not mention the reason why you are here?"

Wait, Lawrence was in on it? The Chevy's death dive was just a ruse to get us to 7th Dimension headquarters? Why would he do that?

"No, sir. Lawrence didn't say a word about it."

Naismith shook his head and smiled. "Ezekiel, this is about your guardianship."

With those words from Naismith, the old guy who was shooting free throws came up short, clanking one off the front of the rim. It was the first one I had seen him miss.

47

I Was Really Piling It On

I took Naismith's words to mean I had somehow been granted a second chance at consideration for guardianship. I hadn't thought that was possible.

"You had better settle in, Ezekiel, we have quite a bit of ground to cover."

At that point in the craziest day of my life, I had nowhere else I needed to be, so Naismith's timing was working out well.

"When we first met, you were still in high school," Naismith said. "You and your associate, Mr. Tuckerman, traveled to this very arena, risking life and limb in an attempt to persuade the Entity to allow Earth to preserve and protect the game. It was an admirable undertaking."

Lawrence and I had accomplished our mission back then to save the game. Nonetheless, I soon learned that the act of violence I had committed at the city finals, when I took a wild swing at Brock and decked a ref instead, had grave consequences on the interdimensional plane as well as in my life. That had caused the 7th Dimension to suspend my nomination for guardianship indefinitely—before I even knew I had been nominated.

I listened intently as the inventor of the game explained that the Entity had timed my intended guardianship to counteract shameful developments in the sport, with violence and corruption threatening its future. "At the time, the 7th Dimension believed that you possessed the requisite fortitude to assist us in returning the game to its rightful state of integrity through proper stewardship," he said.

"I'm grateful for the second chance, sir. What do you need me to do?"

"The 7th Dimension asks that you simply offer, for its consideration, an honest assessment of your previous actions."

I can do that, I thought.

Thump-thump-thump— Whoosh!

The old man tossing up free throws had regained his rhythm. By that time, I had come to realize that there was something uncannily familiar about the way he released the ball and followed through with his wrist. It was almost as if the same coach had taught both of us the mechanics of proper free-throw shooting.

"You might recall our conversation in Springfield, when I told you I was endeavoring to create a new activity that combined elements of physical conditioning, teamwork, perseverance, leadership, courage, self-sacrifice, and integrity."

"Yes, sir."

"Those are the game's seven tenets, the principles and beliefs under which players shall compete. Accordingly, do you not agree that the 7th Dimension should evaluate one's guardianship qualifications based on these same tenets?"

"Yes, of course, sir."

Just then, I realized that I didn't know how well my life might stack up when judged against Naismith's fundamental principles of the game. I had made questionable decisions leading to the moment of judgment I now faced as I stood before him.

I felt my fingers self-fidgeting without warning. I wished I had a ball to spin on my fingertip. That always helped me cope with stress. But the only ball on the court was in the skilled hands of the elder gent who was putting on a shooting clinic from the charity stripe. It didn't seem right to ask him if I could borrow it.

"We will start with physical conditioning," Naismith said as he leafed through several sheets of paper affixed to his clipboard. "According to my notes—and they are quite comprehensive—you once renounced the game. As a result, you all but gave up on keeping your body in good health."

"Yes, sir, that's true." Naismith was right. I recalled walking away from the game when the going got tough.

"We are only on the first tenet. I hope we have not arrived at an impasse. Please consider that renouncing the game may not have been in your best interests."

With that bit of sound advice, the old guy shooting free throws rimmed one out.

My gut was telling me I needed to offer Naismith the details of what had transpired during that dark period in my life. If I didn't, Lawrence and I would be returning to Biffmann Self-Storage sooner than anticipated.

"I had a lot going on at the time," I explained. "Curtis was recovering from serious injuries he sustained after a rogue wave nearly drowned him while surfing at Zuma. Stretch had quit the team at Jefferson to help save the family painting business from bankruptcy. It meant for the first time in my life that I couldn't play on the same team with my best friends. Oh, and my brother, Wade, was killed in action in Afghanistan, my dad had a nervous breakdown and was having visions of my dead brother in his head, my mom was working so many hours at the hospital that I hardly ever saw her, and my girlfriend, Rebecca, broke up with me too."

I was really piling it on.

"I see," Naismith said as he used his pencil to jot down notes.

"That's when I got fired at Chip's and was cut from the team at Jefferson. When Coach Kincaid offered me the position of Jackrabbits team manager, I guess I just gave up. I stopped riding my bike everywhere and drove Wade's pickup truck instead."

I told Naismith it was rec center director Vernon Shields who'd pulled me up short, telling me that I looked out of shape. After that, I'd turned my life around. On my own.

Naismith scribbled more notes while I blotted the sweat from my forehead.

"I think I have what I need," Naismith said as he returned his pencil to the front pocket of his overalls. "Let us move on to the second tenet," he said, "that of teamwork."

A second later, the old dude banged a free throw hard off the backboard and through the hoop. He hadn't called glass, but it seemed inappropriate to say anything.

48

That Is the True Nature of Deckerball

Naismith reviewed his notes.

I wondered what Lawrence would run out of first, patience or gum.

"In looking over your record on teamwork, the aspect of the game that requires the combined actions of sharing the ball and putting the needs of your teammates before your own, it seems as though there may be evidence of malfeasance."

No doubt Naismith was referring to the time I was driving my team downcourt on a fast break in the closing moments of the Southern California Regional Championship in my freshman season at Jefferson.

I explained to Naismith that when I pulled up at the free-throw line, I was down to only two options: take the shot against a tough defender, or dish the ball off to Brock, who had an open look from eighteen feet.

"Perhaps we can revisit those circumstances for a brief moment."

"Sir?"

Just then, a thick blanket of fog descended on the arena from the air vents in the rafters. In a matter of seconds, Naismith and I were shrouded in a thick, impenetrable mist.

When the familiar, thunderous *CLANK-THUNK!* circled the arena, heavy machinery roared back to life and extracted the fog. When it had cleared, I was wearing a Jefferson Jackrabbits uniform and running the fast break at the SoCal regionals.

I caught a glimpse of Naismith out of the corner of my eye, jogging down the court in a referee's jersey and black pants, a whistle around his neck.

I took off downcourt as Curtis speed-shuffled across the hardwood to my right and Stretch filled the lane on my left. Screaming fans rose to their feet as two Westside City College defenders scrambled backward to contain us.

When I pulled up at the free-throw line, my two best options were to take the shot with a defender in my grill, or flip the ball over my shoulder to Brock for an uncontested eighteen-footer.

I chose to take the shot and launched a fifteen-foot jumper from the free-throw line. It was straight as can be, but I airballed it a foot short of the rim, the basketball harmlessly grazing the bottom of the net as the final horn sounded.

When I realized what had happened, I was met by two

muscular hands shoving me to the hardwood. It was Brock, clearly taking exception to my decision.

The foggy-arena process repeated itself exactly as it had happened before, and we were soon standing center court again at Allen Fieldhouse. The old guy didn't seem to notice that we had left and traveled back in time. He just kept dropping in fifteen-footers from the line.

"Perhaps you can explain your decision as it relates to teamwork in that pivotal moment for your team."

Naismith's steely eyes were sizing me up. His records were meticulous. I knew it must have looked bad to the average bystander. Ninety-nine times out of a hundred, I would have hit the open man.

"The regional title was on the line, sir. As captain of the Jackrabbits, I believed the responsibility to take that shot fell on me. I didn't want Brock to have to live with the regret he would've felt if he clanked a jumper off the rim and cost us the title. If anyone might miss, I wanted it to be me. Win or lose, it was my burden to shoulder."

Brock's unhappiness with my decision in the aftermath of that devastating loss only served to reinforce in my own mind that I had made the right call.

Naismith furrowed his brow. He seemed confused as he dug deeper into his notes. As I waited for what he would say next, I noticed that the old guy shooting free throws had one of his attempts circle the rim before it fell through the hoop. I took it as a positive sign.

"It says here that in the identical situation the very next season, when you were once again running the fast break with the championship at stake, you dished off the ball to Mr. Decker rather than take the shot yourself."

"Yes, sir, that's true."

"I am perplexed, Ezekiel. Why did the same principle as before not apply in that instance?"

We'd played that title game only a few months earlier, but it felt like decades ago because so much had happened in my life since then. I hadn't thought about that play in a long while.

"There was a seven-foot defender bearing down on me when I pulled up at the free-throw line, so my chances of getting off a shot with any degree of accuracy weren't so good. I could see that Brock had the better look. Plus I knew what he'd say if I shot and missed again."

Naismith smiled. "According to what I am reading here, there appears to be more to the story."

Naismith had solid intel. He was right.

"I felt it was Brock's time. He'd worked as hard as anyone to be there, so passing him the ball in that situation, in my opinion, was not detrimental to the team. It was a judgment call."

Maybe the older guy wasn't as oblivious to my conversation with Naismith as I had thought because he dropped in another half dozen in rapid succession. By then, I felt like I was almost looking into a mirror at a man who was an older version of me working on his game. And he was even wearing a pair of black canvas high-tops. Just like me.

Naismith scoured his notes. He seemed to be preparing to explore the third tenet, perseverance.

"According to this report, the lines between the first tenet, physical conditioning, and the third, that of perseverance, appear to have intersected for you. It is not unusual for this to happen, as these precepts often cross paths. That is the true nature of Deckerball."

I didn't understand the significance of Naismith's comparison between tenets one and three, but when he referred to the game by its ill-gotten name, my brain jolted against the inside of my skull as if someone had whacked me between the eyes with a two-by-four.

I did my best to shake off the feeling. "Perhaps you can explain that to me, sir."

"A moment earlier, you offered reasons as to why you neglected to care for your own physical well-being. There is no question that the universe gave you much to deal with. I know how important family and friends are to you, so it is understandable that you might stray from the path and lose your way."

"Thank you for understanding, sir." I was relieved that Naismith was willing to accord me a pass for taking the easy way out, in this case neglecting my diet and exercise habits when my world had caved in around me.

"While the Entity may consider your actions to be logical under these circumstances, that same Entity could concurrently and paradoxically denounce them."

Uh-oh.

"Consider that your decision to disregard your own health under such troublesome circumstances, while a normal human trait, was a conscious choice not born out of perseverance."

The old guy at the line was doing a lot of dribbling, but the ball was no longer leaving his hand.

"For the purposes of guardianship consideration," Naismith said, "the 7th Dimension has historically defined the word *perseverance* thusly: steadfastness in performing a task despite great difficulty."

I saw where Naismith was going with his line of thinking. I felt like I had dribbled the ball off my foot and out of bounds.

"I guess that abandoning one's principles when the going gets tough is not in the 7th Dimension's playbook, right?"

"In a manner of speaking, Ezekiel. The Entity views the seven tenets in the context of what can happen on the court in the heat of competition. Consequently, if a player declines to persevere, it would likely be to the detriment of the team."

The old guy picked up his dribble, took aim, and tossed up an airball.

49

I Get It—
Can We Go Now?

I had no idea whether I needed to ace all seven of the tenets in order to achieve Deckerball guardianship status. I left open the possibility that the 7th Dimension might make a combined assessment of my qualifications by factoring in all of my decisions in context.

"I think it would be best at this point if we moved forward to the subject of leadership."

No problem there, I thought. I got this. What better example of leadership was there than captaining a community college basketball team to a regional championship.

Naismith released a heavy sigh. "Leadership can take many forms, but the true nature of leadership transcends any one single act," he said, his eyebrows gathering inward.

"I don't think I understand, sir."

The old guy at the free-throw line tucked the ball under his arm. I recognized that look. He seemed to be standing around waiting for something to happen.

"Perhaps we can step away from here for a moment so that I can show you what the true nature of leadership might look like."

Then it happened again. A dense fog blanketed the arena, followed by the *CLANK-THUNK!* of machinery that pulled out the fog. When it cleared, Naismith and I were still in a basketball arena, but I could tell it wasn't Allen Fieldhouse. I focused my eyes on a familiar banner hanging from the brick wall beneath the scoreboard:

Welcome to Jefferson Community College
Home of the Jackrabbits
High School Basketball City Finals
Southland Central High vs. Mid-City Prep

We were sitting midcourt in the top row of the arena bleachers. I looked at the scoreboard—fourth quarter, twenty-five seconds left to play, Southland Central trailing by a single point.

I focused my eyes on the ten players standing on the court. Brock Decker was in a Mid-City Prep uniform. Curtis and Stretch were there, dressed in Southland Central silks. So was I. The number 23 was sewn onto the front and back of my jersey.

Naismith had dropped us into the closing moments of the

game, when I made the biggest mistake of my life as I swung at Brock and clobbered a referee instead. An error I had repeated on time-travel replay earlier in my wild journey with Lawrence, no less. I was watching myself about to do something life changing, and not in a good way. And I would be witnessing it for the third time.

"I don't mean to be disrespectful, sir, but do we really need to be here?"

"The Entity feels it is important for you to bear witness," Naismith said. "Consider that there is much to learn about leadership, if you are observant."

The Jackrabbits mascot was careening up and down the sidelines inciting the capacity crowd. There was so much noise and excitement in the air that I could feel the rock-hard bench vibrating beneath my butt.

I wanted to be anywhere but there. I scanned the crowd and saw Darla Davenport seated at the media table. She wasn't hard to spot, what with her reporter's notebook in hand and flaming red hair spiked so high that it was possibly obstructing the view of the person sitting behind her.

I lifted my gaze to the top of the bleachers. There he was, Lawrence Tuckerman, standing all by himself, rocking from side to side, arms flapping, sheets of paper everywhere.

Play resumed. One of Brock's teammates inbounded the ball to him. I watched as Brock dribbled all over the place, no doubt in an attempt to run out the clock.

With twelve seconds left in my high school basketball career, I forced Brock to his weak side. When he took the dribble behind his back, I cut in front of him and poked the ball away. I dove on the loose ball to secure it and sprinted down-court on a firehouse fast break.

Curtis and Stretch filled the lanes on either side of me. Brock was hawking me as I approached the free-throw line. I faked the pass to Curtis on my right before whirling a wrap-around to Stretch, who was pounding down the lane to my left. Stretch caught the ball in full stride and went in for a layup, but Brock dropped back and hooked the big man in the throat with an outstretched arm.

Stretch fell awkwardly to the hardwood as the ball sailed out of bounds. Neither referee called a foul. The one with the future broken jaw signaled that it was Southland Central's ball out of bounds. There were three seconds left on the clock.

Brock stood over Stretch and taunted him as he lay on the ground writhing in pain. I watched helplessly as the high school version of me darted over there to defend my friend. I saw me clench my fist, but I hesitated long enough for Curtis to slide in between Brock and me to separate us.

Both refs blew their whistles to restore order. Coach Jackson signaled for our final timeout.

I turned to Naismith. "I get it—can we go now?"

"We can, but if we do, you will never know, at least from a leadership perspective, what might have happened."

It felt like there were two hands ripping my insides down the middle like a muscleman from some TV wrestling match tearing an old telephone directory in half.

I desperately wanted to know how the game would have played out, but at the same time, I needed to turn away from the outcome because I didn't think I could handle it.

"What is your decision, Ezekiel?"

In a moment of clarity, I decided that a real leader would choose to stick around for the opportunity to learn from the experience because any insight gained might lead to better decision-making down the road.

"Let's stay. I need to see this."

I watched as Coach Jackson drew up an out-of-bounds play on his clipboard. When the ref's whistle cut through the din to signal for play to continue, my teammates and I put our hands together in a circle.

"Cougars!"

The ref handed Stretch the ball under our basket. The other four of us were lined up in the key in a stack formation. Stretch slapped the basketball with his hand to signal our team to execute the play.

Stretch had five seconds to inbound the ball. By the time the ref had counted down four precious seconds, Stretch still had the ball, and all of us were covered. The high school Zeke Archer raised an eyebrow before backpedaling for daylight to the area above the top of the key. Stretch found me with a looping pass that was just beyond Brock's reach.

When I caught the ball, Brock was all over me. I knew I was out of my shooting range, so I threw a head fake and darted for the corner of the key, but I couldn't shake Brock.

I glanced at the clock. Two seconds left. Brock was in my grill. I had no choice. I had to take the shot. I elevated for a jumper. As I did, I saw Curtis roll off a pick set by Stretch and scamper for daylight in the corner. I extended my elbow and wrist like I was going to take the shot but whipped the ball over to Curtis instead.

In one sweeping motion, Curtis unfurled a twenty-five-foot rainbow that left his hand just ahead of the final horn. I looked across the gym and saw Lawrence spring to his feet. I turned back just in time to see the downward flight of Curtis's buzzer beater as it splashed through the netting.

When it did, Lawrence pumped his fist in victory.

Ballgame.

Pandemonium.

Elation.

Despair.

Hard lesson.

50

I Was Doomed

I didn't want to ask, but I knew I had to. "Is that really what would've happened if I hadn't thrown the punch?"

"Do you believe that the 7th Dimension only speaks the truth?"

I hadn't expected Naismith to answer my question with a skilled one of his own, but by that point in the guardianship evaluation process, I should have known better.

"Can we go back now?"

"Of course, Ezekiel. I know you would agree that the bedlam you set into motion at the high school city finals may have been an act devoid of leadership. I would like you to consider that assessment if we are to continue with this process."

"Lesson learned, sir."

The fog reappeared. Before long, we were back at Allen

Fieldhouse. The old guy was superglued to the line draining free throws as if he were dropping them down a chute.

"Let us continue," Naismith said. "The Entity believes that a true life of leadership begins with the simple act of leading oneself. I see here in this report that there were times in the past when you may have gone astray."

I understood Naismith's concept of leadership, but nothing specific was coming to mind. I thought my record of perceived self-leadership would stand on its own, but I soon learned otherwise.

"This may seem unimportant to you, but when you were growing up, how many times did your mother repeatedly tell you to wash your hands, brush your teeth, clean up your room, take out the trash, clear the dinner table, pick up your dirty clothes, take a shower, do your homework, turn off the TV, and stop bouncing the ball in the apartment?"

Lots, especially the bouncing-the-ball part. "I see what you mean, sir."

I was learning the hard way that guardianship of the game had less to do with the actual game than I realized. Naismith took another deep dive into his paperwork, so I shifted my gaze to the old man, who was checking the ball to see if it had enough air in it.

By then, I felt disheartened and was wondering whether Naismith might skip past the rest of the evaluation. Then I could get home sooner than expected to share a pizza with the guys and pack up my bedroom. It wouldn't exactly be the pinnacle of perseverance, but since the Entity was likely to reject my application, it seemed pointless to press on.

"So I guess that's everything, sir?"

"Hardly, Ezekiel. We still have three tenets to go, along with a substantial opportunity for self-discovery at the conclusion of the process."

I knew enough about myself to conclude that guardianship would be reserved for people who were of finer moral substance than me.

The next tenet was courage. I believed my track record on that particular quality was mixed at best.

"The Entity views courage as the ability to act when one is frightened, and to exhibit strength in the presence of pain or grief."

The gray-haired man standing at the free-throw line caught my attention when he put the ball atop his right index finger and gave it a spin. The rotation of the ball had a calming, hypnotic effect on me. I mentally checked out of my conversation with Naismith so I could track that whirling orange sphere.

The man pushed the ball into the air with his finger and caught it in the palm of his hand. He tattooed the hardwood with a trio of dribbles before sailing home his next attempt.

"Are you with me, Ezekiel?"

"Yes, sir, I'm right here."

"This report notates but one single significant act of courage."

That was weird. I knew there were many last-second on-court heroics in my playing career. But if the 7th Dimension was looking for quality over quantity, I was doomed.

"It appears you attended one Ernest T. McDerney Continuation School, the institution of higher learning to which you had transferred as a result of your expulsion from Southland Central High School."

"Yes, sir, that's correct."

The only courageous act I could recall taking part in at McDerney was eating the cafeteria's pizza every Thursday. But since Naismith mentioned there was only one instance of bravery rather than many, it had to be something else.

"The evidence here suggests that you carried out an act of valor not commonly witnessed at the high school level. The location was the school cafeteria."

My mind drifted back to pizza and what the cafeteria staff had tried to pass off as pepperoni.

"Your teammate Mr. Decker was causing your associate, Mr. Tuckerman, to experience needless mental suffering."

Of course! That was the day I first met Lawrence. There was commotion in the back of the cafeteria, where Lawrence was sitting alone enjoying a bowl of chili mac 'n' beef. Brock was shouting at him, taking exception to Lawrence's meal choice and threatening to smack him upside the head. I booked it over there and told Brock to back off and leave the kid alone. When he refused, I physically intervened. Vice Principal Littwack eventually had to separate us.

"The Entity places considerable weight on the courageous act of standing up to a schoolyard bully. Furthermore, it believes Earth would be a far better place if everyone exhibited this type of constructive behavior."

Thump-thump-thump— Whoosh!

51

The Act of Building
Your Integrity
Is a Life's Work

I didn't need Naismith to offer a definition of self-sacrifice nor explain its importance on the court.

But he did anyway.

"Ezekiel, the Entity views the sixth tenet, self-sacrifice, as the noble act of a player giving up his or her own wishes in order to advance the cause of the other team members. It considers this type of selfless act to be a true virtue, but only when the player making the sacrifice has no personal expectation beyond the sacrifice itself."

"I'm with you on that, sir."

I was feeling good about that particular tenet because of the ultimate act of self-sacrifice I had offered to Naismith himself at the end of our initial encounter. That was a couple of years earlier, right there at Allen Fieldhouse. Lawrence and I had driven Wade's pickup truck 1,600 miles nonstop from Los Angeles so I could persuade the 7th Dimension to reverse its decision to take the game away because of the violent act I had committed at the city finals.

I took a moment to secretly check the palms of my hands to gauge how sweaty they were and concluded that I shouldn't try to grip a Deckerball anytime soon.

Then I took the initiative to remind Naismith of our chance encounter, which had occurred after I missed the deadline to arrive at Entity headquarters. At the time, Naismith appeared before me as the arena janitor, but he later identified himself as a representative of the 7th Dimension.

"Sir, I am humbled to be here," I said, "but I want to show you that I've got this one. At the conclusion of our conversation back then, I pleaded with you to convince the 7th Dimension to take away my ability to play the game in exchange for preserving it for all others on Earth."

On a self-sacrifice one-to-ten scale, I thought that must be in the upper-eight range, maybe even a nine.

"Yes, Ezekiel, that is correct."

Nailed it.

"It was a virtuous act, indeed," Naismith said, "and a true exhibition of high moral standards, something the Entity views as central to the game's principles."

Phew. It seemed as though I had cleared that lofty hurdle.

Naismith then buried himself in his notes, flipping through pages of charts and graphs until he stopped to study one sheet of paper in particular.

"The Entity has noted here that your act of self-sacrifice was necessitated by your own violation of another of the tenets, that of leadership. I am afraid that under the game's founding framework, and in the context of this evaluation, one act must neutralize the other."

Something deep inside was telling me it was time to stick up for myself.

"With all due respect, sir, I disagree with the Entity's conclusion here. I feel it is only fair that my leadership and self-sacrifice credentials be allowed to stand individually in my defense of my actions."

The old guy with the ball glanced my way and smiled before burying another free throw.

Naismith paused but didn't flinch. "Your keen observations have been noted. The Entity recognizes your individual growth, as well as the care with which you have approached the game."

"Thank you, sir. I hope that my past misdeeds won't be judged too harshly by the Entity," I said with confidence.

Naismith didn't respond to my appeal. Instead, he moved the conversation along to the final tenet, that of integrity.

"The 7th Dimension has a unique approach to evaluating one's level of moral uprightness and rectitude—that is to say, one's integrity."

"Sir?"

"In layman's terms, the Entity seeks to render a judgment on the level of your honesty and the strength of your moral principles."

I had thought I was in fairly decent shape in that regard. The truth was, I had never given much thought to my day-to-day actions until Naismith offered his detailed definition of integrity. I felt as if my life had been on a noble-enough path up to that point, but my gut told me I was about to get a reality check.

"It is important that you not only consider the essence of integrity's true nature, but also why it can be vitally important to possess it at the highest level."

Naismith paused and raised a wary eyebrow. He seemed to be on a scouting mission to determine whether I had understood his words.

Wade had talked about the importance of integrity all the time, so I figured that the seventh tenet was a huge thing, even though my grasp of it was murky at best. I felt my throat closing up as I nodded at Naismith to let him know it was okay to continue.

"Consider that integrity requires honesty and truthfulness in the presence of others," he said.

I took a sharp breath. I could see where Naismith was going with this now.

"Even when the truth hurts," I said under my breath.

"Yes, Ezekiel. Even in those times when the truth can be hurtful to others, it is essential that you consider delivering it with compassion."

I thought about times on the court, in the heat of battle and with the game on the line, when my words to teammates were harsh, even though I meant those words to be constructive.

"I guess it's the best way to gain the trust of my teammates, who are looking to me for ethical leadership." It meant doing the right thing, I thought, even when no one was watching.

I looked down at my high-tops, thinking they might send up some insight. I had more questions than answers about the decisions I had made in my life and whether they were rendered out of integrity or some lesser motivation.

I felt my stomach lining twisting and untwisting itself. I had a better understanding of why it was important to live my life according to a higher standard. I took comfort in knowing it wasn't too late for that.

I stared at the old guy, who was off in his own world working on his form from the line, where games were often won or lost.

I was puzzled. Naismith did a terrific job of defining what integrity was and why it was essential to have an abundance of it, but he didn't say how mine stacked up in relation to my guardianship consideration.

"I think you lost me on this one, sir. I don't know where I stand."

"Ezekiel, your true level of integrity cannot be fully measured and judged until after you have drawn your final breath. That is because the act of building your integrity is a life's work, never complete until others may pause to evaluate it long after you are unable to do so."

52

You Should Brace Yourself

Naismith wrote a few more notes on his clipboard and tucked it under his arm for safekeeping. "This concludes the Deckerball guardianship evaluation process. Do you have any questions?"

Most of my questions were about whether I could have made decisions in my life that were in greater harmony with the game's seven tenets.

For starters, I wished I'd had a better understanding earlier in my life about why I needed to pay closer attention to my physical conditioning, especially the importance of moving forward when the going got tough.

My parents had taught me how essential it was to live my life with integrity, but the concept that the process would take an entire lifetime had escaped me, particularly in those private

moments when I had abandoned what was fair and just, and
instead chose the path of least resistance.

"Just one question, sir. When do you think I might learn
the Entity's decision?"

The old man at the line turned to face us and smiled. He
seemed so utterly familiar to me that I was distracted by his
presence in what should have been a confidential moment
with the game's inventor.

"Soon enough, Ezekiel. The 7th Dimension knows what it
is looking for in an apprentice guardian. I will arrange for you
to learn the Entity's decision forthwith."

Naismith offered his hand to me for what I figured would
be the last time. By then, my handshake came as second nature, and I felt confident as I delivered it.

Naismith wished me well, and the old guy and I watched
as he trekked up the arena stairs. When he arrived at the concourse, he turned back toward us.

"Ezekiel, before you rejoin Lawrence for your journey
home, you may wish to engage in conversation with the gentleman who has been patiently shooting free throws while
waiting to speak with you."

With that, Naismith disappeared through the concourse
exit. That left just me and the old guy with the ball, which
was awkward because we hadn't been formally introduced,
but also weirdly comforting in that it felt like I was hanging
out with a close friend I hadn't seen in a long while.

The guy hit me with a two-handed chest pass, skillfully
executed, with just the right amount of velocity and backspin.

He delivered the ball to the shooting side of my upper body, as if he hoped that his pass might earn him an assist on the postgame stat sheet if my shot could find its mark.

With the exception of my two time-travel drop-ins at the high school finals, the last ball I had held in my hands was the 1890s soccer ball Naismith had put into play for the first-ever game in Springfield. I reflected on how I would be calling that round, orange sphere a Deckerball from that point forward. It made my chest ache as I sent the ball back with a shoulder-high bounce pass.

I thought it would be polite to make the first move. "Hey. I'm Ezekiel Archer, but my friends call me Zeke."

"Pleased to meet you, Ezekiel Archer. Wanna play a game of Horse to determine your guardianship fate?"

I felt my eyeballs bulging from their sockets. "We can do that?"

"Don't I wish."

My mind was sifting through all the dark, murky places where I stashed no-longer-needed information about people I used to know.

The elderly man was about my height, maybe a bit shorter. He had thinning gray hair, a well-manicured goatee, and the kind of gently rounded midsection that declared to the world he had led a comfortable life.

I tilted my head to one side. "Sir, I don't believe we've met." My curiosity was bordering on obsession.

"We have, in a manner of speaking. You should brace yourself."

After traveling through time and apparently across the cosmos, I was ready for anything. "You can just tell me. I can take it."

The old guy went back to the free-throw line and knee-elbow-wristed a high-archer that splashed through the nylon netting as if it had been dropped to Earth from arena rafters in heaven.

"I am your future self."

Excuse me?

"C'mon, mister. Stretch put you up to this, right?"

"Listen to me carefully: I am Zeke Archer, forty-nine years in the future."

I felt the blood rushing from my face, which made me woozy and lightheaded. I went down with a thud onto the hardwood floor.

53

I Knew You Would
Ask Me That

The elderly guy extended his shooting hand and pulled me to my feet. As he did, I caught a glimpse of a faded scar on the inside of his wrist.

I had the exact same scar on mine. I had caught my wrist on the top of a chain-link fence when the guys and I were trespassing at our middle school to shoot hoops during one summer vacation. My mom had to take me to Mikan Memorial Hospital to have it sutured. I remembered that it took seven stitches to close the wound. *Seven!*

"I have it on good authority that this is not the first time you've dropped like a sack of potatoes," the man said. "Are you all right?"

"Yeah. I think so. Dunno. Maybe not." I was trying to shake off the cobwebs. "Ever since I met Lawrence at the McDerney cafeteria, freaky stuff's been happening that I don't understand."

"I suggest you figure that out on your own time. The Entity only allows these meetings to take place for seven minutes."

"What meetings?"

"The ones it arranges between potential guardians of the game and the person they've become—forty-nine years in the future."

My head was spinning. "I don't understand."

"I'll give you a brief explanation, but pay close attention because we only have six minutes left."

The elderly future me said the 7th Dimension sought to prepare guardianship candidates for a life of service by granting an opportunity to contemplate how they might live in greater self-awareness.

"I can ask you anything I want?"

"Yes, of course," said the older me. "There are no restrictions on the type of information you can access. My only advice would be to seek answers in the context of the game's seven tenets."

The clock was ticking. I felt like I needed all six of the remaining minutes just to decide what I wanted to ask. But I knew I had to be mindful of pursuing information from a place of self-sacrifice and integrity, which I believed to be the most consequential of the seven tenets.

That led me to wonder about Curtis. Surfing used to be

his calling, but that had ended when he almost died beneath that monster wave at Zuma. Prior to his accident, I was convinced that Curtis was in this world to learn and grow from the insight he would gain while riding the waves—and to use that knowledge to enhance the lives of those around him.

"Curtis has lost his way," I said. "I don't know how to help him."

"Do you remember what Wade said to us when he was coaching our park league team, that time we melted down when some older kid torched us in the season opener?"

I was so devastated after the game that I wanted to quit the team. I remember thinking my brother would've done me a favor if he had suggested I switch to golf.

"Wade told me, I mean *us*, that the way to overcome our fear was through enlightenment," I said.

"Exactly. Consider guiding Curtis into understanding his fear by suggesting he question it—in this case, ask why the ocean is no longer his faithful companion. The answers, I've learned, can come from within, if you listen for them."

The older me was a pretty smart guy, I thought.

I moved on to Stretch, whose life was consumed by helping his father try to pull the family painting business out of its tailspin. It had Stretch on the verge of dropping out of the criminal justice program at Jefferson, where he'd been laying the groundwork for a career as a private detective, his heart's desire. I told the Zeke of the future that if Puckett Painting went bankrupt, the family would lose everything.

Of course, it also left Stretch with no time for three-on-three at the rec center.

"How can I help my friend?" I asked.

The older me glanced at his watch. "I'm afraid there's no time to design a step-by-step blueprint to address Stretch's sizeable dilemma, so I will simply tell you that the answers might well be right under his nose."

"I don't understand."

"Do you remember what James Naismith said to us at Parkway Fuel & Food, when he validated Lawrence's theory that human consciousness is a form of energy that exists as a fundamental element of the universe and outside the constraints of time and space, and how energy can change form, but it can neither be created nor destroyed?"

That fateful night in the convenience store parking lot was so crazy that it was now all but a blur. However, there was one conclusion Naismith had drawn that stood out, and the memory of it stuck with me.

"He said something like, 'The fruit was already within the seed,' I think."

"Precisely, and that same line of thinking applies here. The answer to Stretch's plight can come from within because it already resides there."

I was hoping there was still time for one more question.

"Can I ask you about Rebecca?"

"Better make it snappy. We've only got a minute left."

Rebecca was—had been—my first-ever girlfriend. She'd eventually broken up with me before transferring from Jefferson to the University of Kansas.

I was about to tell the future me something he already knew: "I still have feelings for Rebecca."

"Yes, I remember."

"Will I ever get back together with her?"

The elderly me bowed his head for a moment. Then his eyes met mine with the kind of solemn stare that conveys unwelcome news.

"I knew you would ask me that."

54

What in the World
Was Going On?

I doubted that a question about my relationship with Rebecca was in any way connected to Naismith's seven tenets.

But I'd elected to disregard the future me's advice to stay between the lines because I was searching for a way to bury the pain of my breakup with her.

"We're nearly out of time. Are you sure this is how you want to spend our final moment together?"

"Yeah, I guess." Might as well go for broke, I thought. Disregarding advice from people who were older and wiser than me had been a hallmark of my young existence.

"Okay, I'll make this quick. Has there ever been a time with the game on the line when you've passed the ball to a teammate without knowing whether he would send it back to you?"

The older me had just answered my question with a well-played one of his own. I guess I had it coming. "You know as well as I do that it happens routinely with Brock."

"Maybe not the best example, but the principle holds true. You've given Brock the freedom to choose—take the shot, or pass it back if you've got the better look. Make sense?"

"Yeah, I guess." Future me clearly knew that it always helped to examine my life through the prism of the game.

"It's all about trust. You cannot force something to happen with Rebecca, let alone with her cement-headed, blowhard stepbrother."

My future self hadn't forgotten what an enormous tool Brock was. No doubt he also knew how things with my former girlfriend would end up, but he seemed to think it was best that I experience the lesson for myself. In witnessing how my life would evolve, I took comfort in knowing that I would get a little wiser as I got older. Plus, my free-throw form would still be solid at age sixty-nine.

"I think I understand."

"Good, because we're out of time. Last thing—be sure to check in with Dad when you get home. Chip Spears, too." I had no idea why he would say that. I was planning to visit my father anyway. "Now if you'll excuse me, I'm meeting up with Brock in a few minutes. We're going bowling."

Before I had a chance to process that, the me from forty-nine years in the future extended his hand. When I clasped it, a flash of light blinded me. My entire body stung as if I'd been struck by lightning. My chest muscles contracted from fear. When I opened my eyes, I saw that a dense fog had filled the arena. I couldn't see more than a few inches in any direction.

Someone grabbed my arm.

"All right, mate." It was William Webb Ellis. "Come with me, then. I've got one job left on the docket."

William Webb Ellis guided me up a staircase, across the arena complex, and out into the clear night air. "My work here is done," he said. "Your mate, Lawrence, is waiting for you over there, next to that grove of trees."

"Thanks for having my back," I said to the youthful, possibly legendary inventor of rugby. "Best of luck on your journey."

I hurried down the concrete path to rejoin Lawrence. As I approached the truck cab, I saw Lawrence's moonlit head through the Chevy's rear window. To my surprise, there was someone else in the Chevy riding shotgun.

I broke into a sprint along the pathway. I felt my heart racing again, and I didn't know if it was happening in response to the need for more blood to circulate through my lungs, or it was simply out of fear of the unknown.

I pulled up at Lawrence's door, out of breath and shaking. Lawrence was holding the dual-heptagon antenna in one hand and pointing toward the gooey, pink hub with the other. I looked past him to the passenger side and saw James Naismith unwrapping a piece of bubblegum.

What in the world was going on?

The two of them were engaged in rigorous discussion and seemed oblivious to my presence. I waited for a break in the conversation. When it finally came, I tapped my knuckles on the glass to get Lawrence's attention. He rolled down his window.

"We're kinda busy here, Zeke," Lawrence said. "Come back later." Then he rolled the window back up.

55

That's No Way to Treat a Friend

The conversation between Lawrence and Naismith continued for a few moments before Lawrence rolled down his window for the second time. "James Naismith has something he wants to say to you."

"Actually, Lawrence, it is best that I say it to you both," Naismith said as he exited the truck cab. "Come with me."

Lawrence climbed out, and Naismith led us several yards ahead to the center of the grove of trees that Lawrence and I knew to be 7th Dimension Earth headquarters. It seemed fitting that if Naismith was going to address us both, he do so with home-court advantage.

"Lawrence was explaining to me how he was able to harness

the principles of Sacred Geometry to breach the boundaries of time and space."

"No big deal, really," said the pencil maven airily.

I admired Lawrence's humility, although I left open the possibility that it had been so simple for him to construct a time machine that he truly thought nothing of it.

"On the contrary, Lawrence," Naismith said, "the Entity did not think it was possible for a mere mortal to harness the undiscovered, combined power of bubblegum, No. 2 pencils, and the cab of a 1965 Chevy Fleetside shortbed pickup truck to traverse the seemingly untraversable."

"I do what I can." As understatements go, that was a doozy from Lawrence.

Naismith blew a sizeable bubble that got stuck in his bushy mustache when it popped. "There is much to do and deadlines to meet, so I must cut our conversation short," Naismith said as he pried the sticky pinkness from his facial hair. "The Entity has rendered its decision regarding your application for guardianship of the game."

"Sir?" Luckily, I was able to squeeze out that one word before my stomach lodged itself inside my throat again. I glanced at Lawrence, whose eyes met mine, which was rare, so I figured he might be trying to gauge my reaction to the news I was about to receive. No matter the decision, I thought, perhaps my response to it would be a learning experience for the penciled one.

"Ezekiel, based on our discussions on the seven tenets of the game, the Entity has approved your guardianship application,"

Naismith said matter-of-factly. "Your apprenticeship begins now."

I felt my eyes well up and a warm glow sweep through my body. I knew that the game would be a part of my life for all my days. Even if it was called Deckerball. Lawrence flashed a look of relief, followed by a wide smile and massive bubble.

"Thank you, sir. I won't let you down."

"I am happy to hear that, Ezekiel, because there is more. For the next seven days, neither you nor Lawrence are permitted to say anything to anyone about all that has happened between you and the 7th Dimension. After that, all memory of your experiences with the Entity will be wiped away forever, and you will no longer be consciously aware of your selection for guardianship. Instead, it will become an ethereal part of your being for the rest of your time on Earth."

Lawrence raised his hand.

"Yes, Lawrence, what is it?" Naismith said.

"Why the seven-day extension?"

"The overtime rule allows guardianship-consideration participants sufficient time to commit the Entity's lessons to the subconscious mind, where wisdom may be accessed during a lifetime of service to the game, and by extension, to humankind."

There was a lot of information in that statement to process, but Naismith didn't give us much time to absorb it.

"There is still more, Ezekiel. Just before you came back to the Chevy, Lawrence had asked if it were possible for the 7th Dimension to change the name of the game from Deckerball back to basketball. I told him that, unfortunately, it would not be possible."

There you have it. I would be stuck for the rest of my days playing a game that was named after a distant relative of my archnemesis.

Lawrence stepped forward. "That's when I asked him if he could make an exception," Lawrence said. "I learned that from you."

I knew how hard Lawrence had worked to undo the unfortunate events he'd set into motion after he had knuckled under to pressure from Brock. But no doubt Naismith had set Lawrence straight, lecturing him on how he was unable to turn back the hands of time.

"Your friend can be quite persuasive," Naismith said. "After spirited negotiation, I agreed on behalf of the Entity to grant Lawrence's request for an exception."

Lawrence stood up a little straighter after those words from the game's inventor. My friend had matured during our journey and enjoyed a higher level of confidence as a result. It filled me with pride.

"An exception, sir?"

"Yes, and a rare one at that. You see, the Entity bestows on me a certain amount of latitude to conduct affairs and oversee outcomes on its behalf. Under the terms of my agreement with Lawrence, he can never again intercept 7th Dimension communiqués or sever the earthly boundaries of time and space. We shook on it because, as you both know, a man's handshake is his word, and his word is his bond."

After those words, there was a brief moment of silence among us, the only sound a gentle breeze dancing through the grove of trees that towered above.

"Want a piece of gum for the road?"

"That is kind of you, Lawrence. Perhaps so."

Lawrence reached into his pants pocket and pulled out his top-secret ingredient for time travel. "Here, take two. They're small."

Naismith, fully and forever restored as the inventor of the great sport of basketball, said thanks to Lawrence before turning to me. "In a manner of speaking, Ezekiel, I will see you on the hardwood."

We watched as Naismith made his way along the pathway back to the arena's main door. Once he disappeared inside, Lawrence took over. "I need to get this thing wheels down at Biffmann Self-Storage before my dad grounds me for life."

I took one last look at Allen Fieldhouse. I knew I would soon walk through that entrance again, but for a far different reason.

Lawrence put the vessel through a preflight check as he tweaked the dashboard controls and clicked the radio on. After I had delivered the countdown, the wunderkind math nerd released the brake, engaged the clutch, and slipped the shifter into first gear.

"Going with throttle up, Houston," he said as he pushed down on the gas pedal.

When Lawrence squeezed both hands onto the wheel, the leathery basketball smell returned.

"Hang on, Zeke! I've identified the wormhole that will take us back to the storage space."

Again, the rocking and humming gave way to strobing lights that settled into a pulsating shade of gray. Again, I felt focused, then mushy, then floaty. The truck cab seemed to lift from the ground and pick up speed. When I felt the familiar G-force pressure, I knew we were homeward bound.

Lawrence spun the steering wheel and adjusted the knobs and controls. Before I knew it, the Chevy thumped and skidded and came to a hard stop. Lawrence dropped us dead center inside space 1046. I knew it because the unit's lone light bulb revealed the rest of the Chevy's parts, exactly where we had left them.

BAM! BAM! BAM!

It sounded like someone was banging on the roll-up door. "You boys in there?"

It was Chett Biffmann, as scheduled.

I jumped out of the truck cab to answer him.

"It's me, Zeke. I'm in here with Larry Tuckerman. We're working on my truck."

"Biffmann Self-Storage rolls up the sidewalks at precisely seven p.m., and the missus don't much cotton to me being late for supper. Come outta there right now, or the next sound you'll hear is ol' Gus chewing his way through this here metal door."

"Sorry, Mr. Biffmann. We were just wrapping everything up," I said as I unlatched the roll-up door and flung it open.

"What in tarnation happened to your truck?"

Lawrence stepped in front of me before I could answer. "Zeke dropped a contact lens," he said. "I was helping him look for it."

"Don't crack wise with me," Chett Biffmann said. "It's late, and I'm hungry."

"We were working on the Chevy, but we ran out of time," I said. There was no need for any behind-the-back finger crossing as that was more or less the truth. "Do you think you could give us a ride home, sir?"

Chett Biffmann grunted and hawked a wad of tobacco spittle into the nearby bushes.

"This won't sit well with the missus on account of dinner being ruined and all, but I reckon I can do that for a long-term customer," he said. "Jump in."

Lawrence piled into Chett's pickup truck while I locked the roll-up door and tossed my bike into the truck bed.

When we pulled up in front of Lawrence's house, Mr. Tuckerman came running out the front door.

"Sherman, thank goodness you're all right."

Mr. Tuckerman had spent a fifteen-year-long lifetime raising his strangely gifted but thoroughly unpredictable son. It was clear this had taken a considerable toll on him.

"Am I grounded?"

Mr. Tuckerman ignored his son's question and turned to me. "Thank you for bringing my son home safely, Zeke. You are a true friend."

"You're welcome, sir. It was no trouble at all."

Chett Biffmann honked his horn long enough to express the precise level of his irritation and hunger. I thought I heard his stomach growling all the way from the Tuckermans' front lawn.

"The mission is complete," I said, holding out my fist to Lawrence. "This is where we celebrate."

Lawrence slapped my hand away.

"Sherman, that's no way to treat a friend." Mr. Tuckerman was trying to negotiate a graceful exit for me.

I extended my fist a second time, but Lawrence slapped it away even harder.

"Sherman, I think you—"

Lawrence's eyes met mine. He beamed with pride as he grabbed my hand and yanked me in for a tight bro-hug that included two jarring backslaps and a double-shoulder shake after the release.

"Good hang, friend," he said. "Let's do it again sometime."

56

The Gunfire Stopped

"Where to, sport?"

I was so exhausted by then, I could barely keep my eyes open. But I remembered what the elderly me had said before he disappeared in a flash of lightning.

I needed to go see my dad.

"The VA hospital, Mr. Biffmann, if that's all right."

Chett Biffmann grunted, which caused his chins to rejiggle. We both knew that the VA hospital was on the other side of town. I wasn't sure where he and Mrs. Biffmann lived, but I suspected it was nearby the storage facility. That meant the favor I was asking for was an inconvenience of the highest order.

Chett clicked on the radio and spun the knob to a country music station while I settled in. The long drive gave me a chance to collect my thoughts.

"Mr. Biffmann, do you mind if I ask you a question?"

"Call me Chett. All my customers do."

"I'm leaving for the University of Kansas tomorrow. What kind of deal can you make me if I pay for a full year in advance?"

"One heckuva a deal, that's what kind."

"Thanks, Mr. Biffmann."

I figured I had just enough money saved up from my summer job at Chip's to cover the space rental and buy a bus ticket to Kansas. After that, I'd need to find a part-time job, pronto.

Chett Biffmann dropped me off in the VA hospital parking lot. I pulled my bike from the truck bed and locked it up at the entrance. Then I went inside to check in with the security guard.

"What's up, Officer Nordquist? How's my father doing?"

"Kenton has been up and around a bit." I took that as a good sign. "But I'm afraid you missed visiting hours by thirty minutes."

Chalk up another blown deadline. That and my solid midrange jumper were two of my more predominant traits. "Do you think the hospital could make an exception?" If it had worked for Lawrence with James Naismith, I figured I had a shot.

"I think we can do that, young man. Want me to call ahead?"

"I've got this, sir. I'd like to surprise him."

I had learned it was easier to gauge my father's mental state when I showed up unannounced. A surprise visit always revealed his true condition.

I worked my way through the hospital's brightly lit corridors. The door to my dad's room was open, which was unusual, and I was surprised to find my mom sitting there keeping him company. She was still in her nurse's uniform, so I knew she must have taken the bus from Mikan Memorial.

"You look tired, son." My mom had a sixth sense for knowing when I wasn't in midseason form.

"I'm okay," I said as I turned to my father, who was sitting in his lounge chair. "You look good, Dad. How's it going?"

"I'm glad you're here, son. There's something I need to tell you." My dad seemed agitated.

There was so much my father had failed to say to me over the years that it was impossible to guess what he might mention in that moment.

"Do you remember earlier today when I told you I see Wade inside my head sometimes when I close my eyes?"

It was hard to forget that my dad had uttered those words. It reminded me of what a long road to recovery he was facing.

"Yes, sir."

"Kenton, why don't we talk about this later." The smile vanished from my mom's face.

"The gunfire stopped."

"Sir?"

"I wasn't able to understand what Wade was saying because of all the gunfire, but it stopped a few hours ago."

"What did he say?"

"He told me to tell you that seven days without shooting hoops makes one *weak*."

THIS WAS ALWAYS ABOUT BASKETBALL

I felt my heart rate spike. My palms got sweaty. Wade used to pester me with that stupid saying whenever I got lackadaisical and walked away from rec center basketball for a few days.

It was our own private goofy joke. We never told anyone else about it.

"What do you think it means?" my mom asked.

My mind shifted to the letter Wade had written me, the one he'd left with Chett Biffmann for safekeeping, just in case.

In it, Wade had promised that if he didn't make it home alive, he would send me a sign when he got there. I took *there* to mean his next destination. Wade had even repeated those words during our ethereal encounter at Allen Fieldhouse, when the perfect fast break I ran in the regional title game gave us one final chance to be together.

"I'm not sure, Mom. It could mean anything." I slid my nonshooting hand behind my back, just in case. "Maybe it's just sound advice."

While what I said was technically true, I knew exactly what those words meant. Wade had made good on his promise to send me a sign when he arrived at his destination, and he had chosen our father to be the intermediary.

There was one more thing I needed to say to my father before I left for Kansas, and it wasn't going to be easy.

"Dad, something happened to my truck today. I'm not going to be able to drive it to KU."

My dad had rebuilt that '65 Chevy pickup with his own hands, part by antique part. He knew every inch of that truck, but he was in no condition to lift a wrench, let alone leave the VA hospital to witness it chopped up into pieces.

Dad shifted his position in the chair, but he didn't say anything. My mom was staring at me. She didn't seem to know what to expect.

"I was wondering—and if this is something you don't want to do, please tell me."

"Just say it, Zeke." It was some of the best advice my dad had given me in a long time—maybe ever.

"I know how important your truck is to you, but since you might not be driving it for a while, I was wondering if I could maybe buy it from you, or something. I could get a part-time job in Lawrence to make the payments."

My dad paused for what seemed like the length of a media timeout during an NBA playoff game. Then he reached inside the drawer of his nightstand and tossed me a jangling bundle of shiny keys. I caught it in my shooting hand.

"We'll work something out," he said. "Remember to change the oil every three thousand miles."

I simply said thanks and gave my dad a hug. Dad hung onto me a little longer than usual before he let go. When he did, I noticed my mom brushing away her tears.

"I promise to come visit every holiday," I said.

"Truth is, that old jalopy of yours was good for getting you around town, but if you're going to be traveling halfway across the country and back for the next couple of years, you'll need a more reliable vehicle."

I knew that my father was doing his best to make up for lost time. I had mixed feelings about taking his truck to Kansas, but it was of little use to him right now beyond the comfort of knowing it was sitting in the hospital's parking lot. The doctors had already told us he might not drive again for a while. Dad seemed to accept his fate, and he had taught me that accepting a kind gift could be as powerful as offering one.

"I'll take us home when you're ready," I said to my mom. We left the hospital room a few minutes later.

I thanked Officer Nordquist for his kindness, loaded my bike into Dad's truck bed, and fired up the engine.

Driving a truck forty years younger than mine would be a new experience for me, one of many I knew I'd have in the months ahead as I moved forward with my college education. Mom and I didn't say much to each other on the way home. I could tell she was sad that I was leaving for KU the next morning.

We parked the truck in the carport, retrieved my bike, and headed for the stairs leading to the apartment. Mrs. Fenner was there to intercept us before we could get far.

"I think it's a little late for that young fella to be getting home, Maude."

"Thank you for looking out for my son, Mrs. Fenner."

"Maybe it's my eyesight in the night darkness, but I have to say that Zeke looks different, maybe a little older."

"Yes, Mrs. Fenner, and I certainly feel that way, too."

Mrs. Fenner reached inside her handbag and pulled out two miniature fuzzy basketballs connected together by a string.

"This used to belong to my son a long time ago. He doesn't come around much anymore, but that's a story for another time. I understand you're leaving for Kansas in the morning.

If you hang this from your rearview mirror, it'll bring you good luck, I'm told."

"Thanks, Mrs. Fenner."

There was simply no time to meet up with the guys for pizza. I spent the rest of the evening packing up my stuff as I prepared to leave home for the first time.

It was well past midnight by the time I finally crawled into bed, spent and exhausted. I tossed and turned for the better part of the night, going over and over in my mind all that I had experienced in the past several hours.

I knew that my life would never be the same, but I had no way of knowing how profound the changes would be or how well I would handle them.

Friends, family, relationships, the move, my guardianship—there was just so much to think about. I felt that my path was clear, and I was looking forward to what the future might hold.

57

I Was Wondering If You Had Sold The Duke

When I woke up in the morning, my mom already had breakfast on the table and a cooler stuffed with food and drinks sitting by the front door.

I felt sad for my mom. The Archers had gone from a traditional family of four to half of that practically overnight, when Wade enlisted in the Marine Corps and my father split for Denver soon after. Now she was on her own in that nearly empty two-bedroom apartment, with Mrs. Fenner as her only ally in the building.

But a mother's job is to prepare her children to the best of her ability for the outside world and then set them free. I had a sense that knowing part of the job was complete wasn't making it any easier for her to see me go. Mom was a blubbery mess by the time she issued her final instructions.

"Make sure you call me when you arrive on campus."

Then my mom opened a kitchen cabinet and set a coffee can onto the counter. She reached inside and took out a wad of cash.

It wasn't as large as the one Brock had pulled from his pocket at Chip's when he was a millionaire for the length of a Darla Davenport follow-up interview. But it looked like a lot of money.

"Here, take this," she said. "I've been saving it for a while."

As I wrapped my fingers around it, my mom gripped onto that bundle of cash with all the resolve of a Chip Spears handshake. When Mom finally let go, she roared in laughter as tears splashed onto her light-green hospital scrubs.

"It's enough to keep you on your feet until you find a job," she said. "I'll put it on your tab."

"I'll pay you back someday, I promise." Mom had never let me down. I had an open account that was impossible to ever repay.

I kissed my mother goodbye and hauled everything I owned down the stairs and into the truck bed. I needed to make a few stops before I hit the open road for Lawrence, Kansas, otherwise known as Sherman Tuckerman's namesake city, as well as the home of KU.

I pulled into the parking lot of Chip's Sporting Goods to turn in my company property and say goodbye to Nathan and Chip.

"I'm going to miss you, rookie," Nathan said. "The basketball section will take a hit, but I'll hire another rookie to follow in your footsteps."

That was weird. Since when was Nathan doing the hiring? He was only the store's senior assistant supervisor.

I glanced at his name tag and saw that he had a new job title.

"That's right, I'm the new assistant store manager. Chip likes to reward stable employment history in his staff."

"Congrats. Where's the boss?"

"He's in his office trying to figure out how soon till my next promotion, so try not to take up too much of his time."

I made my way through the store for what I knew would be the last time until I came home for Christmas break. I took comfort in seeing that all the new basketballs had the word BASKETBALL inscribed on them.

Passing through the rugby aisle reminded me of the time when William Webb Ellis had stopped by the store to check up on me.

The chess and checkers section was immaculate, a tribute to Nathan's commitment to his craft.

Chip's door was open, but I knocked as a courtesy to my soon-to-be former boss.

"I'm here to turn in my company property."

"I'm glad you're here, Zeke. Nathan tells me he wants to expand the store's chess and checkers service offerings. What's your opinion about that?"

"Nathan Freeman is a man with a plan, sir. I think it's a solid move."

"That cinches it. I've always respected your opinion."

I handed Chip my name badge and polo shirt. He tossed the badge into a desk drawer but gave me back the polo.

"What's this for, sir?"

"Publicity and promotion, Zeke. Feel free to wear it everywhere you go on campus. I've been thinking about opening up a branch in Lawrence. Might as well put the wheels into motion."

"If you do, sir, please let me know. I'm going to need a job to help pay for college. Maybe I could be a part-time senior assistant supervisor in the new store."

"I like the sound of that," Chip said.

I had two more agenda items to cover before I left the store. Both had to do with my best friends.

"I was wondering if you had sold The Duke."

"The *what*?"

"Curtis's surfboard. The one you bought from him yesterday for fifty bucks."

"I told Nathan to put it in the stockroom and throw a net over it. I figured Curtis would return for it someday."

"Can I buy it back from the store? I'd like to return it to Curtis."

"Sure thing. I would normally charge a service fee, but I'm going to give you what Nathan refers to as the rookie employee discount. I'll just take the fifty out of your final paycheck, and we'll call it even."

"There's one more thing, Chip, and this one's not going to be as simple."

I explained to Chip about Stretch's dilemma, how his efforts to ward off a financial calamity with the family painting business would likely result in his dropping out of the criminal justice program at Jefferson. And if that happened, Stretch's hopes for a career as a private eye were sunk.

"I have this idea," I said. "What if Puckett Painting added a new product line that offered private detective services for investigating fraud and mediating disputes within the painting industry?"

Chip wiggled one of his bushy eyebrows. "I like the idea. Do you think the Pucketts would consider taking on a silent partner who would provide the requisite venture capital?"

"I think that's doable, sir."

"Then it's settled. Have Stretch and his father contact me, and I'll arrange to draw up the paperwork."

Chip rose from his desk and extended his hand to me. I met his grip and, with friendly sincerity and direct eye contact, reeled off the best three pumps over three seconds I had ever delivered.

"Door's open if you need some hours during the holidays," Chip said as I left his office and went to the stockroom to retrieve Curtis's surfboard.

On my way out, I saw a guy I recognized purchasing a new basketball from Nathan at the cash register.

"What's going on, dweeb?"

Brock's designer cardigan had been replaced by a well-worn Jefferson sweatshirt and the expensive haircut reduced to nothing more than his usual matted bedhead.

"Just tying up some loose ends, cement head. What's with the ball?"

"Old man Shields has been squawking about budget cuts

at the rec center, so I thought I'd put some of the money I owe Rebecca to good use."

"If I see her on campus before she leaves for Senegal, I'll be sure to let her know."

Nathan handed Brock his change and a receipt. I waved goodbye to the boss and walked out to the parking lot with Brock.

"I know we haven't been on the best of terms lately—or, like, ever," Brock said, "but I wanted to say good luck making the squad. The Jayhawks could do a lot worse."

"Thanks, man. Hold down the fort around here, okay?"

"If you land a spot, and KU's nonconference schedule brings you to the West Coast, I'm expecting you to score me a pair of tickets to the game. Nothing special— third or fourth row center court would be fine."

"I'll make a mental note."

I had two more stops to make. I drove to Curtis's house, fished the board out of the truck bed, and knocked on his front door. Curtis's sister answered. When she saw that I had The Duke in tow, her eyes welled up.

"Where's the dude?"

"He's in his room watching *The Endless Summer* on an endless loop. Been in there doing that for, like, days."

"I'll let myself in."

I walked through the house to Curtis's room. There he was, eyes glued to the tube, tan faded, hair disheveled. He seemed surprised to see me.

"Looks like The Duke has made a cameo," I said as I ducked

Curtis's former surfboard through the doorway. "Thought you might want this back."

"Nah, dude, surfing's for chumps. I'm retired."

Curtis wasn't going to make this easy for me. I turned off the TV and told my best friend that he could get back on his surfboard if he took the time to find out why he was afraid to.

"It's called overcoming fear through enlightenment. Some really smart old guy told me about it."

I suggested to Curtis that he haul his board to Zuma, take two steps into the ocean, and plant himself there until he felt comfortable enough to take two more steps. No time limit, just progress, one foot in front of the other. And when he got to where the ocean was too deep to keep his head above water, he could slide onto his belly and let the ocean's current catch him. Then after he was comfortable enough, he could paddle a few strokes out to sea.

"I get it, bro. Baby steps."

"Sorry I flaked out on my own off-to-college celebration."

"Not to worry, dude. Stretch took care of your portion of the pizza."

"I promise I'll make it up to you guys over Christmas break," I said.

Before I left, I asked Curtis to apologize to Stretch for me. I also told him to have Stretch check in with Chip Spears, who had a business proposal he wanted to discuss with our geeky crime-stopper friend.

"The Chipper does have a flair for the free-enterprise system," Curtis said as we executed our intricate secret handshake.

After that, I left for my final stop before guiding the truck onto Interstate 10.

I parked in front of the Tuckerman residence and rang the doorbell. Mr. Tuckerman answered.

"Down the hall to the right. He'll be happy to see you."

The door to Lawrence's stuffy man cave was closed. I knocked. When he answered, I flinched, but there was no slap, just the boy wonder presumably in there plotting his next caper.

"I've got something for you," I said. "Get a pen."

"Will a pencil do?"

Usually, I would have let that slide, but what I was about to do required a pen. Lawrence went to his desk to oblige while I took a look around.

The top of his dresser was covered in chess tournament trophies. Lawrence's twin bed was neatly made, complete with a bedspread that featured the planet Mars floating idly in the lifeless void of outer space. The clock radio on his nightstand was set two hours ahead to Central Time—the time zone in Lawrence, Kansas. After all we'd been through in the last twenty-four hours, I thought it was best to leave that one alone.

Lawrence handed me a pen. I pulled an envelope from my back pocket. Inside was the California Certificate of Title to my 1965 Chevrolet Fleetside shortbed pickup truck.

I signed and dated it, stuffed it back into the envelope, and handed it to Lawrence.

"The Chevy, it's yours now." No reaction. None expected.

I told Lawrence that once he put the truck back together, he should change the oil every three thousand miles and be careful not to grind the gears. "And if I find out you've driven it faster than 125 miles per hour, I'm taking it away and giving it to Brock. I hear he could use a good set of wheels."

I let Lawrence know that I had arranged for him to keep the truck at Biffmann for free for a year, at which point he could either get a summer job and take over the space-rental payments, or store it in his dad's garage.

"It's your call," I said, "but consider that leaving the Chevy with Chett enables him to hassle you in exchange for you giving him your hard-earned cash. Choose wisely, my friend."

We bumped fists, which, by that point in our relationship, had become fairly routine. I was down the hallway and about to turn the corner when Lawrence called out to me from his bedroom.

"Hey, Zeke, do you think this document is more valuable than Dr. Naismith's Original 13 Rules of Basketball?"

"I think what matters most is what *you* think."

Lawrence paused. He seemed to be weighing the decision. "I suppose that conventional mathematics would favor the 13 Rules," he said, "but sometimes you have to throw math out the window and go with your gut instinct. So I'll call it a tie at the end of regulation. We're going to overtime!"

58

Always Go Strong to the Rack

The drive to Lawrence, Kansas, was uneventful—no impossible deadlines to hit or stubborn interdimensional energy beings to reason with.

The hundreds of miles of interstate provided a much-needed opportunity to get my head straight as I was about to venture into the unknown of college life a long way from home.

I moved into my dorm room as soon as I arrived on campus. My roommate, a quiet and reserved freshman named Douglass, was an aerospace engineering major. Douglass knew next to nothing about basketball, but I thought our newfound friendship would come in handy if I ever received a letter from Lawrence that leaned heavier than usual on aviation and space flight.

Registering for classes was a few days away, so I spent all my free time in the weight room, on the running track, and in the pool to prepare for what I knew would be the most challenging goal I had ever attempted to achieve.

I had only one day left before the 7th Dimension would erase the memory of my journey with Lawrence across the barriers of time. I decided to spend that last night writing what had to be the world's thickest diary, a complete recap of everything that had happened since I walked into the McDerney cafeteria for the first time.

James Naismith had told me I was forbidden to *say* anything, but there were no restrictions to prevent me from writing it all down. I had found a loophole in the Entity's directive. It might have been an oversight on the part of the 7th Dimension, but since Lawrence was no longer permitted to communicate with the Entity, there was no way to get an official ruling on it.

That diary would enable me to express to Lawrence how important he was in my life, and how our friendship was bigger than basketball.

The next morning was the first day of basketball tryouts. Douglass had left early to hit the library. I was in the bathroom brushing my teeth when it hit me. I had been thinking about Rebecca's letter ever since I had put the truck on the interstate and headed east. The news of Rebecca joining the Peace Corps had been so sudden. I went from thinking that I might see her around campus and maybe hang out a little, to not even having the opportunity to say goodbye.

I kept brushing my teeth because I was only halfway done. My mother's voice was inside my head haranguing me about brushing at least three times a day. Mom had this dental-health theory: if I didn't take good care of my teeth, they'd all fall out by the time I turned thirty.

I rinsed and turned off the faucet. Then I went to my desk and dug Rebecca's letter out of a stack of important papers I'd brought from home. I hadn't paid much attention to the return address on the envelope when it first arrived, but now it was an important detail.

By that time, I had driven around my new city enough to know how to find places. I threw my stuff into my backpack and drove to an apartment building a couple of miles north-east of campus near Massachusetts Street and East 7th.

I walked up a flight of stairs and rang the doorbell. My stomach was rumbling as if there were a team of butterflies in there running whistle drills.

The door swung open. Instead of Rebecca standing there, it was a guy about my age and height.

But not just any guy.

Colton Banner.

Double gut punch.

"Sorry, I...I must have the wrong apartment," I stammered.

I heard Rebecca's voice in the distance: "Who is it, honey?"

"It's Zeke Archer," Colton said.

That information was met with silence.

"C'mon in," Colton said.

I hesitated for a long second, then stepped inside and im-mediately noticed two large suitcases standing upright in the entryway. The rest of the apartment had cardboard boxes sealed with tape stacked up all over the place.

Colton extended his hand to me.

I shook it.

"Hey, man." I didn't know what else to say.

Colton Banner had been captain of the Future Jayhawks, the team that beat Curtis, Stretch, and me in the finals of the Western Regional three-on-three youth tournament that had been held at Allen Fieldhouse a couple of years earlier. In the waning moments of that one, Colton ran me into a pick and buried an uncontested jumper from distance to earn his team the crown.

I guess you could say he was in a better spot than I was—then and now.

Colton and I had been slated to be freshman teammates at KU before my monumental lapse of judgment at the high school city finals. I had a brief conversation with him after the three-on-three tourney, when he expressed regret that we wouldn't be playing together as we were supposed to. I remember thinking at the time that we would've been great teammates, even though we play the same position.

I had followed the Jayhawks over the past two years, so I knew that Colton had been the starting point guard for KU in both seasons, leading his team to a pair of berths in the NCAA March Madness tournament.

"Coach told us you're looking to walk on with the team. I hope you make it. We sure could use some . . . *depth* in the backcourt."

"Thanks, man," I said to the guy whose place—at least on the court—I had hoped to take. "Guess I'll see you out there."

Just then, Rebecca emerged from the back of the apartment. She waved at me rather than offer a hug.

So that was how the day was going to go.

"I've got to get over to the weight room," Colton said. "Have a safe flight, babe."

Rebecca gave Colton an awkward hug—no kiss—and out the door he went.

"What are you doing here?"

"I guess I needed . . . to say goodbye before you left," I said.

Rebecca was wearing a pair of weathered Jefferson sweats with a faded Jackrabbits mascot on the jersey. Her long brown hair was pulled back in a ponytail. It felt awesome to see her, even if I knew it might well be the last time I ever would.

"I wish we had more time to hang out, but my ride to the airport will be here soon."

"It's weird to see you go. Brock was telling me that everything was working out for you here. Oh—and, speaking of Brock, he told me to tell you that he spent some of the money he owes you on equipment for the rec center."

Rebecca rolled her eyes. "It's hard to explain, Zeke. It's like there's something missing, and all my usual ways of filling up the empty spaces weren't working anymore. I thought that if I truly got away from everything, I could get a step closer to figuring it out."

I wasn't sure how to respond. I felt happy for Rebecca that she was taking steps to get control of her life, but it made me sad to see her so lost and confused that she needed to travel to a different continent to work things out. So far away from me. From Colton too.

"Is there anything I can do to help you?"

"Yeah, you can make the team and maybe look after Colton a little. Be a friend. He didn't take the news very well that I'm leaving."

I knew that feeling.

"I think I can do that."

"Good, because when I told him the other day that you and I used to date, he kind of flipped out. He said it might be awkward sharing the court with you."

Making the team at KU wouldn't be hard enough. Might as well toss into the mix trying to become a good teammate to the guy whose position I was trying to take—oh, and by the way, he and I both used to date the same girl.

"I've got to get to tryouts. This is day one. If I'm late, there might not be a day two."

Rebecca leaned in and kissed me on the cheek before whispering into my ear some well-intentioned life advice that also happened to apply to basketball.

"Always go strong to the rack, Ezekiel."

It was Rebecca's final gift to me.

59

Thanks for Being My Friend

"**R**un it again!"

That was KU Head Coach Bob Worth, reminding everyone in the arena—even returning veterans like Colton Banner—that we all had a long way to go to make the cut.

During a water break, Colton walked over to where I was leaning up against a wall, dripping like a mop and panting like a beagle.

"I'm glad you're here, Zeke. Having another ballhandler on the squad sure would help us this season."

"I'm still trying to get my wind. Coach sets a high standard for physical conditioning." I didn't know what else to say because it felt just plain weird to be sharing the court with someone after kind of sharing the same girl.

Colton seemed to be searching for the right words too. He cleared his throat to get my attention, but that was unnecessary because he already had it. "I guess it's a small world. I didn't know about you and Rebecca until she told me a few days ago."

"It's cool," I said.

No big deal.

Right.

I attempted to take the high road. "Rebecca said she thought we might hang out. Anyway—"

I decided to start over. "Look, Colton, she's gone now—from both of us. So I guess we've got that in common, in addition to . . . trying to survive on this team."

I didn't think it was much of a stretch to say that, since spending time with someone who is unexpectedly thrust into your life often means becoming friends at some level, no matter how weird the circumstances. It was one of those peculiar moments when, all at once, basketball had everything and nothing at all to do with what was happening on the court.

"I'd like the Fieldhouse to be a place where we can both just play our best," Colton said. "How about we start by pushing each other real hard in practice and see where that takes us."

Colton was right. We needed to become teammates first.

Even if my ambition was to replace him as starting point guard.

We bumped fists and got back to work.

I was numb for the rest of practice, physically able to deal with the pace, but mentally checked out maybe just a bit.

"Nice job out there today, Zeke." Those were the first words Coach Worth had spoken to me since inviting me to walk on after the Jackrabbits took the regional title in Los Angeles months earlier.

"Thanks, Coach." I was far too exhausted to offer much else. I realized that while all my biking over the summer had kept me in shape, it hadn't quite kept me in *basketball* shape.

"It seemed like you lost a little focus there at the end," he said. "When you're running out of gas, that's exactly when I need you to clear your head—and learning how to do that starts right here, in practice. You're not going to connect on every pass or every shot this season, but I know you have more to give than what I saw today—a *lot* more."

Great, I had already disappointed Coach, and it was only the first day of tryouts.

"Yes, sir."

Then Bob Worth gave me the *coach's stare* until he had bored a hole through one end of my psyche and out the other.

"You're guarding Mr. Banner like you're getting ready to ask him if you can borrow his car keys," Coach said. "I need you to challenge him, Zeke. No second-chance points. The only way you're going to survive on this team is to make Colton earn every possession in practice. Got it?"

"Yes, sir. Lockdown D. I'm on it."

If Coach Worth had said those words to Stretch, the big man would have panicked before raiding the fridge. Curtis would have run his shooting hand through his sun-bleached hair to draw his focus inward before driving his surfmobile to Zuma to analyze the hidden meaning behind Coach's words.

I chose not to overthink it, instead taking it as fatherly advice to work my butt off.

After practice, I stood under the shower longer than usual, hoping the hot water would somehow wash away the emptiness that had engulfed me since Rebecca delivered the news about joining the Peace Corps.

I got dressed and grabbed my gear. I was tired, but I was hungry too. Hunger usually won out, so I made my way to the student center.

"Hey, champ."

Electricity shot through my body. Those words sounded like they could have come from Rebecca, but the voice was higher and more velvety.

I turned around to find Darla Davenport standing there, reporter's notebook in hand, No. 2 pencil slicing through her shock of coiled-up, flame-red hair. She had on a dark-blue KU hoodie that featured the old-school version of the Jayhawks logo.

"You up for a game of Horse?"

"What are you doing here?"

"Looking for an angle." Darla paused after she said that and gave me a squinty-eyed smile.

Wait, was she flirting with me? I felt myself getting flustered. I remembered her asking what was up with me and Rebecca when she interviewed me before I left for Kansas. At the time, I wasn't exactly sure why Darla was asking, but I had a pretty good idea as we stood together at the student center.

"I transferred to KU because I heard the school has a great journalism program," she said. "I tried to tell you after the interview, but you took off like a rocket, and I didn't get the chance. I figured I'd run into you eventually, what with me covering basketball for the college newspaper and all."

I was dumbfounded. I was looking at Darla in a different light. I was also relieved to have another instant friend on campus, especially one who was cute, awkwardly pushy, and awesome to be around.

"How about we get a slice of pizza so I can tell you all about it, now that you're not running around like a madman?"

I said yes.

Darla led us to the cafeteria entrance. When we arrived, I noticed a blue U.S. postal mailbox near the entrance.

"Can I borrow a piece of paper?"

Darla handed one over, along with her pencil.

"I'll just be a moment."

"Fair warning, Zeke: I'm on deadline," Darla said, her intense green eyes sparkling. "I have lots of questions for you. *Most* of them have to do with basketball. I'll see you inside."

Darla smiled as she walked away, revealing that slender gap between her front teeth that reminded me I wasn't as far away from home as I thought.

I plopped down onto a bench and wrote my best friend a note.

Dear Lawrence:

After I arrived at KU, I decided to handwrite the enclosed record of all the time we've spent together since we met at McDerney. Jeepers, talk about writer's cramp!

Anyway, I wrote what might look from a distance like one of your math textbooks because I wanted you to know how important your friendship is to me. I didn't want to leave anything out, so I think you'll find this written record to be as comprehensive as it is thick.

I know how essential rules are to you, so I'm going to impose one on you myself. You must not read this story until you are en route to Mars. I figure my observations will help you to pass the idle time in between conducting critically important experiments in space for the good of humankind.

If it comes to pass that you're selected as the mathematics flight specialist on NASA's first-ever mission to Mars—and I REALLY like your chances—you have my permission to read the enclosed words during your journey. This story will be yours to keep forever, and you may do with it whatever you wish.

Thanks for being my friend.
Godspeed,

Zeke

I folded my letter in half, the same way Lawrence always had whenever he presented one of his notes to me.

Lawrence operated best when he knew what the game plan was, so I wrote the words *to Lawrence from Zeke* on the outside of the letter and added these simple instructions: *Open the letter first.*

I had already picked up a jumbo manila envelope and a ton of postage stamps from the KU bookstore, so all I had to do was address the envelope to the Tuckerman residence and stuff the diary and letter inside.

I sealed it up and tossed the whole thing into the mailbox. Then I went inside the cafeteria to share some pizza with Darla.

ACKNOWLEDGMENTS

I've enjoyed the good fortune of strong continuity with my editorial and design teams throughout the process of writing and publishing this trilogy, starting with my book producer, Marco Pavia.

Marco has functioned more as a spirit guide than a book-publishing authority as he handled the creative particulars of the book's design, production, distribution, and marketing. It is Marco's deeply rooted desire to see authors succeed that makes him such a joy to work with.

Christopher Caines has served as my editor on this book, as well as my copyeditor on books 1 and 2. From the beginning, he has guided my words with his profound expertise in the language, his keen sense of humor, and his deep understanding of the mysteries of human nature. The extent to which his love of basketball has benefited these stories is incalculable.

Jenna Winterberg, my developmental editor for this book, provided a passionate and insightful aerial view of my first draft that helped to set my course for the steps that followed.

Tabitha Lahr (cover designer), Brent Wilcox (interior page designer), and Sara Dyck and Cecile Garcia (proofreaders) all returned for this final leg of the journey. Many thanks to all four.

Judy Gitenstein, my editor on books 1 and 2, encouraged me to write this third installment by saying that the rising story arc must not go unresolved. Without her wisdom and encouragement, I would never have attempted to venture forth from sequel to trilogy.

I would like to acknowledge three books that helped me to develop my own idiosyncratic, mix-and-match theories on the paradoxical nature and mechanics of time travel. They are *The New Time Travelers: A Journey to the Frontiers of Physics* by David Toomey (W. W. Norton, 2007), *Time Travel: A History* by James Gleick (Vintage Books, 2016), and *Time Travel: Fact, Fiction & Possibility* by Jenny Randles (Blandford Press, 1994).

I gathered many of the historical facts pertaining to Dr. James Naismith and his invention of "Basket Ball" from the book *James Naismith: The Man Who Invented Basketball* by Rob Rains with Hellen Carpenter (Temple University Press, 2009). I also gained insight from *Basketball: Its Origin and Development* by James Naismith himself (Association Press, 1941; reprinted by University of Nebraska Press, 1996), and from *Spalding's Official Basket Ball Guide*, edited by Luther Gulick, MD (American Sports Publishing, November 1897). I gleaned several obscure facts about the first-ever game from

The Basketball Man: James Naismith, by Bernice Larson Webb (University Press of Kansas, 1973).

My research journey into the origins of basketball led me to Jeffrey L. Monseau, the college archivist at Springfield College's Archives and Special Collections Department. Springfield College is the institution of higher education that evolved out of the International YMCA Training School. Jeff was generous with his knowledge of the original building as well as the people and events at the epicenter of Basket Ball's invention.

I would like to formally acknowledge the names of the eighteen student athletes who played in the first-ever game on December 21, 1891: Lyman W. Archibald, Franklin E. Barnes, Wilbert F. Carey, William R. Chase, William H. Davis, George E. Day, Benjamin S. French, Henri Gelan, Ernest G. Hildner, Genzibaro S. Ishikawa, Raymond P. Kaighn, Eugene S. Libby, Findley G. MacDonald, Frank Mahan, T. Duncan Patton, Edwin P. Ruggles, John G. Thompson, and George R. Weller.

Please note that, contrary to what you might have read in chapter 26 here, Lyman Archibald was not actually called away on family business in Boston and subsequently replaced by Zeke Archer when James Naismith's noble experiment required an even number of players to take the court.

I'm grateful to the University of Kansas for granting me permission to use images of the Original 13 Rules of Basketball in the book's graphic design. Tim Gaddie, DeBruce Center operations manager, and Paul Vander Tuig, assistant athletic director for trademark licensing, were instrumental in this endeavor.

I also wish to acknowledge Curtis Marsh, KU's endowment development director, who provided me a unique history lesson on how the Original 13 Rules of Basketball came to be archived at the DeBruce Center on campus at the University of Kansas.

I took a course at KU's Osher Lifelong Learning Institute called Kansas: The Cradle of Basketball from James Naismith to Olympic Gold to Phog Allen, taught by Rich Hughes, author of *Netting Out Basketball 1936* (FriesenPress, 2011). The course offered abundant insight into the formative years of basketball, many of the details of which are woven into this novel.

John Lawrence, a friend and former bandmate, taught me the music theory concept known as the *circle of fifths* on a bass guitar more than twenty years ago when we were playing together in the Johnny Walker Band, a rock and blues cover outfit out of Los Angeles. In the scientific sense, the circle of fifths can best be described as a geometrical representation of relationships among the twelve pitch classes of the chromatic scale in pitch-class space. I'd like to think the concept took root at some ethereal level, opening the door for Lawrence Tuckerman to crack the time-travel code by harnessing the power of Sacred Geometry.

I stumbled onto the concept of Sacred Geometry and its possible application to time travel as the book's central storytelling device during a contemplative visit to the New Camaldoli Hermitage in Big Sur, California, a place where magical things can happen when one's antenna is up.

Rabbi Ronald Hauss assisted me with the Hebrew translation of the name Ezekiel. Rabbi Zalman Tiechtel, director of the KU Chabad in Lawrence, challenged me to find a way to honor my Jewish roots through this work.

Bob Conroy, engineering faculty member emeritus at California Polytechnic State University, San Luis Obispo, made an unprecedented third-straight cameo appearance as my math and science guru and fact checker. Bob certainly had his hands full this time around.

Matthew James Walker offered his expertise on how Lawrence Tuckerman might have used basic hand tools to take apart a 1965 Chevrolet Fleetside shortbed pickup truck.

Bonnie Thurston, senior manager of player personnel at the WNBA, served as a key resource as I was hammering out the initial outline for this book.

Back in my sportswriting days, I had the good fortune to share space in the press box with Dave Caldwell and Joe Soriano, the broadcast team who covered local high school and college sports for radio station KHTS 1220 AM. The vivid pictures they painted with their words made a lasting impression on me as I was bearing down on my laptop with deadline looming. Dave and Joe's unique phraseology and youthful energy can be found on these pages.

I'm often asked how I came up with the name Zeke for the trilogy's main character. Zeke was the nickname given to Los Angeles Lakers Hall of Famer Jerry West in the early 1960s by the team's legendary play-by-play announcer Chick Hearn. Chick often referred to West as "Zeke from Cabin Creek." However, West didn't actually hail from Cabin Creek, West Virginia: he was born about two miles up the road in nearby Chelyan. But that didn't stop Chick from coining one of his notable "Chick-isms," those unique phrases he dreamed up while calling the Laker games I used to listen to on my AM transistor radio when I was growing up in the San Fernando Valley. I always thought that Zeke was a cool name for a basketball player.

I am fortunate to have such a distinguished group of young-adult beta readers who carved out time from their busy school schedules to read and comment on my manuscript. This list includes Hailey Star Dowthwaite, Sam Hertzog, Elliot Lawrence, Bryson Montgomery, Stiles Montgomery, Truman Peterson, Whitman Peterson, Santos Rodriguez, and Drew Weschler.

I've offered Samuel Adam "Shmuli" Weber the role of Sherman "Lawrence" Tuckerman when this trilogy is made into a feature film or TV miniseries. I'm still waiting for Shmu's decision. I really hope he says yes.

I have a sizable group of friends and relatives who've offered love and encouragement throughout the creation of this novel and the entire trilogy. I'm grateful for the support of Lilly Akpobome, Rob Anker, Steve "Junior" Aronson, Mark Baarstad, Michael Benner, the real Chett Biffmann, Stephanie Bluestein, John Blum, Stephen and Suzy Bookbinder, Michael Bowler, Herb Brady, Greg Brown, David Buchan, Brian and Cathy Bunnin, Leo Bunnin, John Burnley, Steve Cantos, Gregg Chisolm, Chris Coppel, Frank Cotolo, Ted Dayton, Bob Dickson, Cheyenne Nicole Dunham, Kerry and Michele Feldman, Ric and Teri Garcia, Joan Gilbert, Theo Gluck and Cindy Goldberg, Burt Golden, Todd and Mary Goodson, Kathy and Andy Gordon, Hope Goss, Fran Graziano, Jeff and Jana Hammond,

Mike Harris, Randie Hauss, Jane Hawley, Joey Held, Mark Hidalgo, Mike Hulyk, Jasmine Ilkhan, Jiggy Jaguar, Max and Audrey Johnson, Larry Jonas, Michael Kadenacy, Scott Kelly, Gary and Donna Klein, Greg Klein, Martine Korach, Bernie Larsen, Neal Laybhen, Alvin Lee, Doug and Jennifer Leener, Jared Leener, Marty Lieberman, Stanley Malone, Tad Marburg, Darryl Mardirossian, Alfredo Marmolejo, Don McLean, Paul and Ellen McLeod, Mark and Ilana Meskin, Jeff Miller, Brian Minkoff, Laura Moe, Brandon Montgomery, Steven Moscowitz, Jesse Muñoz, Mason Nesbitt, Cary Osborne, Vimal Patel, Carol Perata, Bob Perkins, Clark Peterson, Tim Riley, Doug Roberts, Susan Roberts, Fran Morris Rosman, Gregg Sandheinrich, Kurt Schwenk, Steven G. Smith, Kip "Chip Spears" Sears, Doug and Vicky Skane, Jane Stanton, James Stewart, Shirley Strickland, Stuart Toben, Aaron Walker, John and Megan Walker, Dawn Walock, Steve Waugh, Angela Weber, Bob Wells, Reno Wilde, Steve and Sally Williams, Bobbie Yunis, and Irwin Zucker.

My friends Steven and Ann Hertzog, publishers of the Lawrence Business Magazine, have once again served as my ambassadors in Lawrence, where they opened many doors for me as I was conducting research into the origins of the game.

I got my start in the business world as an account executive at KRUX 1360 AM in Phoenix, where my job was to sell airtime at a radio station with weak Arbitron ratings and an even weaker signal. I didn't close many deals, but I sure did enjoy writing those commercials. The station's general manager, Joe Koff, taught me the importance of working as a team to overcome stacked odds.

My friend and mentor, Jim Gentilcore, provided a much-needed clandestine beta read in the early going. His observations and insights helped to keep me on the path.

My son, Zachary, and my daughter-in-law, Erika, insisted that I get out of my comfort zone by looking for unorthodox ways to connect with the reader.

My wife, Andrea, supplied the unconditional love and support that enabled me to win the ultimate battle of man versus blank screen. She makes the fragility of existence seem a little less daunting. Nothing in my life would be possible without her.

JAMES NAISMITH'S ORIGINAL 13 RULES OF BASKETBALL

James Naismith's Original 13 Rules of Basketball are on display at the DeBruce Center at the University of Kansas. The university created the DeBruce Center not only as a shrine to the Rules, but as a gathering place for the extended KU community.

Basket Ball.

The ball to be an ordinary <u>Association</u> foot ball.

1. The ball may be thrown in any direction with one or both hands.

2. The ball may be batted in any direction with one or both hands (never with the fist).

3. A player cannot run with the ball, the player must throw it from the spot on which he catches it, allowance to be made for a man who catches the ball when running at a good speed.

4. ~~The ball must be held in or between the hands, the arms or~~ body must not be used for holding it.

5. No shouldering, holding, pushing, tripping or striking, in any way the person of an opponent shall be allowed. The first infringement of this rule by any person shall count as a foul, the second shall disqualify him until the next goal is made, or if there was evident intent to injure the person, for the whole of the game, no substitute allowed.

6. A foul is striking at the ball with the fist, violation of rules 3 and 4, and such as described in rule 5.

7. ~~If either side makes three consecutive fouls it shall~~ count a goal for the opponents (consecutive means without the opponents in the meantime making a foul).

8. A goal shall be made when the ball is thrown or batted from the grounds ^into the basket and stays there, providing those defending the goal do not touch or disturb the goal. If the ball rests on the edge and the opponent moves the basket it shall count as a

#2.

goal.

9. When the ball goes out of bounds it shall be thrown into
the field, and played by the person first touching it.   In case
of a dispute the umpire shall throw it straight into the field.
The thrower in is allowed five seconds, if he holds it longer it
shall go to the opponent.   If any side presists in delaying the
game, the umpire shall call a foul on them.

10. The umpire shall be judge of the men, and shall note the
fouls, and notify the referee when three consecutive fouls have
been made.   He shall have power to disqualify men according to
Rule 5.

11.   The referee shall be judge of the ball and shall decide
when the ball is in play, in bounds, and to which side it belongs,
and shall keep the time.   He shall decide when a goal has been
made, and keep account of the goals with any other duties that are
usually performed by a referee.

12.   The time shall be two fifteen minutes halves, with five
minutes rest between.

13.   The side making the most goals in that time shall be
declared the winners.   In case of a draw the game may, by agreement of the captains, be continued until another goal is made.

First draft of Basket Ball rules.
Hung in the gym that the boys might
learn the rules — Dec, 1891 - James Naismith
6-28-31.

ABOUT THE AUTHOR

Craig Leener grew up on the hardscrabble basketball courts of the San Fernando Valley in Los Angeles, California. He has studied the game as a player, coach, referee, fan, and sportswriter.

Craig earned an associate degree in liberal arts from Los Angeles Valley College and a bachelor's degree in radio, TV, and film from California State University, Northridge (CSUN). He subsequently worked in the entertainment industry in film operations, postproduction technical services, and human resources management before finding his calling as a sportswriter and young-adult novelist.

Craig sits on the board of directors of the Journalism Alumni Association at CSUN, where he mentors student journalists and serves as the organization's director of scholarships. He is a member of the North Valley Family YMCA and lives in the suburbs of Los Angeles with his wife, Andrea.

Craig purports to be an 87-percent free-throw shooter on his backyard home court, a claim that has never been independently verified.

Printed in Great Britain
by Amazon

83302989R00189